Strangers to Grace

By Sharon Turner

Copyright © June 28, 2014
Sharon Turner
All Rights Reserved

No part of the publication may be reproduced, stored in a retrieval system,
or transmitted in any form, or by any means, without the prior, written
permission of the publisher.
ISBN – 10: 1505378893

My family and friends have been the heart and soul of my book.

To Linda Bryan, Phyllis Butler, and Sue Kerby, dear friends who loved and encouraged me, but are now with the Lord, Larry Brian Radka, a one man operation called The Einhorn (Unicorn) Press, for his help with information regarding Parkersburg during the Civil War, Bill and Laura Morrison who told me I would someday be an author, my sixth grade teacher, Mrs. Long, who said I was special and would someday do great things, my parents who filled me with the stories of our history, my sister, Karen, who proofread and edited my book, my constant cheerleader, my husband, Dan, who happily took over all my responsibilities so I could write, and mostly to my Savior, God, and King who loves each and every one of us, powerfully and eternally, even when we cannot love ourselves, and has made awesome plans for us, even before we knew Him, I owe you a debt of gratitude that could never be paid in this lifetime.

Jeremiah 29: 11

"For I know the plans I have for you," declares the LORD, "plans to prosper you and not to harm you, plans to give you hope and a future."

Table of Contents

CHAPTER ONE 1

CHAPTER TWO 17

CHAPTER THREE 29

CHAPTER FOUR 43

CHAPTER FIVE 53

CHAPTER SIX 67

CHAPTER SEVEN 79

CHAPTER EIGHT 87

CHAPTER NINE 103

CHAPTER TEN 117

CHAPTER ELEVEN 129

CHAPTER TWELVE 141

CHAPTER THIRTEEN 153

CHAPTER FOURTEEN 163

CHAPTER FIFTEEN 171

CHAPTER SIXTEEN 179

CHAPTER SEVENTEEN 189

CHAPTER EIGHTEEN 201

CHAPTER NINETEEN 211

CHAPTER TWENTY 221

CHAPTER TWENTY-ONE 231

CHAPTER TWENTY-TWO 239

CHAPTER TWENTY-THREE 245

Epilogue 257

CHAPTER ONE

December 22, 1861

The cold air rushed in as the massive door slid open, blinding him with the bright light. He wasn't sure how long he had been sleeping, and found it disturbing that he hadn't awakened when the train stopped.

His heart was pounding so loudly he was sure the workers outside the train car could hear it. He had perfected hiding and cowering in fear as a child, and knew instinctively to breathe quietly through his open mouth so no one could hear him panting. As he forced himself to awaken, he took a quick inventory of his aches and pains.

His battered body hurt constantly, having been beaten so often and so brutally over the course of his life, but he was even more uncomfortable now than usual. The cold and hunger he was used to, but he had spent the night wedged between the cold metal wall of the train car, and the heavy feed sacks stacked almost from floor to ceiling, unable to move from his position. His body was stiff and aching, his mouth was dry and he needed to relieve himself badly, but the fear of getting caught outweighed any and all other concerns.

Now was the time. If the men he could hear milling around outside entered the car and began to unload it, he was certain to be found out. But if they walked away, just for a moment, he could escape, and disappear into the world he had been locked away from for so many years.

He strained to hear what was happening for fear they had seen him and had summoned the sheriff, but all he could hear was the deafening roar of silence. When a muffled voice said something about the necessary papers being elsewhere, he held his breath and listened to boots thumping on the old wooden dock as the men retreated.

Ignoring the pain in his back and leg, he began crawling over the bags of supplies that were his only obstacle to freedom. He grabbed the doorframe above him as he prepared to swing to freedom out the gigantic door.

"Whoa!" he shouted out of shock and surprise as he came face to face with a man who was at least twice his size.

Jesse didn't trust his voice to work, but knew he had to respond quickly if he didn't want to arouse suspicion. "Hey! There you are! Got a job for a hard workin' man?"

The man looked for a minute like he was going to call someone, but Jesse interrupted, "Look, all I need is a good meal, mister. I'll unload this whole car for you if you would just feed me when I'm done."

Another pause made Jesse nervous enough to fill the awkward silence with more lies. He was willing to do whatever it took to remain free. "My wife threw me out. Now I can't say I didn't deserve it, but, well, I just need a meal tonight and tomorrow I'm sure she will be missing me, and will let me back into the house!" he said as he climbed out of the car. If he had to run, at least he had that much of a head start.

"I'm fairly good lookin' don't you think? I mean, who could stay mad at me?" The man in uniform grinned a little when Jesse held out his hands to indicate what a completely wonderful specimen of man he was, encouraging Jesse to press his luck a little further.

"Ok, I'll have this unloaded before you can get through all that paperwork!" he said as he nodded at the man who had returned with a stack of papers in hand. He turned and grabbed the first flour sack he could get his hands on, sick with fright. "Now where do you want this, sir?"

To Jesse's amazement, the man said, "Right over there, son. And if you break a bag, you pay for it." The man was not fooled by the stow-away, but, after all, he held little allegiance to the railroad, and the Federal Government paid little attention to costs. He had already calculated the remuneration he could bill for this man's work, and how much he would pocket as a result.

"Yes, sir!" Jesse said with a smile that he hoped looked more sincere than it felt. He turned and let the heavy flour sack fall onto the dock as he leaned against it for support. He tried to breathe and steady his heartbeat but everything seemed to swirl around him. It was days since he had eaten, he had been cramped up in the back of the railroad car, and he was thirstier than he had ever been in his life. But he knew passing out was not an option if he wanted to remain free.

Instead he decided to focus on the flour sack in his hands. As he ran his thumb over the oval shaped label dyed into the unbleached cotton sacks, he was flooded with memories of his mother soaking those labels in Kerosene in an attempt to bleach it out of the material. Although it was a great deal of added work, and a smelly chore to boot, she saw it as a small price to pay for the wealth of free cloth to be used for making them all new underwear, or for quilting, or patching. Not an inch of cloth would be wasted, either.

He remembered watching his mother carefully size and measure twice before cutting the precious material. The last night he was home, she was teaching his little sister, Sarah, how to sew tiny little stitches around quilt pieces, a memory so vivid he could hardly bear it. He fought back tears as he thought of his little sister and wondered what had happened to her. Had they finished that quilt? Were they even still living? And, if so, where were they now?

He tried for the thousandth time to remember exactly what Sarah's little face looked like. Her red freckles, dark eyes, and porcelain skin framed with that dark, deep red hair with blond wisps running through it. He and his older sister had never gotten along, but Sarah thought he walked on water, and he adored her, too, although he would never have admitted it to her. He wondered how she felt about him after what happened the last time he saw her, standing there holding her doll, with tears streaming down her face as they took him away.

He brought his mother's face to mind and tried to see Sarah in it, but all he could picture was his Mama after his father had beaten her: her eyes blackened, nose bleeding, and the cuts on her lip and cheekbone.

"HEY!" The sound made him jump like he was shot.

"Yea?"

"What the hell are you doing, mister?" his employer shouted. "I thought you would be half done by now!"

Jesse thought the fun loving kid routine worked before, so he tried it again. "Oh! About that! Can I buy a couple of these bags for my wife? I was just thinking that if I could get her thinking about making a quilt for our bed…" He allowed his voice to trail off, but wiggled his eyebrows up and down and smiled as if to ask if the man if he had gotten his meaning.

"No wonder she threw you out! You're as worthless as tits on a boar hog from where I stand. Now get to work and don't stop until that car is unloaded or the deal is off!"

"Yes, sir," Jesse said, and with a renewed strength of resolve, he set to the task of unloading and stacking the heavy bags. This was a chore he could have done easily a week ago, but now, in his condition, he wasn't even sure he could finish. With dogged determination, he fell into a rhythm of unloading and stacking that became mindless routine. Darkness was falling, so the likelihood of his being recognized decreased dramatically allowing him to relax somewhat. Despite his exhaustion the rest of the work went surprisingly quickly, because any work is more easily done with the light heart of a free man; even a tired, free man.

Sergeant Lloyd Calvin, his employer and an officer in the Union army, had drawn him a map to his house so he could join them for dinner. Jesse was at the Kanawha Street Depot, and according to the map, all he had to do was go straight up Juliana Street, cross Neale and Court Streets, then make a right onto Harriet and it was the third house on the right. As he climbed Juliana he was amazed at the size of the houses being built there. Having grown up in the ghettos of New York, he had never in his life seen such massive homes for one family, with porches bigger than some apartments.

"Come on in, son!" His boss shouted to Jesse when he saw him step up onto the porch. "You can call me Lloyd, by the way, and this is my wife, Juanita." He pointed to a short rotund woman with sleek black hair pulled back into a bun that sat on top of her chubby neck. Her bright red skirt, navy blue shirt, and bright green shawl with flowers of red, blue, and yellow splashed generously throughout, produced a breathtaking view for Jesse, who had not seen bright colors in nearly a decade of incarceration. She was equally as round as she was tall, and the big friendly smile on her face made Jesse laugh out loud as she threw her arms around him in a big maternal bear hug. He was giddy with freedom and ecstatic to be sitting down to his first home cooked meal since he was arrested.

It appeared to Jesse that Juanita's sole purpose in life was to feed him until he was helpless, which was fine with him. For starters, she plopped a huge bowl in front of him on the wooden table with a thunk, oblivious to the splash of thick soup that sloshed over onto the table. Before he could pick up the spoon, she returned with a plate of large slabs of homemade bread covered with melted cheeses and chunks of roasted garlic. "This is delicious, Ma'am." It was the first word of truth he had spoken since he had escaped from prison, and the pleased Juanita rewarded him with one of her big, warm smiles.

Lloyd was a big man with hair slicked straight back with what appeared to be some kind of grease, but he seemed friendly enough, and for that, Jesse was grateful.

He was also grateful that Lloyd talked nonstop, because it gave him a chance to eat as heartily as he wanted without having to make up more lies. And besides, after the boredom of being locked up, he found he enjoyed hearing about Lloyd's travels, those who tried to cheat him along the way, the bizarre weather he had seen, the high price of goods, and anything else that crossed Lloyd's mind. Jesse ate with a good feeling in his heart, as Juanita filled and refilled bowls.

Jesse was surprised to learn his country was at war, and had been for several months, and that Lloyd was an officer in what he called the Northern Army. Lloyd said, "I have been fortunate to be stationed in Parkersburg since the railroad was taken over by the military." Lloyd entertained him thoroughly with stories of the Northern Army using the same train system to get south, as the Confederates were using to head north, and the fact that there were troops from both armies headquartered within blocks of each other, right there in Parkersburg!

The Parkersburg/Marietta area had become a transportation hub for the war since it had the railroad, two main highways leading northeast to New York, and southeast to Winchester, VA, and the Little Kanawha and Ohio rivers. "The river is jammed with boats of all kinds," Lloyd explained. "There are sternwheelers and military gunboats, supply boats and packets of every size imaginable. That's smart, too, because you can travel by water safer and faster than you can by animal if you know where you're going." Jesse made a mental note of that piece of information for future reference. He didn't care where he was going, but now he knew he could put even more distance between himself and the prison by traveling by water.

Lloyd paused to ask Juanita for a piece of apple pie, and as Juanita hustled off to get it, Lloyd continued with his story with tales of the tent cities that had grown up everywhere, but with a full meal in his stomach Jesse's body began to ache with exhaustion. Just as the last of the adrenaline he had been running on drained from his body, Lloyd stopped in mid-sentence and said, "What am I doing? Talking away while you are falling asleep in your plate! I could offer you the barn for the night if you don't have any place to go. I'm assuming that gal of yours isn't ready to have you back yet." Jesse grinned, and instantly regretted lying to this man whom he now admired.

"You know, son. I wasn't sure you would be able to get that work done with that leg and all," Lloyd said as he nodded toward Jesse's right leg. "But you did a man's job today, and I am proud of you."

Jesse was just as ashamed of that leg now as he was as a boy being teased by the town kids, but the deep humiliation was quickly replaced with intense pride from what was the first genuine compliment he had ever received from a grown man. "Thank you, sir. That means a lot," he said with a heart so full he could hardly breathe. He then turned and thanked Juanita for the fine meal, gathered up the stack of blankets she had offered him, and uttered his gratitude for the use of the barn before he disappeared into the night.

Although the last thing his aching body wanted to do was climb a ladder, he thought the loft would be the safest place to be, up away from the critters. The memory of the prison rats made him shudder, but as he climbed the ladder he realized that tonight, he was a free man. He had choices as to where he slept. He had decisions to make about his life and for the first time as an adult, he was free and making his own way.

He didn't remember lying down on the hay, and he slept deeply and soundly for the first time in years. The night was unusually warm for December, although there was enough of a chill to make him doubly thankful for the blankets Juanita insisted he take with him. He even enjoyed the chilly breezes blowing through the cracks in the barn wood when he would awaken to shift his position, for he had not felt the wind on his face in, well, nearly a decade. Once, when he turned over, he could see the moon as clearly as if he were standing on it but he just breathed the fresh air in deeply and fell back to sleep again.

He had no idea how long he had been sleeping when his eyes opened with a start. His heart was again pounding and his mouth was dry. The moon light was gone and the darkness was so absolute he became disoriented. Where was he? Was he in prison? Was he a child again, hiding from his father? No, he was somewhere else, but where? He was lost until he placed his hand on the floor to push himself up, and the touch of the hay and rough barn wood brought him back to reality. He froze in place, not knowing exactly what he was supposed to do next.

What had awakened him? Had he heard something? He sat up quietly and listened to his heart beating powerfully against his ribs. Why hadn't he thought about the possibility that Lloyd knew who he was and had turned him in to authorities for the reward? How long had he been asleep? And what awakened him? Had he heard someone approaching? Were they below him now ready to put him in shackles and return him to the hell that had been his life for so long?

For what seemed like an eternity, he forced himself to listen for evidence of the presence of men below him. He rolled over silently and peered through a crack in the floor; the darkness was suffocating.

Quietly, he got up, felt his way over to the ladder, turned and lowered himself, rung by rung. He looked out into the dark night and asked himself whether it would be better to leave and risk running into whoever might be out there, or stay there and let them come in to get him, a thought process necessary for only seconds. He was not going back to prison, ever. He would run and run until he died if he had to, but to stay there like a sitting duck was not an option. He took what he thought was the same road he had come up, veering back into the rut in the dirt road when his feet got tangled in the limbs and dry leaves off to the side.

But he had run out of houses far too early for that to be the same street, and soon found himself running wildly through a field with trees and debris. The limb of a tree caught him by surprise, jerking his head backwards with such force, it almost knocked him out. He swung his arms madly, uncertain whether he had been hit by a man who had been in hot pursuit. He began running again with his arms in front of his face, grateful at least that he was no longer banging his shins on the elevated wooden sidewalks. Exhausted, and confident now that no one had followed him, he stumbled across the railroad track and found a place to rest, hidden from view in a grove of trees. After listening briefly to the absolute silence around him, he lay down to await morning. This time, sleep was not restful.

His dreams took him to a time when his father was drinking heavily, and his mother was trying unsuccessfully to fix a meal without making any noise so as to not set him into a fit of rage. He was eight again, hiding under the bed where his mother had hidden him, debating as to whether or not he was man enough to stop the beating of his mother he was sure would come.

Suddenly, the jailer who had beaten him so often in prison, grabbed him from under the bed and dragged him to the judge for the reward that was now on his head. His little sister, Sarah, was watching him in her old tattered dress with tears in her eyes when his fingers suddenly felt as cold as ice. He was dying and turning into a cold corpse, right in front of Sarah! No, he could not let that happen! He struggled to move, to lift his head and speak, and when his eyes snapped open, he realized his fingers were barely in the edge of a huge, ice cold river.

He sat up with a start and saw a woman looking down at him. "Are you alright, sir?" she said with concern.

"Yea, I was just dreaming about… Well, I was, uh…"

"No need to explain, I just wanted to make sure you weren't having a fit. You know, like some poor souls do? I had heard of people swallowing their tongues, and wanted to be certain you were alright, which you seem to be." Immediately after finishing her sentence she abruptly turned and walked away.

"Hey! Where are you going?" he asked. "I didn't even get to thank you!"

She turned and walked back toward him, still keeping her distance. "And what would you want to thank me for? Awakening you from a sound sleep? But your gratitude is duly noted. Now, good day!" she said, turning to leave dismissively.

He hurried to catch up with her, and said, "Well, I just wanted to thank you. That was very kind."

She stopped abruptly, turned to him and said, "I'm sorry, sir, but if I somehow gave you the impression I wanted further conversation with you, I apologize. Please leave me alone."

"Excuse me folks." As careful as Jesse had been up to this point, he had allowed a total stranger to approach him unnoticed, and as he turned he realized to his dismay, that it was an officer of the law.

"Yes, sir?" Jesse turned toward the official and felt his knees go weak. He actually felt the blood drain from his face as he stood in front of a man dressed in the clothes much like those men who had dragged away from his home and family.

"Well, you and the Misses should be careful camping here. This ain't the best part of town you know. You can be robbed blind while you are sleeping in these parts! Someone can come off the river, you know, rob you and be gone before you even know you been took!"

Jesse looked at the woman he had known only a few minutes, hoping she would not correct the lawman's misconception that they were husband and wife, and found her instead stepping closer to him, assisting in the charade. Before he realized it, he put his arm out to draw her near, and to his shock, she stepped closer and stood beside him as if she were his wife. Jesse was caught off guard, but managed to smile down at her, and felt warm all over as she surprised him by returning his smile. *Newlyweds*, the officer thought to himself. He cleared his throat, and said, "Well, you folks need to move on now."

"We're beholding to you, Sir." Jesse said with a smile. "We'll be more careful from now on."

With a tip of his hat, the lawman turned and walked away, leaving the two of them standing side by side, wondering what had just happened. As the officer engaged another group of people in conversation, they stepped away from each other, stared eye to eye for a brief moment, then turned, and tried to find anything to do, except talk to each other. She took inventory of her pack, while Jesse busily cleaned the dust off his pants and shirt. He had no idea what to say to her, so he simply stood there looking at his feet, wishing he knew anything at all about women. When he looked up, she was gone. "Hey! Wait up!" he shouted. Did all women walk that fast?

Just as he was gaining on her, she spun around with a start and said, "Stop! I want nothing more to do with you, and you can certainly trust me when I say, you do not want to get involved with me either." As she turned to leave, Jesse caught her arm, but she insisted, "Let go of me! And do not follow me, either!" She smiled graciously at those around her as she made certain no one had noticed her outburst. But in an instant, her smile changed to a sneer as she leveled Jesse with her eyes and continued, "I appreciate what happened back there, but I am going to go my way and I want you to go yours or I will tell that officer over there you are bothering me."

"No! Don't do that. Just wait a minute, will you? Give me one minute and then we will go in separate directions if you want." Jesse said watching her for any reaction.

By then they were in the midst of a small crowd that was gathering to purchase tickets on a riverboat, and whether she was afraid of drawing more attention, or relished the idea of an opportunity to convince him to go away, she gave in. "Come over here where we can talk privately, but there are still people around just in case you don't agree to go away." She smiled at the crowd as she took him by the arm and led him over to a park bench. "Sit down, but keep your distance. I have had a great deal of experience with being a victim, so I can play one quite convincingly if necessary. I can, and will, have you arrested and never look back." He nodded his understanding and took a deep breath.

Faced with the opportunity to actually speak to a woman who was sitting within a foot of him, his throat became dry. Had she not glared at him and stood to walk away, he may never have found his tongue.

"Wait, please! You said you would give me one minute." She turned and stared at him as if considering her next move, then pulled her carpet bag around in front of her, clasped it with both hands and sat down. "One minute. You may have one minute, sir." As if to emphasize her commitment, she checked the tiny watch pinned to her cape, then turned her eyes to meet his.

He drew in a slow breath and said, "I have no idea what happened back there." She started to stand but he caught her by the arm. "Please? I'm not going to ask you any questions, I promise."

He watched her stare at her hands as he continued, "I don't need to know what was going on back there." She turned and eyed him suspiciously. "All I *do* know is that for some reason, we worked as a team. And because of that, we were safer than we would have been had we been traveling alone. Am I right?"

She looked straight ahead, tipped her head back, and took a slow, deep breath in through her nose which gave her an air of dignity he hadn't seen before. "I agree," she said finally.

"So?" he asked.

"So what?"

"Look, we don't have a lot of time to dance around all this. Can we just be honest?"

"Yes, in fact, and honest man would be quite refreshing," she said meeting his challenge eye to eye. Then she raised one eyebrow and said, "Brutally honest, shall we?"

His inexperience with women was to his benefit. There were no bad habits to break. No lines to try that had worked for him in the past. Brutally honest was all he had. "I don't want to tell you anything about me. And I don't need to know anything about you," he paused to check her reaction. When he saw he had not frightened her off, he continued, "But I'm just thinking it would be better, or safer, if we traveled together." If what he said bothered her, she again gave no indication.

"Well," she said after a pause long enough to unnerve Jesse, "To be brutally honest, I would rather cut off a finger than admit this, but it is indeed, safer for me to be traveling with a man. But what would be in it for you? Because if you are thinking…"

"Oh… NO!" he interrupted, "It's just that, well, that lawman thought we were married, and he treated us with respect, instead of suspicion, and I'm not use to that. Let's just say that for me, there is safety in being a married man."

Whether she actually understood or not, she seemed at least to accept his explanation. It was easier to talk to women than he had guessed, and he loved the way she could hold her own in a conversation. *Women aren't so complicated,* he thought to himself. He didn't know what all those grown men in the prison were talking about. It seemed easy to him to just say what he thought and listen to what she had to say. He could do that.

She was pretty good at judging character, and she assessed him to be a basically kind man. However, she would remain on guard because men were men, and promises made in the daylight were often forgotten at night. That being said, dealing with one man would be infinitely easier than dealing with every man she encountered as a single woman traveling alone.

"Let's say for the moment, that I would agree to travel with you for the day. You must first be absolutely clear on two points." She waited for him to respond with a nod and then continued, "No questions will ever be asked by either of us," she paused and waited for his nod of agreement, then continued, "and you will never, ever touch me again. Agreed?"

"Agreed."

"I mean it," she continued. "If you try to hurt me, or if you actually do manage to do me harm, just remember that at some point in your life you will have to fall asleep. And when you do, I will tangle you up in the bed sheets and beat you to death with whatever I can get my hands on," she paused and looked around the crowd with an astonishingly innocent childlike smile. But when she looked back at him, her expression became deadly. "And do not think for one minute that I *would* not, or *could* not do it." Although there was a faint smile on her face, the stone cold resolve in her eyes betrayed the violent past she was trying so hard to hide, and that in and of itself convinced Jesse that indeed she would, and she certainly could kill a man who hurt her. He found himself wondering if that just might be what she was running from.

After another brief smile to the public, her chin lifted slightly and her eyes narrowed as she turned to look at Jesse, totally prepared for the expected challenge to her threat. Instead, he said softly, yet very convincingly, "I would never, ever, in this lifetime, hurt a woman. And if you are ever frightened of me, just say so, and I will leave your presence immediately." He watched her carefully, and noticed the almost imperceptible relief that crossed her face briefly before she assumed the hard exterior again and dropped her head to think about the situation.

He had no clue as to what she was thinking about him and his past, but was encouraged when she said resolutely, "Well, then. Where are we headed? I, personally, have no plans as to where to go, only to go... somewhere... and never look back." Again her comment was far more revealing than he thought she would have liked. Jesse felt an overwhelming desire to be certain nobody ever hurt this woman again, and at the same time he felt she was quite capable of being his protector if the situation arose. He loved his mother, but this woman had a courage he had never dreamed possible in a woman, and he liked it. And he was pleased he was going to continue in her company.

"I really hadn't put much thought into where I was headed either. But in my opinion the water is a quick way to travel." He looked over her shoulder at the boat that was docked a small distance from where they were seated. "In fact it is quicker than traveling on horseback or walking. And once on a boat, we need only deal with those traveling with us, whereas travel by land could bring us face to face with soldiers who are looting and robbing." He was pleased with himself because he actually knew what he was talking about, and it felt good to speak with knowledge and authority to this woman he suddenly wanted to impress.

But before she could answer him, a man dressed in an old, shabby uniform climbed into a small gazebo that was built for this use, and announced to the crowd that they were about to board the small boat heading east on the Little Kanawha River. Anyone wanting passage could get their tickets from him by just stepping up to the gazebo.

They looked at each other briefly then she shrugged her shoulders, turned and headed for the man who had made the announcement. Jesse struggled to catch up with her as she waved her hand to attract the attention of the captain of the boat who had stepped down from the gazebo.

When the three met, the captain looked at Jesse and said, "Sir, I take it that you and the Misses are interested in the boat going east on the Little Kanawha River? Well, you can purchase your tickets right here."

Jesse hadn't thought about the fact that he would need money for the boat ride. He had gone from being a child, to being a prisoner in a heartbeat, and in both situations, everything had been provided for him, such as it was. Traveling as a single man he could make do sleeping in barns and working for meals, but traveling with a woman was another matter. Out of the corner of his eye, while lost in his thoughts, he saw this fascinating woman turn and speak to him.

"Oh, remember, dear? I put our money in my bag," the woman said as she opened her satchel and pulled out enough cash to serve them very well. Perhaps there were some questions that did need asking, but now was not the time and besides, he had promised to ask nothing at all.

He watched her purchase the tickets, then they followed the captain toward the ramp to board the boat. He wanted to put his hand possessively on the small of her back, but remembered his promise to never, ever touch her again.

CHAPTER TWO

The boat would be boarding in less than an hour. There was a vendor selling boxes of thick ham sandwiches for the trip, and Jesse wanted to ask Sarah if she thought they should purchase meals, but remembered he did not have the wherewithal to buy them. He wished he could march right up, buy the meals for her and say, "Here you are. You bought the fare, so I bought our lunches." But he not only had no money, he had no idea how to get any. His humiliation was complete when Sarah again took the lead, stepped forward and purchased two sandwiches, loaded them into her grip, then returned to stand beside him while waiting to board.

As they stood there in awkward silence, he felt the need to say something to her. "My name is Jesse, by the way," he said shyly as they returned to the bench they had been sitting on before buying the tickets.

She liked that. He had given her his name, leaving the decision to reciprocate up to her. Maybe he was a man of his word, and would ask no questions. "May I, again, be honest, sir?" she asked with a playful tone.

"Always," he said beginning to relax a little, "You may *always* be honest with me."

"Brutally?" she smiled and he thought his heart would explode.

"Brutally," he smiled back at her. Oh, he could get use to this.

Her speech was pointed and deliberate and her face was filled with pain and sorrow as she said, "I do not ever want to speak my name again as long as I live. It haunts me, and fits me like an anchor. It is my hope that I shall never hear my given name spoken again as long as I shall live."

There was a brief pause as he processed the expressions on her face, and recognized the pain. "Well, then it shall be as you wish," he said with a smile and a nod of his head. He now liked the word 'shall' because the first time he ever heard it was when she said it. After all those years of misery, he was beginning to understand why some people actually wanted to be alive, and if this kept up, he would be one of them.

Her laugh was golden, and had he known what love was, he would realize he was falling into it, head long. She straightened herself and said, "I guess the next step would be to choose a new name. Would you like to help me?"

"Well, is there a name you like? Maybe from someone you knew in the past?"

"No," she said emphatically as a forlorn look came over her face. "I would never choose a name from those who are behind me," she said looking up with new resolve. "I want a name that holds no memories for me; a new name that I shall give my own meaning. Do you have a name you like for a woman?"

"Well, for a woman, I am partial to the name, Sarah. It comes from the Bible, and it suits you very well."

She looked into the beautiful blue sky for a second and said, "Sarah!" She stood and walked toward the river boat, stopped with her hands on her hips as if she were looking into her future and whispered, "Sarah." After a brief time, she said, "I like the name, Sarah, very much." She turned toward him with a renewed energy and said, "It does suit me. Honestly, my heart actually feels lighter when I think of myself as Sarah. Thank you, Jesse. Now that I am boarding a boat, and I have a new name, I feel I have been reborn and I have an entirely new life ahead of me."

He envied her, and the thought crossed his mind to change his name as well. "You know, that's not a bad idea," he said quietly.

"What isn't?" she asked.

"I should change my name as well," he said, realizing it would make him harder to find. "So what suits me, ya' think?"

Before she could answer, a scream pierced the air. Somewhere in the woods away from the crowd was a child screaming, "Oh no you don't! Let go of me!" Something inside Jesse snapped and he ran, first pushing people out of the way and then the heavy brush and limbs of mighty pine trees.

Unexpectedly he came face to face with a foul smelling man who would have been a foot taller than Jesse had he not been bent into a permanent curve. As it was, Jesse was looking straight up into the face of a man whose beard had tobacco juice draining through it. His rotten teeth hung crookedly and his tongue worked back and forth feverishly over one of the many sores that surrounded his lips. His eyes were wild with desire and it was clear that he intended to rape this small girl, who looked to Jesse to be only nine or ten years old. Before Jesse could act, the man swung the back of a huge fist into the side of Jesse's head knocking him to the ground. Jesse was first dazed and then filled with a familiar rage. As he jumped to his feet he yelled, "You are going to have to do a lot better than that old man!" as his head made contact with the filthy man's belly, driving him backwards.

"I have been beaten by the best, and you need to know up front that you are going to lose this fight!" He was on top of him now punctuating every phrase with another punch to that disgusting face. The little girl screamed, which told him the sight was frightening her, so he picked up the man like a rag doll, threw him into the brush, and went in after him.

"Jesse! Jesse, stop! Leave him alone! You are going to kill him! He isn't worth going to prison for!" The words hit him like ice water in his face. In an instant he was standing over the man like a witness to the beating instead of the one who had done it. The filthy old man was alive but badly injured, a thought that only pleased Jesse.

He cooled himself down by walking in circles away from Sarah then back again. He dropped to his knees by the river and washed the blood off his hands and face, and was reminded of the blood that was on his clothes for days after he had beaten his father to death. He was drawn back to the time following his arrest when he had to eat bread with bloody hands because they would not let him bathe. He remembered wearing the shirt and pants his mother had lovingly made for him, now soaked in his father's blood, day after day until the smell sickened him.

"Jesse?" Sarah called.

He turned and saw her there comforting the frightened child. Sweet, sweet Sarah.

Sarah? How in the world did Sarah get through all those pine trees and heavy underbrush? He laughed as he peered through the trees and saw a host of people on the other side trying to peek through the branches to see what was going on. Even the men hadn't managed to make it through the entangled limbs of pine trees with that barricade of thick undergrowth and briars! And yet, there was Sarah, standing with her arm around the little girl as if they were calmly posing as an artist painted their portrait. What a very strange woman this was. Beautiful, graceful, soft spoken, and yet hard as nails if need be.

He felt his anger drain at the comical sight, and as he turned back to the river he noticed his hands were clean. There was no sign of blood anywhere. The water had done its job and washed the filth away. "The man is still alive," he muttered to himself with great relief, "thanks to Sarah." Had he killed the man, there would have been an investigation Jesse could ill afford, but as it was, he appeared to be a hero.

The crowd had a pretty clear idea of what had happened, and had begun shouting out words of encouragement to Jesse and Sarah as they prepared to leave the hidden cove beside the river. Some of the men even risked soiling or tearing their expensive travel clothes to help part the trees so the woman and child could leave the scene of near tragedy. A collective gasp was heard when they saw how young the child was, and then cheers and pats on the back erupted for Jesse as he stepped awkwardly out of the woods behind them. He was tired and his leg hurt, but he felt free of the memories of his father's blood, and felt as Sarah said, that he had been reborn.

The crowd quickly dispersed for fear of missing their boat as Sarah dropped to her knees in front of the child and wiped the tears and dirt from her face. "Now, where are your parents?" she asked.

The child stood still, her face giving no clue as to her circumstances.

"Sweety, if you don't take us to your parents we are going to have to turn you over to the authorities! You can't stay here alone." Sarah watched as the girl mulled that problem over in her head.

"Jesse, go get the sheriff," Sarah shouted without taking her eyes off the child. She hoped the threat would prompt the child to speak.

"NO! WAIT!" The little girl looked defeated, as she tried in vain to think of another option. "I'm a norphan," she said, hoping that would settle the issue about finding her parents and they would go away and leave her alone.

"So, who are you traveling with?" Sarah noticed the barely visible slump in the girl's shoulders as her mouth pursed defiantly. Sarah stood and looked around her to be certain no one was listening, led the girl by the shoulders over to a small rock and sat down so they could be face to face. "As long as Jesse and I have known each other, we have agreed that we could always be brutally honest with each other. Because sometimes you just need someone to listen, without judgment, and help you think through a problem. And so far it has worked out really well for us. So why don't you just tell us what is going on, and let us help you."

The girl looked at Jesse and then Sarah, and then at the ground. By now Sarah was beginning to feel uneasy that Jesse might be angry at her for taking so much time, but when she looked at him, she saw only concern for the child in his face.

"But what if you tell?" she asked as she drew lines in the mud with her shoe.

"Well, I think that is a fair question," Jesse said with lifted eyebrows, "don't you, Sarah?" Jesse knew he didn't want his story told, and Sarah, well the fact that Sarah wasn't her real name made his point for him.

The innuendo was clear to Sarah. "Why, yes I think that is an excellent point," Sarah said as much to Jesse as the child. She looked down at the little girl and said, "Look, Sweety. I know you don't know us. But you do know we care enough about you to risk missing our boat in order to see you safely out of here. And we are the ones who rescued you from that horrible man. And it appears to me that you really need someone to trust, and, in all fairness, I think we have proven ourselves to be trustworthy. But I will leave it up to you."

The child looked over into the bushes and thought about her dilemma. Although she realized she had absolutely no other way out of this, she just couldn't bring herself to say so. As she stared into space, tears welled up in her eyes and rolled down her cheeks with no change at all in her expression. She held her breath for just a second and then sighed in acquiescence.

"I runned away from a n'orphnige. Things were 'horble' there, so I told 'em I wanted to go on the next Orphan Train west. But I din't want to be adopted and worked like a dog… or worse!" Her little face looked up at Sarah and an understanding look passed between them that should only have been between two grown women. "So I runned away from the train and hid out. When it was warmer they was fish, and apples, and pears to eat. But when it got cold, I had to figger another way. I was doin' fine, too, until the store owner found me livin' under his danged ole porch. I guess he figgered out who was stealing his food and come lookin' fur me. I clumb that there tree to wait for a boat I could hide on, but I just had to pee, and that is when that horse's ass grabbed me."

Sarah flinched at the language, but locked eyes with Jesse, their faces filled with concern and questions. Silence hung in the air while the child waited to see what her fate would be, as Jesse and Sarah stepped to the side to discuss what they should or should not do about the situation.

"We cannot just leave her here," Sarah said. "She would be fair game for anyone of these men."

"Well, you can take her to the authorities if you want, but I sure don't want any lawman asking me questions about who I am and how I got this little girl," Jesse suspected that Sarah was also avoiding the law but said nothing. He knew Sarah was right, so he continued, "So that means we have to either stay here with her, or take her with us." The issue of the money was implied although not addressed directly.

"Oh, I can well afford the fare. While we are traveling together, you need not worry about funding. The question is, what will we do with her when we get off the boat? *We* don't even know where we are going! And our situation is, well, tentative at best! We are in no position to take on a child!"

Jesse looked over at the little girl, then at Sarah and said, "We seem to have done well just laying our cards on the table, right?" She nodded in agreement. "This child cannot stay here alone, and we can't stay here with her. I personally, can't afford to stay one more day to see her settled. Am I right in that?" Another nod. "So as I see it, her best option is for us to take her with us as far as the boat goes. Surely we can take her to a church, or an orphanage in the next city." Sarah's face reflected the anxiety he was feeling about what would happen at the end of the boat trip so he added for emphasis, "We can't leave her here."

With a deep sigh, Sarah gave in, "Ok, you are right, that is the only option we have."

As they walked back over to the pitiful little girl, Jesse was the first to speak, "Well, young lady, may I be brutally honest with you?"

Her eyes widened as she nodded once in agreement and sheer terror.

"Here is the situation. You don't have any family, and we are not leaving you here alone. So..."

"So," Sarah interrupted, "we are going to get you a ticket and take you with us on the boat if that is alright with you."

She eyed Jesse suspiciously and looked back at Sarah with very clear questions in her eyes. Sarah knew immediately what her fears were and she wanted to ease them, but to be perfectly honest she was a little afraid of the same thing since she had only known Jesse a little less than two hours herself! Although she was feeling better and better about him as the day progressed, she still didn't know him well enough. As she knelt before the girl she said, "You will be traveling as my little girl as long as you want to be with us. We will never leave each other's side and you can even hold my hand all day if you want. But keep in mind," Sarah said nodding toward Jesse, "this guy is the one who risked his own life to save you from that man."

The girl looked up at Jesse and back at Sarah, took hold of her hand and nodded her head.

As they turned to walk to the boat the girl stopped and froze in place. "Uh..." They both looked back at her standing there completely covered from the neck down with a filthy dirty, ill-fitting cape that surely had been a hand-me-down, or stolen, from a girl two sizes larger than she.

"What's wrong, honey?" Sarah asked.

"Uh... Could I be 'brully' honest with you two?"

Sarah just looked surprised, but Jesse grinned from ear to ear, dropped to one knee so he could be eye to eye with the child, and said, "Always! You can *always* be brutally honest with us."

After a deep sigh, the child turned and looked at the same bushes she had been staring at before and whistled a short tone with the pitch going higher at the end.

To their surprise, the thinnest, dirtiest little boy they had ever seen crawled out from under the bushes. He was so weak he could barely bring himself to his feet. There was no fear in his face, only a look of resignation as he watched his sister for his cue.

Jesse immediately recognized that face of sorrow. He instantly felt exactly what the boy was feeling as it all came flooding back to him in a tidal wave of emotions. The deep sorrow, exhaustion, and malnutrition, mirrored the lack of hope he felt during those first months of prison. There was nothing left to fear because the worst had already happened. He would never see his family again, and he was locked into an existence of lack: lack of food, lack of warmth, lack of loving family, lack of any kind of comfort, and worst of all, lack of protection, for in that prison, he could be both beaten and sexually abused and no one on this earth cared. And now, there he was, standing right in front of himself, in the body of another child.

Jesse ran to the emaciated boy and scooped him up in his arms. With the child's head on his shoulder he whispered in his ear "It's ok. Everything is going to be ok now." He didn't trust himself to say anything else, or to look at Sarah as he limped through the grass toward the gazebo. If Sarah wasn't comfortable with taking this child, he would find a way to repay her later, but there was no way he was turning his back on this starving and exhausted boy who reminded him of himself in that stone cold prison.

If Sarah begrudged the ticket she purchased for the boy, she didn't show it, as the four of them boarded the boat without speaking. Jesse looked for a place for them to sit down, and pointed to a space near the front of the boat. Sarah maneuvered the child to the seat next to the wall and sat down beside her, shielding the little girl from contact with any other passenger.

Jesse just needed some space to regroup. He was breathing long deep breaths in an attempt to hold back his overwhelming emotions, while he paced the floor with the boy lying as still as a corpse on his shoulder. He kept rubbing the child's back, not certain whether it was to comfort the boy or himself, and noticed he could clearly feel each of the boy's ribs, a fact that only deepened his sorrow.

Finally his arms began to tire, and he took a seat on the opposite end of the boat from Sarah. As he sat down, he twisted the boy around and placed him on his lap so he could look into his face. Dear God in Heaven, what had this child been through? He was so gaunt his head looked too big for his body, and he was little more than a skeleton underneath the thin shirt he was wearing. Jesse wanted desperately to take him out of the hell he was in, and knowing he wasn't in the position to arrange for that to happen made his heart actually, physically hurt.

He ran his hands down over the boy's arms and felt nothing but bones and cold, the boy was so deeply, deeply cold. Jesse took off his coat and wrapped it around the boy, pulling the collar up to warm his ears.

Benji locked eyes with Jesse and for just an instant Jesse saw a flash of something unrecognizable pass over his face, then he said, "Where's my sister?"

"She's right over there with Sarah," Jesse said, indicating the direction of the two of them. Benji looked over at his sister and then back. With eyes devoid of emotion, he stared into Jesse's face as if he could see clear into his soul, then got off his lap and walked away.

The boat ride was uneventful for the most part, and took the better part of the day to complete. Sarah seemed comfortable having the two children beside her, so Jesse kept his distance. Neither female wanted him too close by, and the boy seemed just as wary, so he decided to wander around and look at the scenery.

It was the first time in his life he had seen a river, and he was captivated by it. His mother had forbidden him to go anywhere close to the docks where the men worked, so he had had an image of the river being something very dangerous, like having a 30 foot cliff, or raging waters that reached out like a rope to snatch little boys off the riverbanks, dragging them to their death.

But this was quite nice. The water was very peaceful and calm and it seemed to be just what the doctor ordered after all he had been through in the past few days. There appeared to him to be surprises at every turn of the winding waterway. Birds he had never seen, the vast varieties of trees, open fields and yet mountains so high and so close to the river he felt he was bumping into the center of them. And the joyous colors! Only someone who had spent years in prison looking at drab grey and khaki, could appreciate all the fantastic colors of the fallen leaves, the shiny, thick, green leaves of the Rhododendron, and the deep, deep green of the pines. It was as if, having been blind his entire life; he had just regained his sight, and found himself devouring all the different shapes, smells, and colors in the world hungrily.

But what soothed him the most was the water. Calm and ever flowing, they were traveling along at a relaxed pace and he found it to be very healing. Water was easily scooped up in his hand, and yet it was strong enough to support this massive boat and carry it along in complete silence. And oh, how he did love the silence. Oh, there were the soft murmurings of private conversations going on behind him, but not the shouting of his father, nor the screams and arguments he had heard from his jail cell. Never had he experienced this feeling of safety, in this wonderful, peaceful silence.

He turned and looked at Sarah sitting there with the children and unwrapping the sandwiches she had purchased from the vender. She lifted one to him as an offer, but knowing there weren't enough sandwiches for everyone, he just shook his head. He watched the children eat hungrily and realized that Sarah, herself, was not eating and admired a woman who could give that selflessly. He knew they would be fine. She had the money to care for them, at least until she could find them a home. And without him along, her money would go even further. He felt a twinge of guilt over adding the boy to her burden without discussing it with her, but he hadn't forced her to buy him a ticket! Of course the girl would not have come without the boy, but…

He turned back around, and with his elbows on the rail, looked back at the banks of the Little Kanawha River for the peace he had been feeling before his thoughts ran away with him. He had only been a free man for about three days, and although his life had gotten a great deal more complicated since he met the woman, he was feeling lighthearted and free.

Maybe he was beginning to understand what the men were talking about all around him in the prison, and he needed to think about his attitude toward women. It occurred to him that they just might be a lot more trouble than they appeared, but so alluring, that a man could not help himself

CHAPTER THREE

Just as the sun began to burn him through his shirt, the boat slipped into the shade of massive trees whose limbs hung heavily over the river. He thought the shade to be more pleasant than the sun at this one particular moment of cool reprieve, but at first he couldn't see the fish as well as he could when the sun was beating down on him. However, once his eyes adjusted, he discovered there were actually more sights visible to him in the shade.

"Over there!" someone shouted from behind him. He turned to see men, women and children running to the starboard side of the boat, pointing and shouting at something he couldn't see.

"What is it?" he asked young woman holding a baby on her left hip while using her right hand to shade her eyes.

"A bear! Right on the edge of the water!" She pointed and he tried to follow her cues to find the location of the animal.

His first problem was that he had never actually seen a real bear, and from the many books his mother had brought him from the nearby library, he had assumed they were the size of a small child, certainly bigger than dogs, but about half the size of a full grown man. He held this belief until the enormous boulder he had been focusing on reared up on its hind feet and roared mightily through its cavernous red mouth, and bared teeth.

"I think we surprised him," the captain said. "He had his head down drinking when we rounded the bend, and I think we just snuck up on him. Boy, he's mad as a hornet, though! Just look at 'im!"

The women pulled their children away from the rail protectively and a man with animal pelts slung over his shoulder shouted, "Don't worry ladies, he ain't boardin' the boat!" He turned to the men around him laughing loudly. Clearly, the comment was more to impress his cronies than to comfort the women.

The captain motioned to one of his crewmen who turned and went inside, and said, "Don't be too sure of that. If he charged us there is no tellin' what might happen." The crewman appeared with a muzzle loaded musket ready to shoot if necessary. "Excuse me, excuse me," the captain said to the crowd in front of him. "I just want to get this man to a place where he can get a clear shot if necessary."

One well-dressed gentleman with a pocket watch secured with an expensive watch fob, stepped forward and asked, "What kind of bear is that, sir?"

"It is a black bear," the captain answered. "They are thick in these Virginia woods."

"How much do you think that bear weighs?" His voice showed the respect he held for the size of the animal.

"Oh, I'd guess two to three hundred pounds. He's standing about six feet tall would be my guess. In the summer he'll weigh probably closer to four or five hundred pounds I'd figure. But he has been hibernating I'm sure, so he is down in his weight some."

"I was not aware that bears awakened from hibernation in the dead of winter, sir! Would something have frightened him out of his sleep?"

The captain laughed out loud, "Oh, I don't think there is anything out there that could scare a bear out of anything! But sometimes when it is unseasonably warm, like it has been this winter, they will stir and come out and wander around for a while." Although the captain appeared to be engaging in idle conversation, his eyes were clearly focused on the bear.

"If he charges," the captain ordered his crewman, "fire one shot into the air. If that doesn't scare him off, shoot to kill." As if on cue, the bear charged, splashing his front feet in the water, more as an intimidation tactic than an actual attack. BOOM! The first shot was effective in driving away the bear as well as the entire passenger load, had they had anywhere else to go. The bear turned and ran up three or four leaps up the river bank and then slowly disappeared into the thick underbrush between the trees, leaving a well entertained group behind.

Thanks, Lloyd! Jesse thought to himself as he remembered his words about the safety of traveling on water. He was glad he had listened to what he had to say, and grateful for the man's input. His father could have been helpful to him as well, had he not been a drunk. As those memories flooded back, he felt his new found joy turning into the bitter resentment he had lived with for so long.

Suddenly, he remembered Sarah's willingness to put her past in a trunk, label it, "those who are behind me," and move on. He decided that just like he learned from Lloyd, he would learn from Sarah as well, choose a new name, and become a new man. Making decisions as to what kind of human being he would want to be was a new experience for him, but right now, with nothing to do until the boat came to a town, it seemed like a good time to think about those things.

He knew for a fact he could never hurt a woman or a child, but so far that was the only proven element of his character. He knew he could kill a man, and almost did again this morning, so that was something he would watch out for. He vowed he would never again allow his temper to go unchecked, and not only because he would surely be returned to prison, but because it was wrong, and he knew it was wrong. He guessed he knew it was wrong to beat his father to death, although the years of pent up frustration, and the image of his mother lying there on the floor, injured, was enough to... *Stop!* He said to himself as he brought his hands up top of his head. *I'm not going to waste time thinking about 'those who are behind me,' anymore!* He was perilously close to spiraling down that road to the past that had haunted him night after night, day after day for so many years. He wanted to, and needed to let go if only to preserve his sanity.

Instead of carrying a head full of sorrow, he decided he was going to fill his thoughts with everything beautiful he saw and heard. He sat down and leaned against the wall, his head back, resting on the rail. He thought about his gratitude for Lloyd and his hospitality, his good advice, and the delicious meal Juanita prepared for him. He remembered her colorful clothes and that smile that lit up the room, and decided those would be his first memories. From now on, his life began in Lloyd's house, eating Juanita's fine cooking.

He was stirred from his thoughts by the slowing of the boat. People were up and milling about, looking for their children, gathering luggage, and saying their farewells to their new friends. He pushed his way to the front of the boat where he found Sarah and the two children standing and watching for him.

"Could I have your attention, please?" The passengers stopped their chatter and turned toward the captain. "We have gone as far as you can go on this boat," he continued. "We are at Creston, Virginia, so if that is your destination, please be sure you have all your parcels and watch your step as you go ashore." The chatter arose again as he repeated the announcement, although no one could hear what he was saying by then.

The captain waited until the line formed and gave the signal for the crewmen to put the ramp in place for the passengers. "For those of you wanting to continue your trip, please… "

"What? What is he saying? I can't make it out!" Sarah shouted above the crowd.

"I don't know. I just know there is a way to continue traveling if you want to, but I can't hear what he is saying about it."

"Let's wait until the crowd dissipates and we shall go ask him!" Sarah shouted again.

All Jesse heard was the part about waiting, but that was fine with him. Having no idea where you're going sure does reduce your sense of urgency.

When the bulk of the people had gone, Jesse and Sarah had a moment to talk. "I do not want to stay here," Sarah said simply.

"Oh, good. I don't either," was Jesse's reply.

Neither had given their reasoning, and neither asked as was their agreement. But for Sarah there were too many men there. The group of rowdy trappers had gotten off the boat in this town, as well as several soldiers, and she had no intentions of being stranded where she had to face them even once, and there was no way she could survive in a town where she had to deal with them repeatedly. She would live in constant fear. No, better the next town she didn't know than the one she did.

Jesse was still making his escape, and he didn't want to live in a town where all those people had seen him beating that man, and had watched him travel the river with them. He knew that if the law did catch up with him, it would be because of his leg and the easy mark of identification his limp would provide them. Unfortunately, anyone watching him struggle to keep his footing on deck would have a memory of that event etched on their minds forever, especially since they knew he was the man who had saved the little girl.

As they stood there, lone passengers on a very large, very empty boat, the captain came up to them and asked if they were interested in going farther. "Yes, sir," Jesse said. "But how would we go about that?"

"Well there are a couple of ways you could go," the captain said patiently. "You could buy some horses here and go by land, or those fellers over there have a small bateau they will take up that way if you want to go by water."

Sarah had no intentions of running into a bear, and Jesse had never been on a horse in his life. Sarah nodded as she looked up at Jesse, feeling certain they agreed on their next step, and said, "So, do you want to go on?"

"Yes," he confirmed. They guided the children off the boat in what appeared to be the picture of any other family. Sarah, with the girl beside her, and Jesse walking with the boy, went toward the two men beside the small boat.

Apparently, the word "bateau" meant "push boat." It was a little flat boat, almost like a raft, that men stood up on, and used poles to stick down into the ground beneath the shallow water, and literally push the boat upstream to the destination. They had four crates nailed to the center of the boat for passengers to sit on, which Jesse did before they began. He wasn't afraid of walking on a boat with sides on it, and a rail to hold on to. But he wasn't about to attempt walking on this flat boat and falling off, because getting wet at nightfall just didn't seem like a smart idea.

By the time they got to the end of the line, it was getting dark, and the two children had long since fallen asleep. He and Sarah had decided the first thing they would do was find a church where they could leave the children in capable hands, and then they would rent a room for the night. They had decided to stay in the same room. Even Sarah had to admit it was safer for her to have him near. He had given his word he would sleep on the floor.

As the bateau slipped out of site, they turned to find nothing but darkness in front of them. They climbed the river bank and found a few tents, glowing with lantern light. Jesse walked up to one of the tents, cleared his throat loudly and said politely, "Excuse me." He was welcomed with the barrel of a gun slipping out between pieces of canvas, and a woman's voice saying roughly, "State your business!"

"We just arrived," Sarah said, hoping to disarm the holder of the weapon. "And we are looking for a place to spend the night. Is there a hotel, or a boarding house somewhere?"

The woman in the tent must have decided Sarah was harmless, dropped her bead on them, and emerged from the tent. She was less than five feet tall but wiry and gave the distinct impression that she was not to be messed with. The hard lines in her face were softened with the laugh she was getting out of Sarah's request. "A hotel! Here? Well, not yet, little Missie!"

"There are some homes around closer to Pine Bottom that might rent you a room for the night, but I figger they've all settled in. The Braxton's might still be up. They got eleven kids and I don't think they got room for 'em all to sleep at once! If you want to go, I can have my man drive you up there since you got them kids and all."

"That would be wonderful," Sarah replied with a smile. "Is it far?"

"Naw! Just up Leafbank! Give him a minute to hitch up Doc."

"Doc?" Jesse couldn't imagine what animal would be called, "Doc."

"Yea, he's our mule. Call him Doc 'cos my husband's back hurt him for twenty-three years. The day we got that mule, Jeb leaned over to pick up his shovel and that mule kicked him clean through the wall!" She laughed with unexpected joy, considering it was her husband who had been injured. "Got up the next day, and Jeb was dancin' a jig! His back ain't hurt him since. Ole Doc here is the only doc in town, too!"

Jeb emerged from the tent, pulling up his pants by the suspenders. As he hooked them over his shoulders, he grabbed his hat from the wooden box beside the fire, and said, "Follow me!"

He entered the shed and patted old Doc on the rear. "Yea, I'm back here you old son of a bitch! So don't you be gettin' ornery on me!" He grabbed a contraption from a nail on the wall, and slipped it over the mule's nose. Sarah had never seen anything like it. It seemed to be small homemade halter/bridle sort of contrivance that had the reigns already attached to it. In all her years of riding, she had never seen anything quite like that. It was incredibly easy to put on and worked most effectively.

He then placed a harness around the shoulders of the animal with one swift motion, and proceeded to lift what looked like a large fan with two long handles, off nails on the other side of the shed. With one hand, he pulled the large fan around the back of the mule while the other hand was busy patting the rear of the animal in the hopes that it would not kick. He snapped the two handles into the holes in the harness, grabbed the lantern and turned old Doc to walk out of the shed.

"Hop on!" the old man said, as he threw his leg over the mule and mounted it. "Grab those blankets and spread them out on the travois there. It'll hold you!"

"Get one or two more of them blankets and cover up with 'em. They ain't purty, but they're real warm. Them kids there look like they's all skin and bones. Should fatten 'em up some if you want 'em to make it through the winter's here. Although this winter ain't been bad a'tall."

As they plodded along, Jeb spoke of the blessings an unexpected warm December had on old bones, and offered the problems that came with it as well, such as the inability to "keep meat froze." The muddy road at the river and in the camp where the grass had been worn away soon turned into pleasant traveling along fairly even land. After a day of being confined to the deck of a boat, Jesse enjoyed walking. In fact, he could not remember the last time he had the freedom to walk, and walk, and walk wherever he wanted to go. His stomach growled with hunger, and he had no idea what tomorrow would bring, but tonight he was a feeling blessed, walking along side ole Doc and looking at the moon, and thoroughly enjoying the simple freedoms others took for granted.

Even Sarah fell asleep from the rocking rhythm of the mules' pace. It was completely dark when they pulled up to the Braxton's house, but Jeb assured them that the Braxtons never turned children away, and if they would just knock, the house would "light up like wildfire."

Sarah awakened the children and removed the warm blankets from them; Jeb was right, they were incredibly warm. Jeb walked the mule ahead of them and turned it around, then stopped and said, "You can keep them blankets. Them youngin's gonna need 'em worser than we do." He waved his hand behind him as he rode off without looking back.

"Keep them here," Jesse said as he watched Sarah wrap the children against the cold once again. "I'll go knock on the door.

Just in case everyone around here greets folks with a rifle, I don't want the children down there."

"Alright," Sarah said, and then without thinking, added, "Be careful." Oh, why did she say that? It was something a wife would say, and she had no intentions of ever being a wife again. She made a mental note not to get carried away with playing that role with this man. She had to be aware, every minute of every day, of exactly what she was doing, and not fall back into the comfortable trap of relying on a man for anything. She thought about speaking to him about what she had said, and then thought that would be worse. She must remember not to let herself be that careless again.

Jesse wished he had a lantern as he scooted his feet along the path in an effort to remain upright. The last thing he needed was to turn an ankle. Finally he connected with the heavy wooden steps that led up to the front door, held onto the rail as he climbed the steps, then crossed the immense porch and stood in front of the door. He wasn't happy about waking a family of thirteen, but it had to be done, so he made a fist, held it in midair until he could gather his courage, and knocked sharply three times.

No response.

He knocked again and turned to see Sarah's reaction, but he couldn't make her out in the dark shadows.

Again, he knocked and Sarah shouted, "I don't think there's anyone home!"

"I think you're right," he shouted back. He stepped to the left and looked through a window that opened into the living room. There was no fire in the fireplace. To the right of the door was a window that went into a bedroom that was also empty. For a brief moment he considered breaking into the house, building a fire in the fireplace and disappearing into one of those big feather beds for the night, but thought instead, "What kind of a man do I want to be?" He considered the possibility of starting to build his new character first thing in the morning, but something in his heart told him he did not want to add breaking and entering to his list of offenses, even if he didn't get caught. He turned back toward

Sarah and shouted, "There is nobody here! We are going to have to move on, find some place that will turn weather and hole up for the night."

"But where are we going to go?" She was understandably upset, but appreciated the fact that he didn't even suggest they break in. It bolstered her hope that he was a trustworthy man.

"Well, first things first. I'm goin' lookin' for the outhouse," Jesse shouted in the hopes that she would take that as a cue not to follow him around back of the house.

"Me, too," Benji said as he trotted after Jesse. He didn't mind goin' in front of his sister, but he wasn't going to in front of this strange lady.

"Well, we are not staying here alone!" Sarah said. "Let's go together and we will all wait our turns." She didn't want to mention the bear, but it was on all their minds and they all felt safer as a group. As they crossed the creek on the tiny boards that were a makeshift bridge, they were extremely careful not to get their feet wet. It was slow work, and hearing the trickle of the water didn't help the situation. The children agreed they could both go in together, and then after what seemed like an eternity they both came out.

Sarah was next and the brief thought of using the outdoor john as a shelter quickly left her mind after sitting in there for a minute. The smell was "horble" as the girl put it. She smiled at the memory of the first time she had heard that word, and then thought, *Was that only this morning that all that happened? It seemed like years!*

As she came out and shut the door, twirling the small oval shaped piece of wood held onto the door frame with a single nail, around at an angle so as to lock the door, Jesse stepped out of the woods where he had relieved himself. "All done?"

"All done!" they chimed in unison.

"Well, where should we go from here?" Jesse asked.

"Sarah, what are your thoughts?"

"Well, I don't know…"

"I know," the little girl volunteered. To her surprise, both adults looked at her as if she were someone who might have something to say, making her feel very important. "The last place you want to be in the middle of the night is beside a road. No tellin' whose gonna come along. I think we should head up where the creek is comin' from. That way, we can stay near the creek for drinking water, and we won't wander off and get lost. And maybe we will be able to see a town or sompthin' from up there."

Sarah and Jesse looked at each other with surprise. "Now that is a good idea, Sissy! I'm glad we have you along," Jesse said. Without realizing it, he had called her "Sissy," the nickname he had used for his little sister so many years ago.

The girl rolled her eyes behind them at the silly name, as she led Benji up the trail. The moon had come out from behind the clouds so the going was a little easier. They kept climbing, in the hopes of finding another house, or a small cove where they could sit or lie down away from the steep banks of the creek. Although neither of them voiced it, both Jesse and Sarah had grown up in large cities, and both felt foolish for assuming there would be anything less than a city, with city conveniences, such as hotels and diners, awaiting them at the end of their trip.

It had begun to rain, and Sarah was glad they were climbing above the little creek. She had never actually seen a flash flood, but she had heard enough to make her want to avoid being in that position. As she now led the group up hill, she kept her eyes on her feet to be certain she didn't step on a rock that would turn and send her sprawling. After several minutes of stumbling through the trees, Sarah looked up, and stopped suddenly, when she saw trees and dried leaves, surrounding a huge gaping black hole, like a mustache and beard around a very large open mouth.

"What is that?" she said to Jesse who was now behind Sissy, carrying Benji on his shoulders. As he stood Benji down on the ground, he quickly passed Sarah and went on to investigate. For a brief moment, he disappeared into the darkness: then stepped out waving his hand and shouting, "Come on in! It's a cave! It's not cozy, but it's a cave nonetheless." The floor of the cave dropped down a bit and then up again to the wall. Scattered along the floor of the cave were the remnants of old fires. The stones used to make one fire pit had been moved around when an attempt was made to scatter the ashes, but there was some dry wood left that hadn't completely burned, so they were encouraged.

The children began to explore while Jesse repaired the stone ring and arranged the fire wood, smallest on the bottom, like he had set the fires for his mother's wood cook stove, and Sarah began to dig through her satchel for her Lucifers. This was one of the first things she had thought about packing when making her plans, and was happy when her hand made contact with the small tin box she had filled with them. She found comfort in knowing no matter where she went, or what happened to her, she could keep herself from freezing to death if she had those magical sticks that burst into flame when struck on almost anything. She hated the smell they made, but that was a small price to pay for the comfort and security of a warm fire.

As they gathered around the fire wondering about the age and use of this cave, they began to notice the markings on the cave wall and ceiling. Theirs was not the first fire by far, and as they began to explore, they found at least five distinct patches of soot as evidence of prior use. Over closer to what appeared to be the other end of the cave, the wall was completely covered with soot, making both Benji and Jesse very curious.

Jesse carefully picked up a burning stick and carried it over to peer behind the huge boulder under the left side of the opening. He had to duck, but there was a separate room back there, hidden by the enormous stone. Building a fire on the ground under all that soot, afforded those in the hidden room privacy and safety from animals. Although not ideal because of the water trickling in on one side from overhead, it was much safer from predators than the yawning gap of the overhang.

Jesse decided there would be enough room for Sarah and the children to sleep in there without getting wet, and he would stay out by the main fire. He would get more of the wind, but as soon as the stone heated up a little bit, he thought it would be warm enough wedged between the fire and the cave wall.

He returned to the fire and realized as his own stomach growled, how hungry the children must be. He had no idea how to feed even himself, let alone all these other people, and wished he had left the company of Sarah and had gone on his own before all this happened. Alone he could have sought out work somewhere until he found out the lay of the land. He realized now that traveling with a woman and children was a hindrance he could ill afford, but leaving would not be easy. He would see to it that they were safe and settled before going, but a deal was a deal, and he had only promised her one day.

CHAPTER FOUR

The cave kept the rain off them if they stayed in the back of it, but for shelter, that was all it offered. The wind whipped in through the open mouth of the cave, threatening, not only to blow out the fire, but to scatter the logs and ashes as well. Jesse decided he would spend most of the night making sure the fire didn't go out, because if a bear came by, he wanted to see it before it saw him.

"I found a place for you and the children to sleep," he said. "Over behind that boulder is a perfect place for the three of you. You will have to be careful not to get under that drip, but if you can manage that, you should all fit. I will build another fire at the entrance of that little room and you should be quite comfortable."

But Sarah had other ideas. While he built the small fire, she picked up another stick with a big enough flame to last while she made up the children's beds. "Come on children; let's get you down for the night." And upon her return, Jesse encountered a completely different woman.

"You and I need to settle some things," Sarah said bluntly in the loudest whisper possible.

"SHALL we be brutally honest?" He replied mockingly, completely unaware of what was bothering her, and irritated with her sudden change of attitude.

"You seemed very happy to leave me with those two children all day and then again to pack them off with me tonight, leaving them completely in my care. Well, in case you haven't noticed, these are not my children. And as much as you would like to think I will take them under my wing like a mother hen just because I am a woman, I will not! Yesterday I didn't have a clue as to who you were, and I still don't know you other than you call yourself Jesse, and now you are handing me full responsibility for the two children *we* brought here!"

"Well, at least Jesse is my REAL name!" he shouted back in an even louder whisper!

She wanted to scream at him and go off and find her own cave, but reason brought her back to her senses. "One argument at a time, if that's alright with you! We are discussing those children and what is to become of them. I did my part in saving them from the city, but the point remains I am not going to get caught because of them. And you are *not* leaving me with those children, as if they are only *my* responsibility!"

"What do you think I can do with them? At least you have money! When we get to town, you can buy them breakfast! I have *nothing* to offer them!" He was pleased with himself for presenting his argument so effectively that she was suddenly dumbstruck; clearly an amateur's mistake.

When she finally did speak, her words were so slow and deliberate, she actually sounded a little lethal, "So you don't deny that you were planning on leaving them with me?"

Uh, oh.

She turned her back on him, knelt and began digging through her bag again. He hoped she didn't have a gun in there, 'cos if she did, he was about to get shot. Without speaking, she pulled out a long dress and two petticoats, sat down by the fire, wedged her satchel behind her, knowing full well that the stone was cold all the way through, and would only make her colder as the night wore on, and proceeded to cover her legs and shoulders with the more than ample clothing.

Oh, yea. He should have listened more closely to the men in the prison. He had a strong feeling he should say or do something, but he had no idea what. Instead, he turned to look out the opening of the cave. It was about fifteen to twenty feet high and the downpour of rain dripping from the top rim of the cave created a sort of curtain of water, like being behind a waterfall. As he stood there looking out, he felt as if he had gone from one prison to another, the brief illusion of freedom far too fleeting.

Through the pitter patter of rain, he heard something that sounded like a kitten mewing. "Meew." He so doubted his hearing that he turned to see if Sarah were reacting at all. She furrowed her brow and sat up, turning her head in effort to hear. "Meew," the muffled sound came so softly that neither was sure they had heard anything and looked at each other with confusion on their faces.

"What was that?" Jesse asked as he headed toward the children to see if they were alright.

Sarah threw her dresses back and stood up, brushing the shale off the back of her skirt. "Maybe one of the children is crying," she said as she followed him into the smaller room. Jesse got there first but stepped aside to allow Sarah to enter. The room was lit with the fire they had built outside the door and there between Benji and Sissy was the tiniest, weakest little human being either of them had ever seen.

"Is that a baby?" Sarah screamed! "Where did you get that?" The girl was certainly too young to have given birth, and besides they had been traveling together all day and there was no baby! "Where did you get that?" Sarah screamed again. But without waiting for an answer, she shouted, "Did you *find* that in *here*?" She was in shock and babbling. This was not happening. Finally she was ready for an explanation. She breathed deeply and said, "Where did this infant come from?"

Sissy lifted her head as if daring Sarah to hit her. "She's mine," she said unapologetically.

One look at Benji's face and she knew his loyalties were with the girl, and he had no intentions of being forthcoming.

"Alright, get the baby wrapped up, and let's all move out by the fire and we'll talk about this."

Jesse went out and looked for more firewood. There was only one more log and it looked too big to catch from this little fire, but he threw it on in the hopes that it might light. As he turned it around he discovered the side was burned out of it, and realized he was not the first to try to burn this monster.

The four of them sat facing the fire, exhausted, yet vibrating with tension. Sarah tried to be welcoming as she looked at Sissy and said, "Alright now Sissy. Why don't you start by explaining the presence of this infant?"

"My name ain't Sissy, so stop callin' me that!"

"Alright then, what *is* your name?" Sarah asked with sweetness dripping off her lips in an attempt to hide her fury.

The girl wouldn't speak, but Benji said, "Tell 'em, Oddy!" Silence.

"Is that it? Oddy?" Sarah asked as she bent over and tried to make eye contact with her, though the child's hair covered her face as she looked down at her feet.

"Oddy'll do," she said dryly.

"Ok, Oddy. We need to know where you got that baby," Jesse stated the truth in the hopes that it would be straightforward enough for her.

"It's mine," she repeated.

"'It's mine' because you stole it? 'It's mine' because you found it in this cave? 'It's mine' because it is your little sister and you weren't as brutally honest as you led us to believe? What do you mean, it is yours? And when did you intend to tell us about it?" Sarah was almost screaming now.

"One argument at a time," Oddy said slowly and deliberately. "Ain't them your rules, Miss *Sarah*?"

The way she accented her name told them Oddy was quite aware now that Sarah was not her real name. Jesse and Sarah glanced at each other in embarrassment. They should have been certain the children were asleep before discussing their problems.

"Alright. Where did you get that baby?" If Oddy wanted to play by the rules, so be it.

Strangers to Grace

"It's mine," Oddy started, but when she saw the frustration on their faces she added, "I birthed her."

"YOU birthed her? How old are you?" Sarah asked.

"Thirteen I think. Fourteen the day after Christmas."

The prolonged silence that followed her confession gave Oddy ample time to begin fearing they might get angry and leave her there for allowing so many lies to come between them, and they might even take Benji. It was just them against her and they could do whatever they wanted to do with her. She thought maybe they were finding it hard to believe she was old enough to have a child, and said, "We're little 'cos they din't feed us nothin'. Benji is almost ten, but he don't look it. And I done the best I could with this little sprite, but she just won't grow none," Oddy said sadly, clearly carrying the weight of the world on her shoulders.

"How old is she?" Sarah's compassion was replacing her anger. What ungodly events had happened to this child? Even fourteen was far too young to have a baby.

"Well, me and Benji runned away the night before school started. We waited 'til they gave us our new school shoes and clothes, and we runned off that night. We got into a train car to wait for mornin' so's we could tell 'em we were there for th'Orphan Train. But we didn't wake up until it was too late."

"Had you had the baby by then?"

"No. I kept the days by measuring Sunday church bells. It was four Sundays and a few days later that I got real sick. I had no idea what was happening to me, so I made Benji go down to the river until the next morning 'cos I din't want him to see me die. And then after a time there was a baby. I done the best I could with it, but I din't think it was mine. I kept waitin' for someone to come get it and take it from me. But no one never did come, so, then I figgered it was mine."

They sat in silence as they let the dust settle. There was a lot to think about. Finally Jesse broke the silence, "So, you had this baby with you all day? And we didn't know it?"

"Yes, sir!" Oddy smiled, "I had her right here under my cape the whole time, just a suckin' away at my teets! She had messed the inside of my cape real bad, but me and Benji cleaned it up when we was goin' in the outhouse."

As they sat there staring into the campfire they all realized through their exhaustion that it was too late to ask all the questions, and there were no answers to be had anyway, so they all went back to bed, welcoming the reprieve from having to find solutions to their troubles… at least for the night.

The next morning they awakened tired, cold, and extremely hungry. Sarah had already made a trip into the woods and was rolling her clothes up to put in her bag when Oddy and Benji came out and headed for the woods. Jesse had broken up the fires and spread the ambers so a new fire wouldn't start up after they had gone. But everyone was too numb, too tired, and too hungry to say anything, so they organized and left without a word.

Sarah walked out first, stood with her hands on her hips, looked to the left and headed around the cave and up the side. She was hoping to be able to see the town from the top of the hill they were climbing, and everyone else just followed without question. At one point Benji turned around and looked back at the hill they had climbed and shouted, "Look! You can't even tell there is a cave back there!" It was true. Had they been traveling the other way, they would have walked straight over the top of the entrance and fallen twenty feet without even seeing the opening, something they all needed to remember if they came back that way. They all turned at once and continued their climb.

Nobody wanted to ask where they were going, because they all knew there was no answer for that. They just kept walking over one, two, and three small hills, and slowly, just when they thought it couldn't get any worse, it started to snow, making the leaves wet and slippery. *What next?* Jesse thought as he kept putting one foot in front of the other. *And what are we going to do when we get to wherever we sleep tonight?* Both he and Sarah were thinking about the mess they had made of their big plans to escape, and Sissy was not pleased either.

The snow was pounding down on them now, a snow so heavy you could actually hear it hitting the dry leaves that were

Strangers to Grace

still hanging on the trees. They had to find shelter or hopefully a family that would take them in for the night. Jesse stopped to see if he could locate the telltale smoke of a fire anywhere now that they had climbed to the top and could see pretty far. There was no smoke, but he thought he had seen a small shack or barn in the distance. As he turned to announce his findings, he saw that Benji had fallen far behind and ran to get him. "Come on!" he said as he scooped Benji up in his arms, "It isn't much farther! Right over there! Is that a cabin or something?"

They were encouraged by the sight and hurried with renewed determination to get to the shelter in front of them. It took a kick from Jesse, but the front door finally gave way and swung open, breaking the top hinge and allowing the door to swing awkwardly back against wall. "It's going to be ok now." He stood Benji down on the floor and went back to wedge the door shut tightly. As he rubbed his hands together to warm them up, he took inventory of the room he was in. This had been someone's home long ago! There was a fireplace that was made to cook in, a stack of dry wood and a badly broken chair in this main room. As he walked behind the fireplace he found old cupboards on the wall with their doors either gone or hanging at odd angles, like a mouthful of missing and crooked teeth.

To the left was what they discovered to be a bedroom. It was small, but there was enough room to walk around the bed, and there were nails on the wall at the foot of the bed to hang clothes.

"Could I have one of those Lucifers? I want to get a fire started," Jesse spoke directly to Sarah for the first time since their argument. Without speaking, she got into her bag and handed him one. "There's a bed in that room," he said tauntingly, "how 'bout the kids and I take it, and you sleep in here on the floor?" he asked her with a sneer on his face.

He had worked hard for the glare he received from her, and he enjoyed every minute of it. He lit the fire and blew softly to get it burning. He wished he had some paper to burn in order to heat up the chimney so it would draw, but he didn't, so he just kept fanning until the flames were self-sustaining. The wood was dry...

49

too dry. So although he was happy it caught so quickly, he knew it would burn up just as fast, so he would have to break up the chair to burn, and even that wouldn't last all night. He would have to go out later to see what he could find.

"Hey, look what I found!" Sarah shouted, "I found a gallon jug half full of dried beans! If we can find a pot, we will have dinner!" That bit of information sent all four of them scrambling noisily to find a pot. Apparently, this cabin had been used upon occasion. There was the large jug of beans, a small cast iron pot and a larger one, a coffee pot, a glass jar with coffee in it and another one filled with candles and Lucifers. There was a smaller jar with something bitter smelling in it which Sarah determined to be tea, and six tin coffee cups and plates, each with its own spoon.

Their spirits were lifted as they hurried to ready the bed and get the beans on, and before long the house felt downright homey. The baby was resting near the fire in a big pile of Sarah's dresses, exhausted from crying most of the day because of her sore bottom. Having been under the watchful eye of Sarah on the boat trip, Oddy hadn't the chance to clean the baby properly and she was now covered with painful little blisters. They had melted snow and warmed it so they could bathe her, and then placed her, naked onto Sarah's clothes with the baby blanket folded under her to prevent her from making a mess. The fresh air would help her bottom heal while the warmth of the fire would keep her warm.

The meal was as fine as any meal had ever been. After the long two days, they were starving and cold, and the beans met both those needs, rendering them exhausted and ready to relax. Oddy had gone out to fill another pan with snow and set it by the fire to melt, and the cool water was a perfect contrast to the hot beans while the adults enjoyed their coffee.

Each of them sat in silence as they stared at the fire, watching the snow fall outside the window as darkness fell, and it occurred to Sarah that although to an outsider they may look like a normal family enjoying a winter evening together, there was nothing normal about them. Each person in this room was living one day at a time, expecting nothing and needing nothing but enough food and warmth to get through the day. Tomorrow they might all go their separate ways, and none of them would care. In fact, Sarah thought the sooner they had the children placed in someone's care, the better. She could say her good-byes to Jesse and resume her journey to freedom. As she looked around the room, she decided not to dwell on the situation, stood and said, "Well, good night all. I'm going to bed," and went into the bedroom with a backwards smirk at Jesse.

"Come on, Benji, let's go to bed," Oddy said as she walked by the baby and followed Sarah into the room. Benji followed her into the room without even looking toward the baby, and shut the door behind him, which Sarah quickly reopened saying, "We have to leave the door open for the heat. Go hop in the bed beside Oddy and I will be right back."

Although she enjoyed having the upper hand as do most people, she was being unfair to Jesse, and knew there was no room in her bed for her rudeness. He was a good man, and in her heart she knew he was carrying his own burdens. Besides, being cruel to him was not going to repair the damage done to her by the previous men in her life.

"Jesse," she said softly as he looked at her. "I do appreciate the company as I travel, and how protective you are of the children. It is true that am angry with you for many things, but in all honesty, I need you to know that I see what a good man you are, and I appreciate that. I am still angry with you," she said with a hint of a smile, "but I do not want to be unfair."

"Thank you, Sarah," he said. He was actually surprised at her comment, as well as pleased. What a difference her kindness made in his mood this evening. He made a mental note to remember to tell people about the good in them, even those he felt no kindness toward.

He felt like he, the grown man, was now rearing the child inside him who never had anyone to guide him, and he was grateful for the lessons learned from Lloyd, Juanita, Jeb, and now Sarah.

She turned to go to bed, and he retrieved his socks from in front of the fireplace. They were now completely dry and warm on his feet, so he put on his shoes, got his jacket from a nail beside the door, and readied to go outside to find firewood. When he opened the door he was surprised to find nearly a foot of snow packed tightly against the door, and when he looked up into the sky he saw no end to the snow. He was grateful for the beans, the fireplace and the coffee, but he couldn't help worry about what they would eat tomorrow and wondered again what they had done by taking on the responsibility of the children.

CHAPTER FIVE

Before he went to sleep that night, he checked the baby. Her feet and fingers were cold so he covered her up and tucked her in, marveling at how tiny her little ears and fingers were. He remembered that the day his sister Sarah was born, she was much bigger than this baby and her cry was bigger still. The gentle mewing of this baby would never awaken him, so he drank several cups of coffee and a glass of water before bedding down. He might not awaken when the baby cried, or if the fire died and frost formed on his week old mustache, but there was no ignoring a full bladder.

He got as comfortable as he could on the hard wooden floor, turning this way and that in an attempt to keep his bones from bruising, but his belly was full and he was at least warm, so he reckoned he had a lot to be thankful for. He crowded out the hateful thoughts that crept into his mind whenever he was alone, by going over his daily recollection of things that brought him a smile. Again, he remembered Lloyd's hospitality, Juanita's colorful dress and fine cooking. He said a silent word of thanks to Lloyd for his good advice before going on to the memory of meeting Sarah and the boat ride. He decided to pick and choose his memories, like packing and unpacking for a trip. Surely, if he gave time only to the good memories, and trained his mind not to focus on the bad, he could change his way of thinking and put himself on the road to being a healthier man.

The sun hadn't come up yet when he reluctantly admitted he had to go outside. As he threw the covers back the cold air notified him that the fire had gone out, so he pulled on his boots and started the fire again. He decided to just leave his socks behind, grabbed his coat and shoved on his untied shoes to answer the call of nature, and made a mental note to check the fire and the baby again before he went to back to bed. But just as he touched the door knob, the baby began to stir. It'll be a minute before she wakes up hungry, so I will just go ahead quickly, he thought.

By the time he returned the baby was fully awake and doing her best to rouse the entire household. A little rest had gone a long way to making this baby stronger, and he smiled as he heard the loud commotion. "Oh, it's ok there little girl," he said as he picked her up. She felt to him like a tiny China doll, smaller than many newborns, but her little voice had grown from a kitten's mew, to a real baby's cry. He held her head and back in his left hand and her tiny butt in his right, and bounced her up and down as he went to the bedroom. He thought the cries would at least awaken the mother of the child, but when Oddy didn't come out, he stepped around the corner and slipped up beside the bed to find her.

He found Sarah sleeping on the right side, so he quietly made his way around the bottom of the bed and up the other side. He felt the top of the bed for heads and immediately touched someone's face. Benji sat up with a start. "Sorry, Ben. The baby needs her mother."

"She ain't here," Benji said.

"What do you mean, 'she ain't here?' Where could she possibly be?"

"She runned off, sir."

"She did what? When? When did she go?" Jesse was frantic. It was freezing out there and the snow was far too deep for her pitiful little shoes. Her legs would be frozen with that cape and dress riding up on the snow behind her like a sled.

"Sarah! Wake up! Take the baby, Oddy ran off!" Jesse left the room and the house pulling his coat on as he ran.

"What is going on, Benji?" Sarah struggled to sit up and pull the covers around herself and the baby.

"Oddy told me last night we was leavin'. She said you two was up to no good, that you din't even know each other 'til yesterday. She said you was runnin' from somethin' and she was afraid Jesse would come to her bed the way Mr. Dunge did. She wanted me to go, but I said I din't want to. She said, 'FINE!' and said I'd be ok here if I din't want to go. And she figgered the baby would be better off with you anyway, so she left off by herself."

"Benji, who is Mr. Dunge?" The thought of any man coming to the bed of a child sickened Sarah to the pit of her stomach. Whoever he is, he must be the father of this baby.

"He was the headmaster at th'orphnige, Ma'am." Benji just looked down at his hands making him look even more pitiful, and Sarah realized he had seen more misery in his short little life than most adults had.

Oh, what a mess they had made of things. Every word that boy said was like a knife in her heart. She knew by now, that God had completely given up on her, but she also knew he loved children because of the scriptures that told her so, so she began praying with all her might.

"God, I know I am not worthy to come begging favors, but I am not asking for myself. I am asking you to send angels to help this child, Lord. Keep her safe from predators, and most of all, Lord, don't let her fall over the cave entrance. Line your angels up, Lord, like a fence around that cave and keep her from falling over it. I am begging you, Lord; I am begging you on behalf of that child."

When she opened her eyes, Benji's face was covered with tears. His tough guy act dissolved as he threw his arms around her neck and cried, "I should'a went with her! I could'a kept an eye out for that cave!"

When would she learn that the children could hear her? She should have prayed silently. She must remember not to speak in anger or fear when the children were close by. "Oh Benji, you are not responsible for this. Oddy decided, on her own, to run away. You were smart to stay here. This is not your fault!" she said as she swayed back and forth rocking him and rubbing his back.

"But I stayed behind 'cos it's cold outside, and I am tired of bein' cold. I let my sister go out there alone because I din't wanna get cold."

"You are brother and sister? I didn't know that!" Again he sobbed, seeming to get more upset by the minute. Sympathizing with him seemed to make matters worse, so she decided to try the authoritarian approach. "Alright young man, you leave the worrying up to Jesse. He saved her once and he is determined to save her again. So I want you to lie down here, right next to me and go back to sleep. Maybe you will awaken with Oddy's cold fingers on your neck," she said smiling in order to soften the tone the conversation had taken. She lifted the covers and he snuggled down under them to wait.

Sarah knew Jesse and Oddy would be freezing when they got back, so she placed the baby beside Benji, slipped out from under the covers and put the water on to boil. It wasn't much, but the hot coffee and tea would at least be a beginning toward thawing them out. Shivering with cold, she returned to the bed, scooted down until she could get her shoulders under the blanket, then placed the baby, in her right arm, facing her, and eventually fell asleep.

Jesse's feet were freezing. Without the socks, his feet had nothing but cold leather against them, and his untied shoes were packed with the heavy wet snow and looked like two snow balls at the ends of his legs. He regretted having left the cabin to relieve himself earlier, without putting on his socks. He made a mental note never to leave the cabin again without being fully dressed, because nobody knew what might happen next. As he stumbled along, he thought he had gone across three hills, but he wasn't certain, so he decided to go down into the valley to see if he could find the Braxton's, and locate the cave from there. It was the only place he could think of that she might go. The problem was, the top of the cave was not only invisible to the naked eye, it was sloped, so by the time one realized where they were, it would be too late, especially with snow on the ground. He paused, trying to collect his thoughts, and keep his wits about him. He had to trust that he had crossed three hills, and assume he was above the cave.

He knew what he was planning was dangerous, but he had to try, because she might be lying in the ravine below the cave at this very moment, and that thought went through him like a knife. Running toward the cave as his instincts told him to do, was foolishness, so he decided to proceed carefully no matter how slow and frustrating his progress seemed. He dropped his head so he could pull his collar up around his ears, and with his arms crossed he headed down the hill, watching right in front of his feet for any indication that his next step might be straight into mid-air. When he looked up he discovered that within ten paces, he would be engulfed in a heavy, blinding, swirling fog, a phenomenon with which he was unfamiliar.

Clearly, to walk forward was to march to his death. There was no way he could progress any farther safely, and getting himself killed would not help anybody. His feet had almost stopped working, he couldn't see where he was going and she might be home by now for all he knew, so his new plan was to return to the cabin, warm up while putting on his socks, get one of the blankets to put around his head and shoulders and another to put around Oddy if he found her alive. He hated the thought, but he had little confidence in his abilities to survive in the outside world all by himself, let alone save another. He was painfully aware of his lack of skills in surviving this world, and wished someone else would have taken the children into their care.

As he tried to retrace his steps, he became a little alarmed that he couldn't clearly see his own footprints. Since they were on the top of a hill, the wind howled almost constantly and was blowing the snow across his tracks, erasing them almost the second he lifted his feet. "Calm yourself," he said to himself as he felt panic rising within him. "You have to keep your wits about you or you are going to get lost out here." The sound of his own voice made him feel a little more in control.

He noticed finally that although his footsteps were gone, there was a small continuous indentation in the snow, like the times he had dragged his finger through the sugar in his mother's sugar bowl. He quickened his pace as he became fearful the slight indentation might be erased by the wind as well and he would be completely lost. Fortunately, the sun was coming up making the shadows more severe, outlining his route home more clearly. But just as the cabin came in sight, the path he was following broke into two, one veering off to the left, and the other toward the cabin. It appeared that someone had walked this path and had gone behind the cabin instead of following it to the front door. Perhaps Ben had gone looking for Oddy, or maybe Sarah, so by now they may have two people lost. Tempting as it was to go inside and warm up, he needed to see where the path led, and was glad he did. It didn't go very far at all, in fact, it led rather quickly to an old outhouse. Banging on the door sharply he said, "Oddy?" Are you in there? Oddy?"

The door opened and a very ashamed little girl's face peered out. "Get out here," he shouted more angrily then he meant to. As she stepped out and he could see she was ok, he felt raw anger well up inside him. He had not asked for this. It was like prison all over again. He still had no freedom at all, with every decision being based on what was best for these children, knowing one mistake could even cost them their lives. "These children aren't even mine, so why am I taking care of them?" he shouted angrily. It wasn't that he didn't care about their welfare, he loved children, but did that mean he had to walk around in the woods in the middle of the night half frozen when he should be putting distance between himself and the prison?

His feet were numb now, so he extended his hand out to touch her shoulder and guide her into the house. In an instant, her arms went up to protect her face and she crouched to brace herself against the blow, but to her credit, she did not run. He withdrew his hand and stared in disbelief and pity. Her arms dropped, her legs straightened, and her face became the embodiment of defiance.

Strangers to Grace

He would have laughed had he not been so cold, and frustrated, and angry, and relieved, and shocked, and tired, and… "Get in the house!" he said with a calm that betrayed his real feelings.

"But I got to get the bean pot," Oddy said as if it were perfectly logical. Jesse just stood there staring at her, speechless, as she opened the door, entered the outhouse, and then emerged with the pot of beans from the night before. As she stepped out of the outhouse she set the hot cast iron pot down in the snow to pull her cape around her against the wind, and with a loud "POP" the pot broke in half, sending the beans oozing out onto the snow in a hiss of steam.

Both stood there in complete incredulity staring as the lid of the pot slid slowly down the slow moving volcano of bean lava. Slowly, Oddy lifted her eyes to Jesse's face to see if she could find a hint of what was going to happen next. He simply stepped back and waited for her to walk by him while he shook with anger.

They were met at the door by Benji, who threw his arms around his sister, snow and all. She was smiling down at him with rosy red cheeks as he asked, "Where did you go? Did'ja go all the way back down to the cave? We was scared you was gonna fall over the cliff!"

Jesse sat down on the floor with his bare feet facing the fire place, rubbing them in an attempt to get the blood flowing again, and held his socks up to the flame knowing that in just a few minutes he would have nice warm socks on his achingly cold feet.

The two children headed for the bedroom but Jesse shouted, "Just a minute you two!" He looked at them over his shoulder, "Get back here right now!" He turned around and saw the terror on their faces which angered him more, "Get over here!" and pointed to the floor beside him. "Sit!"

They sat down so close to each other they looked like one child. "Stop that! Stop cowering like I am going to beat you! I don't beat children, ya' got that?" Not surprisingly, that thunderous proclamation did nothing to ease their fears. Here was

59

this mad man screaming into their faces that he did not beat children, and even he realized it was counterproductive. He paused a minute to regroup as the children waited in silent dread. He remembered hiding under the bed when his father was angry, and vowed once again, never to frighten any children as his father had done.

"Ok, here is the deal. Did I hit you, Oddy, when you told me there was another child to take with us on our journey?" He waited for Oddy to shake her head. "Did I hit you when we discovered the baby? That little something you had failed to mention when you were being brutally honest with us?" Again, a no.

His eyes turned to Benji, "Ben, did I hit you this morning when you told me Oddy had run away?" Benji didn't take his eyes off Jesse as his head turned slowly left and right. By now the entire scene had just become comical to Jesse and he turned back to the fireplace grinning, he knew he had lost his edge because he had lost his anger.

Oddy was the first to speak, "So. . . ?"

"So what?" Jesse replied.

"Ain't this where you tell us you never wanted us in the first place and that we need to get goin'? Or that you are leavin' us here and goin' off on your own? Well, you can't leave us with her 'cos she don't want us neither. So…" she folded her arms and said, "go on, tell us what you're gonna do about it."

Sarah was listening from the other room and had to admit she found this interesting and a little amusing. She thought briefly, that she should go in to help Jesse, but the baby was still asleep in her arms, and she was warm and toasty, and besides, she wanted to hear what Jesse would say.

Jesse thought about what he wanted to communicate to these children, took a deep breath and said, "All I was going to say was that, after us going to all the trouble of saving you and bringing you out of that hell hole, you ran off and caused even more trouble! Why didn't you talk to us or at least Sarah about all this? Running away only caused more problems, it didn't solve anything!"

"Well, why are you runnin' then?" Sissy said defiantly. "You and Sarah both from near as I could tell. 'Peers to me runnin' is fairly fancible in these parts, so whatcha gotta say about that?"

Jesse was not expecting that, but knew if she succeeded in putting him on the defensive, he belonged to her like Doc belonged to Jeb. "My life is none of your business, young lady! You are children here under my protection and you will answer to me, not the other way around."

Oddy was up on her knees waving a finger in the air, ready to scream her rebuttal when the door swung open crookedly letting in the snow and cold. Jesse got to his feet just as a large figure filled the door frame, and he staggered backward as it approached him.

"Good morning, neighbors! And Merry Christmas to you all!" Benji thought for a moment it was the Santa Claus he had heard about but had never experienced, but was quickly distracted as another figure came in stomping the snow off his feet just inside the door. As he turned, Jesse could see the man was carrying some bundles hidden under a folded blanket.

"I'm Midgie and I live just over yonder hill from y'all. We saw the smoke in your chimney last night and were just tickled pink to see light coming from the windows. It's been a 'coon's age since anyone lived here, and it just warms our hearts to see fire in the fireplace. You must be friends of Oaky's and if you are friends of Oaky's, you are friends of ours!"

She didn't stop to breathe it seemed as she continued, "I knew that movin' in so late, you'd be tired, so as a Christmas treat, I brought you a pan of biscuits and a big pot of sausage gravy! Then this here is a basket for dinner. Now I'll set it over by the fire and it should stay warm." The children jumped up to take the food and Midgie continued, "Oh land's sakes you got babies!" She bent to hug them both, lifting them clear off the floor. Without missing a beat she said, "We got eight of them little darlin's, and one on the way! Well, look at you! You look to be about my Ira's age, how old are you boy?"

"Nine, Ma'am."

"Well, will you listen to that boy's manners!" Midgie stopped, put her hands on her more than ample hips and continued, "Ma'am, huh? Well I just think a boy with manners is half on his way to bein' a grown man! And what about you, girl? Are you about twelve? I got a girl about your age, too. Her name's Bessie and she is the sweetest thing." Midgie was making a loop inside the little cabin taking inventory of everything that was going on and as she passed the bedroom door, she saw Sarah lifting the baby off the bed and squealed, "Oh my stars and garters! You have a baby! Oh I do love babies!"

Sarah came out of the bedroom carrying the baby and looking rather bedraggled herself. As Midgie crossed the floor and took the baby out of her arms she said, "Oh! This is a newborn! Why this child can't weigh half of what my babies weighed when they were born! Are you alright, little doll?" With the baby in her left arm, she shepherded Sarah back into the bedroom with her right hand on her back as she said; "Now you just turn around and get right back into that bed! Go on, and don't you give me no sass now!" She gave Sarah little choice as she gently guided her over to the bed. "That's it, now just lie down there and, where's your pillow?"

"Uh, we don't have any pillows, we uh…"

"Now don't you say one more word about that. There's no shame in bein' poor. Most of the folks here are dirt poor, but we don't stay that way for long, 'cos hereabouts, if you got neighbors, you got family, and if you got family, you're rich."

And just like that she was gone. Midgie tucked Sarah and the baby in, made sure they left the biscuits and sausage gravy, patted the children on the head and turned to leave. "Let's go Abram!" she said to the man who had stood there in complete silence, examining the broken hinge on the door, "the kids are bound to be gettin' cold in that wagon and besides we are fixin' to be late for church."

Strangers to Grace

Boom! The door slammed with a thunk, then bounced back again because of the broken hinge.

They stood in stunned silence as they all tried to process what had just happened. Then from the bedroom doorway they heard Sarah say in Midgie's vernacular, "I don't know about y'all, but I'm afixin' to eat me some biscuits and gravy!"

When they pulled the blanket off the box holding the biscuits they were delighted to find a bowl of butter, a large jar of strawberry jam, and a quart of apple sauce. What a feast Midgie had prepared for them! They ate until they were helpless and ready for naps and there was still more left in the pan than they had eaten.

The children and Sarah went back to bed to get warm and rest up from their travels, but Jesse was too concerned about needing firewood to rest, so he went outside to look for more. Although there was snow on the ground it was actually fairly warm outside. He found it stimulating to walk around, go where he wanted to go, and explore his surroundings. He saw the sleigh tracks in the snow and decided to follow them in the hopes that he could peek over the hill they were on and see the house where Midgie lived, but he walked a half a mile before turning back. "I think our nearest neighbors aren't as near as we first thought," he said to the four of them as he stomped the snow off his feet.

They had prepared dinner while he was gone and it was kind of nice coming home to such a happy scene, but this wasn't his family and he could not afford to stop running this close to the river. He needed to get farther away, and nothing was going to stop him.

He had enough wood collected outside the door to last them through tomorrow, and a dinner feast of biscuits with butter, sausage gravy, apple sauce and strawberry jam for desert waiting for him inside the door. These were just more good memories for him to call up and think on before sleeping, and he began going through the list again, just so he would remember. He had no idea what would happen in the future, but for tonight he was truly grateful for these past few days.

They sat quietly after the meal and stared into the burning fire. They noticed the many colors of the flame as it burned different woods at different temperatures, and watched the wet wood hissing as the water inside it boiled and oozed out the ends in a foamy steam. With full stomachs and a safe place to be, the fire provided all the entertainment they needed.

"So what do we do next?" Jesse asked the other three. After all, they were all equals except for the fact that Sarah had all the money and Oddy had all the smarts. He smiled at the thought of what a character Oddy was. How did she survive that night out there? And why did she have the bean pot?

They all looked his way as he sat up and turned to Oddy with a silly grin on his face. "What on earth were you doing with that bean pot last night?" Oddy's face broke into a grin the minute she realized he was no longer angry with her. It did seem a little odd to be sitting inside an outhouse with a pot of beans.

"What bean pot?" Sarah asked.

"When I found her this morning, she was in the outhouse with the bean pot! Why did you take it with you into the outhouse, Oddy?"

She looked at him rather sheepishly and said, "Well, I wasn't about to go out there with nothin' to eat again and it weren't like I could make a samwich!" All four of them laughed at that as Oddy continued, "And it's a good thing I tuk that bean pot, too! When I got in that outhouse, it was a little warmer 'cos there weren't no wind blowin' on me. So's I clumb up beside the 'go' part and squatted down with my cape pulled around me over that hot bean pot. I stayed good and warm. It was right tolerable in there."

Sarah and Jesse laughed at her funny way of telling of her good fortune, but they also marveled at her resourcefulness, and thought her to be really clever. Then Sarah began to question what had happened. "So you got up, took the bean pot and ran away to the outhouse so you could squat over the bean pot for warmth all night?" That was less than believable.

"No," Oddy said, "I runned away to go back to the cave."

Sarah shuddered as she thought of the fall Oddy could have sustained, and remembered her impassioned prayer in the night, "What stopped you?"

"I found the right hill, and found the tree I used as a marker to tell me where to go down to the cave, but I couldn't see the valley at all. There was a thick fog a layin' in the valley, and I was too afraid of fallin'. So's I clumb back up the hill and… well, I was afraid to come back in the cabin, so's when I saw the outhouse, I jus' went in there instead."

"That explained the trail that split," Jesse said. He felt ignorant for not looking for footprints the minute he left the cabin. He had so much to learn about living outside the prison, and he just hoped he could figure it all out before anybody got hurt.

"Weren't the beans cold?" Sarah was having trouble wrapping her mind around the events as they unfolded.

"Well, I heated 'em up 'afore I left off, I had to make water. So I put the pot down in the coals and went out to do my business. Then when I come back in, I sat there and nursed the baby while the beans warmed up, and then I took the beans and left off."

As they laughed and talked about all the events that had happened in the last 24 hours, they felt fortunate to have survived it. There were long minutes filled with a comfortable silence, and then someone would remember something that would send them into gales of laughter all over again. The snow that had threatened to end their lives yesterday now protected them, since no one in their right mind would have followed the trail they had blazed. At least for this one day, they were free to enjoy life, without looking over their shoulders.

CHAPTER SIX

"Ok, we all need to talk about something," Jesse said finally, "and we have to be able to talk to each other honestly. We have to trust each other because we are all in this together. I will go first and speak only for myself. Just like you kids, I am running away from something, you're right about that Oddy," Jesse suddenly felt very vulnerable. Could he trust his entire life to a child? And did he have a choice?

A hush settled over the room, this was risky business and the gravity of the moment had them riveted to their seats.

"Like it or not, we are going to have to get out of this mess together. I don't see us leaving here while the snow is on, do any of you?" Sarah looked around the room for reactions to what he had said. Everyone was looking at the floor, their lack of response speaking for them.

"Do you have any ideas, Oddy?" Jesse was beginning to have great respect for her ability to manage the outside world and he was actually hoping she had come up with a plan to get them out of there safely. But her shrug indicated otherwise.

"So we're stuck here, at least for now, within a community that knows we are here," Sarah sized it up pretty well. "And they think we are a family," she continued, "so maybe that would be our best cover."

"Well you ain't bossin' us around," Oddy said. "We been doin' for ourselves since our Mama left us at th'orphnige and ain't nobody gonna start bossin' us now."

"You are still children," Sarah said, "You need guidance and limits. And it is important for all of us that you do not behave in a manner that attracts attention, so..."

"You ain't bossin' us around," Oddy said, "we can leave any time, and we will, too. I got things I won't abide!"

Jesse had a feeling he knew what she was afraid of. "May I be brutally honest?" he said with an easy smile and a gentle look toward Oddy.

"Just what the hell does that mean, anyway?" Oddy asked.

Sarah ventured carefully into her role as guide, "Oddy, I do not like hearing that language, and to be honest, it is the kind of thing that will get us caught. I cannot see Midgie's children using that kind of language, and it may cause folks around here to wonder about your background." She was pleased with the way that came out because it appealed to Oddy's top priority--freedom.

Oddy's mouth puckered up indicating just how distasteful it was that Sarah was right, but after looking at the floor for a moment, she conceded that it might get them caught, and the last thing she wanted to do was go back to that orphanage.

"I'll work on it," was all she said. Jesse and Sarah looked at each other and then looked away quickly for fear that they would laugh, which would not have gone over well with little Miss Oddy.

"But I thought the rule was, one argument at a time!" she said, riveting Jesse with a look and continued, "I asked you what in the...," she glared at Sarah and started again, "What does 'brully honest' mean?"

Jesse thought carefully about the definition he wanted to give. It had to fit the circumstance under which it was uttered. "Well, there are times when you have room to dance around the truth, and then there are times when your life depends on being completely honest, whether the truth hurts or not. Do you understand that?"

"I ain't stupid!" Oddy was feeling a little defensive. She had always been the voice of authority with her brother and now she was in the position of having to be 'explained to,' and she didn't like it.

Sarah recognized the defensive tone Oddy was using; she didn't feel she was getting the respect she deserved. She recognized her attitude as one she had felt many times as a woman living in a man's world where no matter how intelligent she was she was treated like an ignorant child. Sarah spoke carefully, "We aren't asking you if you understand because we think you are stupid, Oddy. We know better than that. We are aware of how well you cared for your brother and the baby. Neither one of us could have done better, and we are adults."

Oddy looked up in surprise. That could have been true. Sarah had money, and most folks with money couldn't function without it. And Jesse seemed to be less than smart as far as survival was concerned. Oddy looked at them both through narrowed eyes and decided it was at least worth listening to the point she was making, "Then why did you just ask me if I understood?" she asked suspiciously.

Jesse said truthfully, "I wanted to know if I had explained it well enough. If I hadn't made myself clear, I was going to try again. I am not accustomed to speaking to others and explaining myself, so I may not be very good at it, yet." The group appreciated that new point of view, and sat in a hush as they processed it.

"I think the issue is respect," Sarah thought of a new approach. "I don't mind learning new things and hearing other's ideas. I just don't want to be treated like I am not very smart. I happen to be just as smart as any man, and yet I have, or had no say whatsoever in my life. Decisions were made and I was told I had to live with them. You have no idea how frustrating it is to be treated like a child, and a stupid child at that!"

"I agree!" Oddy shouted at Jesse. Oddy scooted closer to Sarah and they shared a look that caused Jesse and Benji to lock eyes in alarm. They were both seeing a side of women foreign to them prior to this very instant.

"Ok, so it is agreed that everyone in this room is to be talked to and treated with the respect that all people deserve, right?" Jesse hoped he had calmed the women or those words might be his last.

Their posture relaxed somewhat, and after a brief moment of staring at him, they looked at each other, then back at him with conciliatory nods.

"So," Jesse continued, "then are we clear on the meaning of 'brutally honest?'"

Sarah and Oddy again made eye contact. "I guess," said Oddy.

"Well, I want to say something else about being brutally honest." He said the word 'brutally' slowly and deliberately so Oddy could hear it without his having to correct her. He did not want to embarrass her. "We can't be totally honest with each other if we are afraid."

"Afraid of what?" Benji asked.

Jesse continued, "Well, for one thing, as Sarah and Oddy pointed out, we can't be honest if we are afraid of being treated like a child. I can't speak for Ben, but I have a great deal of respect for both Sarah and Oddy and for Ben here." Benji's eyes widened as he realized Jesse was calling him a more grown-up name, rather than the nickname he now considered childish. He sat a little taller as Jesse continued, "We are all survivors and that takes intelligence and courage. Right?" Everyone nodded their heads as he continued, "The second thing is that we can't be honest if we are afraid what we say in this room will be told to others."

Sarah then took the lead, "Yes, we all have things we don't want other people to know. That is why I changed my name, because I don't want to be found out. I would not have told you, had you not overheard, that Sarah wasn't my real name for the exact reason we are bringing up now. It could mean death to me if any of you told that." All three listeners immediately identified with the seriousness of what she had said.

"Me, too," Oddy said. "If anyone comes around here looking for a girl named Oddlaug someone just might point right their finger right at me."

"Oddlaug! Your name is Oddlaug?" Jesse and Sarah tried not to laugh at such an unusual name, until Oddy shouted in her defense, "It sounded like angel music when my Mama said it!" Her eyes filled with tears, and her bottom lip began to quiver. They knew she was about to lose that tough façade she so desperately tried to maintain. Jesse and Sarah felt immediate remorse and Sarah rescued the situation by saying very seriously, "It is just such an uncommon name that people would definitely point right at you. Are you thinking of changing it?"

Oddy quickly regained her composure with a sniff and said, "Yea, but I don't know what name I want to pick."

Jesse suggested they call her "Sissy" until she decided what her name would be and Oddy decided she could live with that, although the named sounded silly enough.

"Ok, we are making some good decisions here, aren't we?" Everyone nodded in agreement, even the newly named Sissy, who felt very much respected in the conversation.

"So we have decided that everybody gets treated with respect, right? We all get to have a say in what goes on, and nobody is treated like a child. We also decided it is imperative we keep each other's secrets. No matter how angry we get with each other, we cannot tell anything that could cost someone their life. Are we agreed on that?" Their sincerity was reflected in their demeanor as they nodded in agreement.

"And third, there is enough fear and grief out there in the world. We all need to feel safe inside this house and with each other wherever we are." He looked at Sissy and said, "And this is what I was talking about when we started this conversation. Now let's try this again; may I be brutally honest with you?"

"I guess so," Sissy said sheepishly.

"Your brother told Sarah you were afraid I would come to your bed like some Mr. Dunge did." He paused while Sissy glared at Benji and backhanded him across the chest. Before Benji could protest, Jesse said, "No, it was a good thing, Sissy. If you are afraid of me, I need to know it. In fact, I am aware that both the women in my life right now have just about the same fear," he said without looking at Sarah.

Sarah blushed from the ends of her hair to the bottom of her feet, but again, before she could protest, he simply stated, "No! We need to be honest here. I am aware that living in this house affords me the opportunity to at least try to take advantage of you." His hand gesture included the boy because his own life had taught him that boys were not out of harm's way when it came to sexual abuse, and he wanted to be perfectly clear to Ben that he was safe as well.

"I was hurt, a lot, as a little boy," he said patting his bad leg, "and that is all I am going to say about that. But you can be sure I know what it feels like to be hurt, and taken advantage of, and I would never do that to another human being. Now, I know it will take time for you to trust me, but I guarantee you, that I will never watch you dress or undress, and I will never come to your beds for anything untoward, and now that's all I am going to say about that as well." He let that settle in their minds for a second and then added, "And while we are on the subject of fear," he added, "I do not beat children. And it makes me feel like hell when you cower when I try to touch you."

Sissy inhaled sharply at the 'bad' word, and looked at Sarah. Hiding her smile, Sarah took her cue and said, "I'm sorry, Jesse, but I do not like that word and would appreciate it if you would never use it again."

"Yes, Ma'am," Jesse said obediently as he rolled his eyes from Sissy to Ben as if he were a scolded child, and they all started giggling like children.

"Jesse, what about your name? You mentioned changing it. Have you given it any more thought?" Sarah continued the discussion of important events.

"Can I be 'brually' honest?" Benji said cutting the conversation short.

"Sure, Benji. Go ahead," Sarah said smiling at him. He was normally so quiet she was curious as to what he had to say.

"Is Santa Claus real?" The question hung in the air while everyone struggled to change thought processes without bursting into gales of laughter. Although the question wasn't really in the spirit of being brutally honest, Sarah and Jesse knew it was important to Benji, so they needed a minute to think about their answer, and more importantly, to compose themselves so they could treat him with great respect. This was as important a question to a little boy as any of the questions they had posed, and they intended to treat it with great import.

Jesse felt a reprieve as Sarah asked, "Why do you ask, Benji? I mean what did you have in mind?"

"Well, we was talkin' about names, and I thought… well, I was thinkin' 'bout two boys I knowed at th'orphnige." Sarah was amused at his combination of the two words.

"What two boys?" Sissy asked.

"You know, Thomas and Willie," he said dismissively as he rolled his eyes at his sister as if to say, shut up and stop embarrassing me!

"Go on, Ben," Jesse encouraged. "What about those boys?"

"Well, they was Juniors," he said as if that would clear up the entire mystery.

"I still don't get it," Jesse said totally confused.

"Ok," Benji said as he took a deep breath. "I guess what I would say if I could ask Santa Claus for somethin'… ," he took another deep breath to steel his courage, bent his head low to look at the floor, and softly said, "was to be like Thomas and Willie, 'cos, they gots a father same name as them. I guess I would like a father named Benjamin, like me." He stared at his feet, because he couldn't bear to see their reactions. If they laughed, or if Jesse said, "But you're not my son," he thought he would die right there on the floor of that cabin.

It seemed like an eternity before anyone spoke and it was Jesse who broke the silence, "Ben, I don't know what to say. I would be so proud to choose your name as mine, but are you sure? I mean, you have no idea who I am," Jesse wanted to please this little boy, but knowing his own past, he felt badly about allowing him to bear the name of a murderer. And besides, he didn't want the boy to get attached to him if they were going to split up soon.

Benji's head snapped up and he looked at Jesse as if he adored him. "You are the best man I ever met. Kinder to me and her than anyone else ever been," he announced with pure hero worship on his face. Enormous tears filled his eyes, rolled down his cheeks and dripped off his chin as he jumped into Jesse's arms. Jesse had never experienced this overwhelming love that filled his heart to the point of breaking. Benji pushed himself back so he could see Jesse's face and said, "They can call you Benjamin and me, Ben, right?" he said pausing to wipe his nose on his sleeve, "I know it ain't forever. But while we're here at least?"

"Well, I would be honored to bear your name, Ben." The boy hugged his neck again then turned and said, "You can't call me Benji anymore, Oddy, I mean, Sissy. Benji's a baby's name, right P...?" Ben's face went ashen and it took a second for Benjamin to figure out that Little Ben almost called him, "Papa."

"Ok, that is another topic of discussion for the four of us to decide," he had everyone's undivided attention. He said, "The community would expect you to call us Mama and Papa, and I want to know how you three feel about it." When he finished speaking, he leaned back to listen to what they had to say. This was a great way to run a family for someone who had never had one that worked. He did not have to have all the answers, everyone felt respected, and he was enjoying hearing what they had to say.

"I like it," Benji offered. "I always wanted a Mama and a Papa, and I think we should call them that, Sissy, if they don't mind." He turned his eyes toward Sarah and Benjamin to see what they had to say about it. He had been so encouraged by the response to his last request that he had become downright bold.

Sissy had dreamed for the last several years, of calling out for a Mama in the night, and having a Papa to walk her to school, but she was reluctant to give up the role of mother to Benji. And she didn't like the idea of Benji ordering her to call him Ben. He was her little brother and she had no intentions of sharing her authority over him.

Sarah sensed her hesitation and added, "Think about what Midgie would think if you called us Sarah and Benjamin?" It was just what Sissy needed: a way to agree without losing face.

"Ok, but just until the snow melts and then me and Benji," she said looking angrily at her brother, "are leavin' off from here."

"Alright, then it is settled," Sarah said as they all fell into silence as they processed all the changes that had occurred. "Mama and Papa it is."

"AND, only when there's people around!" Sissy added defiantly.

Jesse and Sarah instantly and simultaneously replied with a resounding, "No!"

"This has to become ingrained into our minds, Sissy. We cannot afford to slip up," Sarah said with great feeling.

Ben quickly agreed, "We can't get into the habit of calling each other one thing in the house, and another in public, because the stakes are too high. If we forget, it could be the end of this little family."

He was about to explain that he did, indeed respect Sissy's opinions, because at least at this time it didn't appear that he did, but she hadn't argued with the outcome of her suggestion, so he continued, "It is important that we think of each other as real family if we are going to pull this off."

Unexpectedly, Ben looked up with a smile on his face and said, "This is the best Christmas I ever had! I never got nothin' before." He was proud that he had the courage to speak what was on his mind about his name, and was extremely satisfied with the results. He sat as close to Benjamin as he possibly could, and began imitating his mannerisms, sitting like Benjamin sat, gesturing like Benjamin gestured, and even agreeing with every point he made as they talked.

In the silence that followed, Benjamin began thinking about his own Christmases and thought this might be the best Christmas he had ever had as well. He looked around the room and found Sarah to be uncharacteristically quiet, while Sissy just stared at the floor, breaking Benjamin's heart. He thought of the hardships his own sisters and mother had endured, and wondered if the lives of all women were as hard as those he had come to know; his mother, his sisters, and now Sissy. And Sarah, sitting there quietly subdued… what had she been through that made her come this far at great personal risk?

Benjamin looked at Sissy again and said, "What would make Christmas good for you, Sissy? What would you like for Christmas?"

She struggled for a time, as if she had never allowed herself to think about such matters. She looked at him with a puzzled look, and then scratched on the floor with a pebble she had found. She shifted from sitting cross legged, to one where she threw her feet forward and leaned back on her hands. Finally she looked up and said, "Well, you know how you walk by a house at Christmastime and see a tree in the front window, and hear people laughin' and talkin' inside?"

Benjamin nodded.

"Well, I would like to walk by a house like that…" she paused then continued shyly, "and know I was welcome there. All those times I walked by houses like that, and knew not one of them folks cared if I lived or died, an' it hurt. I thought about all them other little girls gettin' dolls for Christmas. It weren't fair they had them nice houses and dolls!"

Sarah leaned forward and put her hand on Sissy's shoulder, wishing she had something to say that could fix all the pain the child had suffered.

"And if I lived in a house like that, I would want my own room, but only if I was safe in there. I guess what I want most is just to feel safe for a while. I can't remember the last time I felt safe."

Benjamin knew that feeling, and he also knew no words could make her believe he would never hurt her; it would take time to earn her trust. He turned instead toward Sarah and asked, "What about you Sarah? What is your daydream for a perfect Christmas?"

"Well, when I was a little girl, I dreamed of having a small house with a big stone fireplace with a large wooden mantle, big enough to hold pine branches and candles. Then I would drape a red ribbon across the front of the mantle with red bows at every point where the ribbons came back up to the mantle. And behind that I would have a mirror so big it would reflect all that candle light so at night it would light up the whole room."

"Where you lived before, you never had a fireplace?" Ben asked.

"Yes, but, uh… we'll we didn't decorate for Christmas." She smacked her hands back and forth as if to brush off some imaginary dirt, shot a look at Benjamin that said she would tolerate no further questioning, and said, "But enough about me, it's your turn, Benjamin. What is it that would make Christmas good for you?"

It was Benjamin's turn to think. His only wish was to see his sister again, but he knew that would never happen. So he began to wonder what kind of life he was expecting. What did he want his Christmases to look like? What he wanted had nothing to do with gifts, instead, when he daydreamed about the perfect Christmas, he saw himself sitting down to a turkey dinner with yams, and cranberries, and big slabs of homemade bread, surrounded by people who were happy and content, and as he shot a look at Sissy, he added mentally--and safe. He wanted everyone around him to feel safe.

When he told them about his wish, they all realized just how hungry they were, and jumped up to retrieve the forgotten basket Midgie had left for supper. Under a stack of dish towels they found a tender, moist roasted chicken with boiled potatoes, a jar of home canned green beans, a loaf of bread, and an apple pie. In the side of the box, wrapped in feed sack material that had been cut to size and dyed a beautiful red, were two small packages and one larger one. Benjamin handed each of the little packages to Benji and Sissy, and the bigger package to Sarah to open as he pretended to dig around looking for more. Sarah's package held a large bag of coffee that brought smiles from both adults. The children discovered they each had received a Gingerbread Man cookie, decorated with icing that gave them faces as well as a dress on one, and buttons on the other. All of them were at a loss as to what would compel someone who knew nothing about them, to bring such valuable gifts, but they were oh, so, grateful.

    The meal was a feast indeed because for this one night, they were safe and warm, and it was each one's first Christmas spent free from their own individual prisons. They slept deeply as the wind howled outside this little makeshift home of theirs, because all four had gone to bed safe and happy for the first time in years, and some, for the first time ever.

CHAPTER SEVEN

The week passed quickly. Sarah had worked diligently with their grammar, and pronunciation of words, and to her delight, the children had responded positively. Not only were they eager to learn, they were quite bright, and often corrected themselves before she had to.

The next task, however, was not met so positively. Sarah insisted the children bathe and wash their clothes, so the task at hand was to get the snow gathered and melted in the one big cast iron pot they had left. When the time came for Sissy to bathe, Sarah threw the two Bens out of the house and sent Sissy to the bedroom to undress. "Here is a blouse of mine you can wear as a robe," Sarah called out to Sissy.

Sarah had ripped up a layer of her petticoat to make wash rags, and decided to use two of the blankets Jeb's wife had given them, as towels, since it was early morning and the blankets would have time to dry before nightfall. The room was as warm as they could manage to get it, but still Sissy shivered as she stepped out in just the blouse/robe. Sarah excused herself and retreated to the bedroom to give Sissy some privacy while she bathed, and to pick up Sissy's clothes and check them for mending needs before washing them, but returned almost immediately to get her sewing things from beside the window where she had been mending Little Ben's shirt.

She smiled as she realized that somehow over the week, they had become Ben and Little Ben and was amazed all over again that Little Ben was not in the least upset by the name. In fact, everyone had become so comfortable with their new names, that Sarah would feel quite comfortable attending church with the community tomorrow. Midgie hadn't even asked if they wanted to attend, she just sent Abram to tell them they would be 'round to get 'em a little after daybreak.

As she retrieved her sewing supplies, she turned to go back into the bedroom, and saw Sissy standing with her back to her, naked. The way the light shone on her back, it appeared she had some kind of shiny marks. As she moved forward, Sarah gasped. Sissy had been beaten. Her back was scarred with whip marks, some so deep she was certain her ribs had been exposed. She felt herself getting dizzy and hurried into the bedroom to gain her composure. What kind of a person could do that to a child? It was amazing Sissy was as sweet as she was, and realized that all her love and caring for this child would do nothing but add to Sissy's pain when the time came for them to part.

Sarah looked over at the sleeping baby and felt a flood of relief that the child would not grow up in that environment. She was pleased the baby was healthier and had more color, and more weight. It was a blessing, because the first night they saw her, Sarah feared the infant would not survive.

"Sissy, I've laid out one of my dresses for you to wear until your things have dried. Come on in and get dressed, and then come out to the fire so we can talk." Sarah busied herself emptying the wash water, and hanging Sissy's wash rag and towel up to dry on the makeshift clothes line Benjamin had made. She almost took the cast iron pot out to dip up more snow, but remembered how the smaller pot had broken in half when it hit the ice cold snow, and set it aside to cool.

When Sissy stepped out into the room, she had wads of cloth gathered up in her arms. The dress did nothing but cover her nakedness, since it didn't fit any part of her body. She might have been as comfortable wrapping all of the blankets around her and trying to keep them there for the day. Sissy laughed the bubbly giggle of a child as she stepped out into the main room and it warmed Sarah's heart to hear it. Sarah laughed as well as the oversized dress wafted into the room with only the top of Sissy's head visible.

"Alright now, sit here by the fire so you don't catch a chill. The last thing we need is for one of us to get sick," Sarah said as she draped another dress around Sissy's shoulders and rubbed her shoulders and arms vigorously in an effort to get her blood flowing.

Sissy watched as Sarah sat down on the floor next to her, and proceeded to begin the badly needed mending of her tattered dress. "Is that what Mama's do?"

Sarah looked up and said, "What?"

Sissy nodded toward the mending and said again, "Is that what mothers do? Mend your clothes? Make you take a bath and rub your shoulders to keep you warm?"

Sarah smiled and thought about it for a minute. She pictured her own mother mending her clothes and the clothes of others in order to put food on the table. They didn't have much while growing up, but they always had food on the table, and a roof over their heads, and she relished the very fond memories of her childhood. "Yes, that is what mothers do for their children, among other things. Things you have done for Ben. You know, finding him food, watching out for him." Sarah paused briefly, then asked, "Do you remember much about your mother?"

Sissy enjoyed the memories of her mother as much as Sarah had. A warm thoughtful smile came over her face as she told of her mother's beauty, "She had long blonde hair and the bluest eyes you ever did see. The sky only gets that blue about twice a year, but Mama's eyes were that blue all the time. And she had the pertiest smile I ever had the pleasure of seein'. Trouble is I don't remember much about her 'ceptin' that day she left us at th'orphnige. Oh, I've tried, but I can't remember nothin' 'cept her tellin' me she loved me, over and over, and over." She stopped to wipe her eyes with the sleeve of the dress, and then continued,

"And how sorry she was she couldn't take care of us no more. She was sick when she left us. She was scared she'd get down and couldn't take us there later. So she took us to th'orphnage and left off to die on her own."

Sarah couldn't help herself; she pulled Sissy into her arms. When she put her hand on the side of her face to draw her near, she felt tears and knew Sissy needed to cry. "Go on! Let it all out, Sissy. It's ok to grieve."

"No it ain't. I got Little Ben to watch out for, and that dern baby." Instantly she regretted saying that, sat straight up and looked at Sarah shamefully. Sarah allowed her words to hang in the air for a minute, then hugged Sissy to her tightly again.

Finally, Sarah broached the subject cautiously, "Sissy, I noticed that when you ran away, you didn't take the baby. And you said that as soon as the snow melted, you and Little Ben were going to leave, but you didn't mention her then either. How do you feel about the baby?"

Sissy seemed distressed and defeated at first, then she looked up at Sarah with resolve in her eyes and said, "Can we do that bru'lly honest thing?"

Sarah took her cue from that night with Jesse and said, "Always. You can always be brutally honest with me. You never even need to ask."

That was Sissy's undoing. Sissy laid her head back down on Sarah's shoulder, her shoulders slumped as she let go of the burden she had been carrying. She took a deep breath and then just blurted out the truth, "I don't want it." Sissy stared at a spot on the floor and said, "I know I should, but I don't. I will feed her until she can eat real food, but after that... "

Sarah was at a loss for words. In all her years, through all the good times and bad, she had never met a mother who simply did not want her child. She did not want to condemn Sissy, but this was so foreign to Sarah she was just taken aback, and at a loss for words.

"You think I'm horble don't you?"

"No. No, I do not think you are 'horble.'" She adored that word and couldn't help but smile when she said it. "I admire you for all you have been through and managed to survive, Sissy. I don't know what would have become of me had I gone through everything you have been through," she said as she realized how comfortable their embrace was. It had been too long since she had experienced the innocent embrace of someone she cared for. She had become hard and remote, her heart permanently withdrawn behind a façade of barricades. But as she held Sissy and rocked her back and forth she felt a refreshingly genuine rush of wonderful feelings wash over her soul. For years, she had experienced love only in the memories of her mother. But now, holding Sissy in her arms sent a river of warmth and love through her, restoring life to every suffocating cell of her being. Lifted, for just a moment, out of the past horrors they had both experienced, they paused together in that tattered cabin to heal and rest in each other's arms. Sarah rocked Sissy back and forth and was grateful when she felt Sissy relax against her.

THUD! THWACK! It sounded like someone was trying to break in the door. Sarah shoved Sissy aside protectively and ran to open the door; ready to face any intruder. THUMP! Another assault on the door brought her to her senses and she stopped short and turned to look out the window instead. There in the snow, a good forty feet away, stood the two Bens armed with a pile of snowballs, waving their arms and shouting. She moved to the door, opened it and shouted, "What on earth are you doing?" She was baffled by their bizarre behavior.

"Well, the men folk want to come back into the house before we freeze to death, but we do *not* want to intrude on your privacy!" The sweetness of that gesture overwhelmed Sarah. Both she and Sissy had been frightened of this man who now stood afar throwing snowballs and asking for permission to come back into the house. She had to smile as she stood there looking at him, arms full of snowballs, and Little Ben beside him squinting to see if she were going to wave them in. Not only was he treating them with respect and understanding, he was also teaching Little Ben a lesson that would serve him well throughout his life. Little Ben could do worse than being reared by this man.

Sissy had joined her at her side and was staring at the two Bens as if they had grown horns. "What on earth?" Sissy looked up at Sarah's smile and continued, "What are they doing out there?"

"Well," Sarah explained, "they knew we were taking a bath and didn't want to invade our privacy by coming to the house to be let in. They are standing out there throwing snowballs in order to ask permission to come back in where it is warm. What do you think? Should we wave them in?"

They both shook their heads in disbelief and smiled as they turned to the boys and waved their arms shouting, "Come on in! You look like you are freezing!" As the boys approached, the girls ran inside so as not to be covered in the cold frozen snow they were dragging in and giggled when the boys managed to unwrap their heads enough for their red faces to be seen. Big Ben's mustache had ice crystals on it where the warm, moist air from his nose had frozen solid. They stomped their feet and an avalanche of snow tumbled from them into piles melting on the floor.

Sissy ran to get the old ratty broken broom someone had cut the handle off of, and Sarah put the coffee on to heat while the boys began the process of unwinding the blankets from around their legs and bodies. Some of the blankets were frozen into a permanent circle where they had been wrapped around the bottoms of their legs and tied with ropes. Sissy and Little Ben wondered how cold it must be outside for the blankets to have taken on that shape. Benjamin warmed his fingers over the fire while Little Ben and Sissy chattered about the day's events.

As Ben stood there, grateful for the fire now warming his fingers and face, he watched Sarah bustle around in an effort to make him coffee. This kindness, from a woman he had known less than a week, completely overwhelmed him. He panicked as he realized there were tears in his eyes about to run down his face, and his nose was running, requiring a gesture from him that would make his crying evident to everyone in the room. He put his head back and looked at the ceiling in the hopes that he wouldn't have to sniff, but when he looked back down, tears dripping off his chin, he was looking into the face of a very bewildered Sarah.

He quickly wiped his entire face with one swift movement of his arm, and thanked her for making the coffee. "You are quite welcome," she said still not understanding what exactly was going on, but clear headed enough to embrace the opportunity to also express her gratitude, "and thank you for the privacy and respect. It meant more to me than you will ever know."

As she turned to walk away, his world doubled in size. Prior to meeting this woman, his head was filled with only *his* thoughts, *his* regrets, *his* nightmares, and *his* perspective. But this woman fit so comfortably into his thought processes, and was always so full of surprises that he wanted to share his every thought with her. Here he was, embarrassed by his tears, grateful for her comfort without a clue in the world as to how to express it, and she just turned to him and said something that made him feel valuable and honorable.

How did she do that? How did her presence make him feel like someone had opened a window and shone a light into his otherwise dark existence? It felt good knowing both of them had given the other something of value; he had given her a sense of security, and she was making him coffee, and that was enough. He felt a smile well up from inside him and brighten his entire day, and he knew his happiness had a lot to do with this woman. Before he fell asleep that night, he tried to recite all his blessings he had received since the night he had dinner with Lloyd and Juanita, but found instead that his mind kept wandering to Sarah, and the pure joy he felt in her presence.

CHAPTER EIGHT

That night, Ben drank his coffee and watched the fire die down. It was quiet since the children and Sarah had long been asleep, and he was enjoying the snap and crackle of the fire in this peaceful little cabin. He realized he needed to make a trip to the little woodshed to chop more wood for the night, and wished he could figure out why some of the wood they were burning burned up so quickly. Sometimes the same amount of wood would last for a day and a half, and other times, like tonight, it burned up before dawn. He wanted to know more about living out in the real world, but there was nothing he could do about it but muddle through.

He went out into the night, grateful for the full moon, and stood looking at the blue glow the snow gave off in the moonlight. He looked from left to right at the peaceful landscape and remembered the calm waters he had seen from the boat. The pure, clean and cleansing, liquid water that had soothed his soul was now comforting him in the form of white frozen water that was this glistening snow. "A man could get used to living here," he said aloud, and like a shot, a frightened deer ran from his left, startling both man and beast as it fled. Ben looked around him with a new awareness as he remembered the bear and chastised himself for his foolishness. He made the trip to the woodshed as short as possible and hurried back into the cabin, remembering not to relieve himself in order to awaken early for church. The last week had been fun, interesting, and relaxing, but now he was becoming anxious at the thought of meeting all those people at church in the morning. There were so many things that could go wrong, but he decided this was their lot, and they had to see it through.

The room was still warm when the call of nature awakened him. He had lain the fire so late last night that it hadn't even begun to burn out. Before he stepped outside, he set the coffee onto the fire to heat. It made him smile to think of being able to offer Sarah hot coffee as she had done for him, and the very thought of it warmed him as the icy winds rushed into his face as the door opened.

The household was abuzz when he returned with an armload of wood. Sarah had cut down one of her dresses to make a new dress for Sissy and was making last minute alterations, while Little Ben finished his bath in the bedroom. Sarah wished she had packed more sewing supplies and made a mental note that this week when Midgie's boys came for her grocery list, she would order more thread, a pack of needles, some dress cord for pulling the sleeves closed around at the cuffs, and a better pair of scissors.

When packing to escape, she had thought her needs would be only that of repairing her own clothing and was unprepared for actual dress making. She needed to budget, however, because her diminishing funds would not last through many large purchases, and once again, she wished she hadn't deposited the remainder of her money in a bank in Parkersburg. She immediately pushed back the panic she felt at the thought of how they would get along in the future. "Things are not so bad here," she thought to herself as she walked over to her satchel to retrieve the small pin cushion and realized just how much she liked living in that little cabin, and dared to hope for the future to be as kind as the present.

"Am I clean enough?" Little Ben asked as he stepped out into the front room completely naked and arms held out. Sarah blushed and turned away from the naked boy as Big Ben laughed a deep belly laugh, rushed across the room, turned Little Ben by the shoulders, and ushered him back into the bedroom. Sissy thought nothing of it, of course, and really thought they were making a very big deal out of nothing as she stood listening to Big Ben's boisterous laugh and watched Sarah's scarlet face as she busily tucked, stitched, and twirled the girl in an effort to "fix" the dress that no longer needed "fixing."

When the bedroom door opened, Big Ben came out completely subdued. He understood Sarah's embarrassment and wanted to respect that, but as she turned to him, the silliness of the situation hit both of them and they both burst out laughing until tears came to their eyes. "What do you want the boy to wear today?" Big Ben asked trying to stifle another round of laughter.

"Here," Sarah said as she handed Ben the underwear, pants, socks, and shirt that had been washed within an inch of their lives the day before. "Give him these, and tell him to get dressed before he comes out, please." Her eyes told him that she was enjoying having that carefree moment between them. She was not one to fall over when pushed by life, he was sure of that, and he liked the feeling of being in the presence of a strong woman.

They heard Midgie's voice before they heard the horses or the massive sleigh filled with singing children coming toward them. "When I can read my title clear to mansions in the skies, I bid farewell to every fear, and wipe my weeping eyes. And wipe my weeping eyes, and wipe my weeping eyes I bid farewell to every fear, and wipe my weeping eyes." The song had a Scottish lilt to it and they were all sure that Heaven itself was filled with her joyous sounds!

"Come here Little Ben," Sarah said as she knelt down to help him dress. I made you a vest out of the same material I made Sissy's dress." As he slipped it on over his summer shirt, she thought how handsome he looked and said so, much to his chagrin. But she clearly made a lasting impression on the boy when she presented him with a coat made inside and out of a dark blue material and padded with layers of her petticoats. She hadn't had time to make pockets, but promised him she would add them

89

as soon as church was over. He stood there looking as if he were fighting back tears when suddenly he threw his arms around her neck and said, "Thank you, Mama." The appreciative hug of this child was just delicious to her soul. The coat was thrown together in a way that would have embarrassed a boy who was use to nice things, but for this little man, it meant the difference in freezing to death and living. But more importantly it meant the world to him that his Mama had made it for him.

Sarah was proudest of the swaddling clothes she had made for the baby. Her old petticoat had been put to good use. Although the infant needed very little as far as a blanket was concerned, she had made one out of big squares of cotton that had been the bulk of the garment, and used the lace from the edges of the petticoat to form an edging for the little blanket. The sleeping gown had been made out of the leftovers from the dress she had cut up to make Sissy's outfit and Little Ben's vest, with a little lace around the bottom and collar from the lace on her petticoat. The child would be warm and clean under her cape as they traveled, and yet would be adorable in the church where the little gown could be exhibited.

The scene was heartwarming until fear clutched Benjamin's stomach. He realized that although this seemed like a great excursion, it was a very serious matter indeed. Before opening the door, he turned to the group and said, "Listen to me, all of you. We cannot forget who we are today. We must remember to call each other by our correct names, and let nothing slip about our pasts. No matter what happens, we must stick together, for if one of us gets caught, we all get caught," he looked at their saddened faces and knew they were all feeling as he did. If only they were a real family like Midgie's, going to church like regular folk, putting down roots that would last throughout their entire lives. But they weren't. They were here for a day, or a week, or a month. They were nobodies, and it was good to remember that. "Remember who you are," Ben reminded them sternly as they walked out into the sun, to greet their singing neighbors, their carefree mood now greatly subdued.

Strangers to Grace

Everybody knew what that meant. Remember, you are not one of them. Remember, you could be caught and sent back to a life of hell. Remember, all the mistakes you have made and how these people would see you if they knew. "Remember who you are," was a knife in the heart of those four people who were just getting the bitter taste of a life they could never have.

It was surprisingly warm as they took their places beneath the woolen blankets on the sleigh. The sleigh was nothing more than a large flat bed with small sides on it and runners on the bottom instead of wheels, that was used for taking hay out to the cows in the winter, bringing in the fall harvests, and, of course, transporting the large family from place to place. A small girl named Maxine, handed each of them two hot baked potatoes to keep in their pockets for warmth. "These'll keep your hands warm!" she said as she smiled a toothless smile and added, "then you can eat 'em for lunch!"

"Thank you," Sarah smiled at the little girl with the big copper colored bow in her hair. "How very thoughtful of you!" She watched the little girl blush at the compliment, and then glance at Little Ben, looking at the two potatoes wondering where to put them since he didn't yet have pockets. After a thoughtful moment, Little Ben simply held them up to cover his cold ears, which made Maxine giggle joyously, and set him off on a mission to make Maxine laugh even more. When his antics led him to stand up in the sleigh, Sarah told him to sit down before he fell down which Little Ben ignored. Instead of obeying her, he mocked Sarah and made a face like hers to mimic her, solely in an effort to make Maxine laugh, until a loud "CRACK," broke the silence as Big Ben snapped his fingers and motioned for him to sit down. Little Ben's eyes widened and his butt hit the seat before the sound cleared the air. The rest of the trip was made in complete silence.

"Here it is! Our little church!" Midgie said with great pride. Obviously this church was the center of the lives of the people in the surrounding area. There were men and women gathering and talking outside the log building, while children ran and played games, throwing snowballs and making snowmen as quickly as they could before being called in to the service.

Abram and Midgie knew everybody and made their way through the folks asking about births and deaths, the health of those they knew and loved, and, of course, rumors about the war. The bitter cold brought them indoors rather quickly where Rev. Morrison had a roaring fire going in the potbellied stove that sat right in the middle of the room. "Come in! Come in!" the Rev. shouted as his congregation paused at the door to rid themselves of extra snow. After much foot stomping and sweeping, their clothes were pretty much free of the snow that would melt and render their clothing wet, a dreaded event when traveling in wintertime. Keeping dry could mean life or death, and getting as much of the snow off you as possible went a long way to meeting that end.

To keep the children from having to answer any questions by well-meaning folks, Sarah and Ben put them between them when they sat down in the pews. Sarah took Sissy's cape and folded it inside out so no one could see the many repairs that had been made. Ben took Little Ben's coat and placed it on his lap along with the two potatoes Little Ben had begun playing with and even banging together. Ben didn't want the long hair in the pew in front of them to be covered with bits of potato if Little Ben became a little too enthusiastic in his games, exploding the potatoes in the process. Little Ben had thought about defying his Papa, and began to reach for the potatoes, but with only one raised eyebrow, Benjamin stopped him dead in his tracks.

"I want to open our services by reading the 23rd Psalm," Preacher Morrison's words created a flurry of activity as Bibles were brought out from under capes, taken from the backs of the pews and passed from adult to child. Preacher waited until the swishing of paper stopped as the pages were turned to the scripture they all knew so well. As he read, it struck Ben that although all Bibles were open, and turned to the right page; nobody looked at the books as they recited Psalm 23 from memory.

"The Lord is my Shepherd, I shall not want," they said in unison.

Strangers to Grace

"How many shepherds do we have out there?" The Preacher asked. Several men and boys held up their hands.

"Are your sheep smart?" he asked, followed by laughter as the shepherds shook their heads.

"Do they make mistakes?" he continued.

"Yes, they sure do." They all agreed and smiled as they looked at each other with knowing looks as Rev. Morrison continued.

"Like we make mistakes?" Preacher said pointing to himself.

The crowd began to sober and soft replies of "Amen!" and, "I sure have!" were heard as people confessed in whispers.

"And when your sheep make mistakes, do you abandon them? Or when one wanders away, do you leave the others to go find it? To bring it home? To feed it, care for it, and return it to its place of safety?"

"Yes, Preacher," they said, nodding in agreement.

Preacher pointed out one of the men and said, "How about Luke over there! Has he made mistakes?" Poor Luke laughed good naturedly as those around him pounded on his back and nodded their heads. "And yet our Shepherd brought him right here, into the fold."

He looked out over his congregation in silence as they thought about how blessed they were to be loved and cared for, and then he read again, "The Lord is MY Shepherd. I shall not want." He hit his fist on his chest when he shouted the word, "MY," to indicate the personal relationship they all had with God. Sarah had attended church every Sunday of her life, and had never heard a Preacher raise his voice, but continued to shout, "He is MY Shepherd, and YOUR Shepherd. He loves and protects and provides for each and every one of us as if we were his own children, because we are his own children. Even if we make mistakes!" He paused for the congregation to absorb what he had said before quietly leading them in the reading of the scripture.

In unison they all continued, "He maketh me to lie down in green pastures," again the Preacher paused. "How many of you have had the pleasure of lying down on a beautiful sunny day, surrounded by green pastures, looking up at that beautiful blue sky, and feeling peace? The peace that passeth understanding! How many of you?" They all raised their hands. "Then why do we fear God? If leading us into green pastures is what he has in store for us, then why do we doubt him? Why can't we trust him completely?" He paused for a moment before continuing.

He looked briefly at his Bible, a signal to them that they were to continue. "He leadeth me beside the still waters. He restoreth my soul." The words hit Benjamin full force. "He leadeth me beside the still waters." His head began to spin and he felt lighter, almost as if he were going to float out of his seat. "...beside the still waters." Wasn't that where he had found himself? Didn't he find healing and peace beside the still waters of the Little Kanawha River?

His breath became light and his heart felt relieved of a huge burden. He had come to believe God did not love him because of what he had done, but in this moment, he was experiencing a blessing that was indescribable.

"He restoreth my soul," Preacher repeated. That is what had happened to him. He suddenly heard someone sobbing and crying, and realized it was him, and one by one, he felt hands touching his back. One, two, three, then dozens of hands touching his back, shoulders and head in encouragement, love, and acceptance. He began hearing prayers being said with his name in them. "Lord, Bless brother Benjamin in his walk, Lord. We aren't worthy, Lord, of your love and protection, but you gave your son so that we might be forgiven and we thank you, Lord. We praise you, and lift up Brother Benjamin to your care."

The prayers subsided and Benjamin looked up and realized he felt complete peace in his soul. It was as if he had been given a new spirit; a clean spirit, free of burdens, and free of sin. He was elated, a feeling foreign to him, and he hoped the feeling would never go away. He tried to think that maybe someday, God would remember who he was and turn away from him, but the thoughts wouldn't collect into a sentence. He just kept hearing, "He leadeth me beside the still waters, He restoreth my soul," over and over in his head as they continued to read the rest of the Psalm. He felt as if God were looking him in the eye, smiling at him and saying, "Do you understand now? I have always loved you, and I brought you to this place of peace."

He found it difficult to stand still when he heard, "Surely goodness and mercy shall follow me all the days of my life: and I will dwell in the house of the Lord forever." What a glorious thought! To have goodness and mercy following me! He looked down at the children in his care and saw the questions in their faces. Right here, he thought as he looked at them, and then at Sarah, right here is pure goodness. And he wondered if God had put them in His life. Was he being shepherded before he even knew God loved him? I know for a fact that He did lead me beside the still waters, Ben thought. He did restore my soul. He paused to be grateful for that wonderful feeling and then continued, and there is a great deal of goodness in my life now with Sarah and the children.

But what about mercy? Would there be much mercy handed out to him if they ever found out who he was, and what he had done? The question haunted him, as fear does, and then there was peace again. An unshakable peace had permeated his entire being and he found it impossible to worry about anything.

Suddenly, the tone of the service changed, getting Ben's attention. "And now, we would like for our newcomers to stand and introduce themselves. Although everyone here has already heard all about Ben and Sarah, and know they came right before Christmas to the old Oak Butler homestead out by Abram's and Mildred's, many of you have not had the privilege of meeting them yet in person." It was the first time they had heard Midgie called Mildred and it surprised them somewhat. Maybe because the name, Midgie, suited her, and Mildred seemed a bit formal.

The spotlight was on them, and as Benjamin stood up to introduce his little family, he realized they hadn't discussed a last name, and it was too late now. He would have to come up with one on his own and hope they didn't object. There was no way he could use his old last name, and he hadn't heard any of the others, so as he brought himself to his full height, he said, "Good morning! My name is Benjamin Waters, and this is Sarah," he said as he gestured toward her. She stood up and he realized what an incredibly breathtakingly beautiful woman she was. Full of grace and dignity, she just radiated a wholesomeness that made him unbelievably proud to be with her.

As Sarah motioned to the children, they stood up and blushed at all the attention as she said, "This is Sissy and Little Ben." Little Ben's tiny hand went into Benjamin's, just as Sissy's hand went into Sarah's. "And of course," Sarah continued, "there is the baby. She is a tiny thing, but growing like a weed." They needed to pick a name for the baby, they all realized at once. Hopefully no one would ask.

As they sat down, Brother Dale walked to the front of the church and said, "Now there is no sin in being poor. All of us have stood here in need from time to time, isn't that right?" All heads were nodding in agreement as he continued, "So Brother Benjamin, we would ask that you and your family allow us to serve you in the way Christ taught us to do by accepting our gifts today."

Benjamin looked at Sarah and wondered what he was supposed to do. One by one, the members of the church came forward with jars of canned fruit, pickled corn, green beans, pickled eggs, beets, apple sauce, a few pie apples, loaves of homemade bread, bags of dried apples and fodder beans, a large sack of potatoes, and more coffee. They were speechless, and tears came to Sarah's eyes as the food piled higher and higher on the pew in front of them.

And with each delivery came a smile and a "God bless you," or "Bless your souls," or "Welcome to our community." Every gift was given with a smile and words of encouragement, and not one ounce of resentment. Sarah and Ben stood in awe at the outpouring of gifts. Never, had they experienced such blessings from anybody, let alone people they did not even know.

"How can we pay you, for this?" Ben said as he spread his hands to cover all that had been given. "For all of this?" Benjamin asked.

Reverend Morrison stepped forward and put his Bible under his arm so he could shake hands with Ben; a hearty handshake with his huge left hand covering both their hands as they gripped in fellowship. He looked Ben in the eye and said, "You know, Jesus said, 'As you do unto the least of these, you do unto me.' Sometimes, someone who is on top of the world has a fire, or a death in the family, and soon they find their lives have been shaken to their roots. Then it is time for all of us to step forward and do what Christ asks us to do. So it is our privilege to serve you, on behalf of Jesus Christ, by helping you get a good start. Someday it will be your turn to help, and I think Benjamin and Sarah Waters will step up to the challenge." His big smile was comforting, as he pounded Ben on the shoulder good naturedly.

With that, Preacher turned and lifted his hands, his black Bible in one of them indicating it was time for the Benediction. A hush fell over the room as they all bowed their heads, "Lord we thank you for your grace and forgiveness," he paused for a brief time of praise, then continued, "For without it, we would never find the still waters." A pause gave time for whispers of agreements. "Without it, we would never find the green pastures, because without your unconditional love and grace, we would all be lost… and we know that. We praise you our Lord and King, for loving us enough to be our Shepherd. In the name of Jesus, we pray all things, Amen."

It suddenly became noisy as everyone crowded around to see the baby and shake the hands of Sarah and Ben. Between the adults, the children were making their own introductions and invitations, until Little Ben crawled under the pew to make his escape. Sarah saw in Sissy's eyes that she was about to follow him, so she stepped out into the aisle to allow her to go. The children ran out of the church with parents shouting to put on their gloves and scarves. Ben and Sarah's eyes met and between them passed the unspoken questions. "Why would they do this?" "How will we repay them?" And, "How are we going to get this home?"

But before they actually spoke, Midgie appeared out of the crowd with six of her eight children who began filling their arms with food and carrying it out to the sleigh. Obviously, they had worked together as a team many times, because without a word, they emptied the pews and carefully packed the sleigh so nothing would get broken, and they did it without any adult supervision. It was a light hearted group that rode home that day, singing and laughing, celebrating being alive with carefree hearts.

Ben and Sarah were excited and had a great deal to say to each other when they were alone, but for now all they could do was meet each other's eyes and smile. A great burden had been lifted from them. With this food they would be able to feed the children, and buy enough time to figure out what they were going to do next.

Upon arrival, the children jumped out of the sleigh and proceeded to unload it with unequaled precision. Without being told, Sissy and Little Ben fell into line completely emptying the sleigh in a matter of moments. Benjamin turned to Midgie and said, "Thank you so much, for everything you have done for us. We don't know how to thank you for…"

"We all work together here, Mr. Waters," it was the first time they had heard Abram speak. He stepped forward and offered his hand to Benjamin as he continued, "We share what we have and look out for each other. Someday it will be your turn to give, and it is then, that you will understand. Receiving is very humbling, I know. There have been many times when Mildred and I needed help. But nothing compares to the feeling you have when you get to give."

"Well, I will look forward to that day, and I trust you will call me if there is ever anything I can do."

"Will do, Mr. Waters," Abram said with a smile and a tip of his hat.

"Please, call me Ben."

"Alright then, Ben it is. And please, call me Abram. Well, we had better get going. There is a big snow coming and we don't want to get caught in it."

Ben remained outside and watched the sleigh disappear over the hill. He looked up into the sky wondering how Abram knew it was going to snow. He thought about the blue sky yesterday and noticed the difference today. There were heavy, thick, grey clouds gathering menacingly and the temperature was dropping quickly. It was much colder now than it had been when they left the church. He tried to memorize these signs, so the next time he saw them, he would know there was snow coming without having to be told.

He turned up his collar to the wind and took one more look over the hills as he turned back into the house, but stopped in his tracks when he saw something dark in the distance in front of their cabin. As it came closer, he realized it was another sleigh. Someone was coming to their cabin and they had no defense if it proved to be someone sinister. He opened the door and shouted for Sarah who came running. "Take the children back into the bedroom and stay there until I come get you." Sarah started to ask a question, but caught view of the approaching stranger, turned and gathered the three children exactly as Ben said.

It took several minutes for the sleigh to arrive, but long before that, Ben noticed there was another sleigh following behind. What if they were coming for the children? What would they do? How could they stop them? Or worse, what would happen to the children and Sarah if he was their target? Fear was beginning to get the better of him, when the driver of the first sleigh called out, "Brother Ben!"

Ben assumed it was someone from the church, but knew it wasn't Abram because they were coming from a different direction. "Yes! What can I do for you?" Ben tried to sound welcoming, but the fear in his chest made his words sound stilted.

"We have some things for you in the sleighs here," Homer said. "Boys!" he shouted, and eight boys threw back the blankets they had been riding under and jumped out, ready to go to work.

Ben stepped inside and called for Sarah to come out which she did, followed by Little Ben and Sissy. She stepped back away from the door just in time to see the boys bring in the first of the boxes, filled with pots and other cooking utensils, blankets, pillows, bags filled with 'hand-me-downs' for all three of the children, four chairs that didn't match, a table that was crudely made and yet surprisingly stable, a load of lumber for patching the cabin, and a small box with Lucifers, herbs, salt, mismatched silverware, milk for the children, and two child sized tin cups. The two men who had been driving the sleighs struggled as they brought in a huge feather tick and a bed frame with ropes woven within the frame to hold the tick, as one called for a boy named, Denzel, to go get the wicker bassinet.

When the sleighs were unloaded, most of the boys climbed back in under the blankets, but the tallest two boys came back and leaned some tools against the little cabin. A much needed axe and saw for cutting wood, and a small box holding some nails and screws, a hammer, pliers, a screw driver, and finally a hinge just the right size to fix the front door. That must be from Abram, Ben thought to himself as he remembered Abram quietly inspecting the door that day Midgie came through the house like a windstorm.

Upon reflection, he now realized that Midgie had an agenda that day, covering every room with a watchful eye, on the lookout for any and all needs. Ben had never had the opportunity to be a betting man, but he would have gambled that Midgie was the organizer of all this, and although he was grateful, he also was feeling a debt to these people who had been so generous in their giving when he knew he had little to give in return. It gave him a great deal to ponder, and it was not easy thinking. He couldn't help but compare himself and his former life, to that of the good people in this community, bringing down an avalanche of depression and self-loathing that threatened to destroy him. He doubted his ability to continue playing the role of father and husband, and yet he had no idea where to go, or how to survive if he did leave. In addition to that, for some unknown reason, he felt responsible for this new family he was pretending to have.

Suddenly, the past had trapped him in a nightmare from which he could not awaken.

Every thought he had was incomplete, circuitous, and resulted in hopelessness. Instead of accepting the outpouring of gifts in the spirit they were given, his mind struggled with his past, like a man lost in deep woods. Every time he thought he found a way out of his dilemma, he would discover he had simply wound up at the beginning of the same thought process with which he had begun. He could continue to play the role of Benjamin Waters, but knew he was not worthy of this community. It was only a matter of time before they saw him for what he was. These were fine people he was lying to, a fact he had trouble living with, but what option did he have? He couldn't leave because he had no idea how to fend for himself, especially in this weather. But if he did stay, how would he ever pay these people back the debt he owed them. Sarah had money, but if she paid them, he would just be in debt to her. Around and around in circles his thoughts traveled, always returning to dead center with no answers.

And what about Sarah and the children? He was feeling responsible for their care, and yet they didn't belong to him. As comfortable as it was by the fire inside that cabin with his 'pretend' family, the truth of the matter was that he had no idea how to support them, and besides, they might leave him there someday. They owed each other nothing. So, if he decided he was not responsible for them, why didn't he just leave them? And there he was, back at the beginning again. Every option that arose in his mind, ended with the same self-imposed despair, and his inability to decide what to do, was rendering him paralyzed in one spot, as much a prisoner as ever. He tried to regain the feeling he had inside that little church, but panic and self-loathing had seized his spirit, sending him spiraling, and he could find not one comforting thought to calm him.

CHAPTER NINE

Benjamin remained outside, wrestling with his inner demons, but inside the cabin, Sarah and the children were having fun unpacking boxes and finding surprise after surprise. Sissy and Ben were thrilled at the prospect of having a home of their own, so they dragged the table to the center of the floor in front of the fireplace, and quickly placed the chairs around it. Each retrieved one of the "new" child sized tin cups from the box and sat at the table pretending to have coffee. As they fought over where everyone should sit, Sarah was busy going through the hand-me-downs for the children.

She was pleased to find that almost everything in the bag was a perfect fit for the children. She smiled as she imagined Midgie sizing up Ben and Sissy and knowing instinctively which of her children's clothes would fit them. Her heart was grateful for each pair of warm pants or long dress that came out of the bag. The children now had warm socks and long johns, mittens and scarves, and best of all, there was a winter coat for Little Ben that was truly a God-send. The clothes for the baby had some stains on them, and were well worn and Sarah found herself wondering what it would be like to give birth to eight children and lovingly dress them in the same clothes their sisters and brothers had worn. She imagined Midgie's sorrow as she said goodbye to the little baby gowns her wee ones had once worn. In the bottom of the box, Sarah found a fine little dress made out of large lacey handkerchiefs. It was as lovely as anything she had seen in Paris with its tiny handmade stitches finely lined around each seam. It must be a Christening gown, Sarah thought as she held it up so she could see the full length of the delicate garment.

The door opened and a Benjamin she had never encountered entered the room. The children's chatter seemed to irritate him and he began roughly stacking the boxes into one corner, tossing the items they had removed from the boxes on top of the stack carelessly as if it all were in his way. "There's no point in making a mess in here!" he said angrily, looking no one in the eye. "This cabin is small enough without pulling out all that clutter all over the floor! A man has to be able to walk through here!"

At that, the children stopped their play and began picking up the last of the items remaining and placing them on the pile. A glance at Sarah told him only that she could raise her eyebrows just a little bit without moving the rest of her face, and the fact that he had no idea what that meant just irritated him even more. He wanted to scream. He wanted to run. He wanted to go on a rampage yelling at the three of them until they all felt as miserable as he did.

He suddenly saw himself in his father's shoes, reigning terror down on everyone he should have loved and cared for. He looked at the children and saw himself standing in front of his older sister protectively like Sissy was doing with Little Ben and he hated himself even more. He had to do something or his head was going to explode, so he turned and grabbed the front door and began to wrestle it off its hinges. He pounded the working hinge with a hammer, and then slammed the door shut over and over, daring it to fall off. He went outside and again slammed the door repeatedly until he was exhausted, then giving it a kick, he took a deep breath and decided to try to figure out how the hinges actually worked.

It finally occurred to him that there were two separate pieces of metal involved. There was the one nailed to the door, and the one nailed to the wall. He decided it was pure brilliance the way they were made to interlock like fingers around a single pin, and he retrieved the hinge from the box and stood amazed at the puzzle that lay before him in that simple hinge. He had just happened to pick it up the correct way, so when he turned it over, the pin fell out. He had to fish around in the snow to find it and then headed over to the door to see if he could figure out how to take the door down. After nearly half an hour, he managed to remove the remaining hinge pin and separate the door from the cabin. He was so engrossed in his work that he didn't realize it was almost dark, it was snowing harder than he had ever seen, the cabin had no door, and nobody inside the little house had said one word to him about it.

Little Ben quietly put more wood on the fire, while Sarah began making coffee and warming up the soup someone had given her earlier in the day. "Sissy, would you please cut the bread for us and put it on the table?" Sarah said as she looked at Sissy's cheeks, red from the cold. "And go put on your cape and a scarf from the pile of clothes over there. I can't have you catching a cold." Her words were like a knife in Ben's heart. He felt quite foolish when he realized the situation he had put them all in. And Heaven help them if a bear came along! He felt like a complete fool, and yet the work was extraordinarily satisfying! He now had something to do, a direction to go in, and by God he was going to finish it!

He carefully measured the door and soundly nailed the part of the hinge that was to be attached to the door, onto the door. Then he measured again and attached the other part of the hinge to the door frame. Now all he had to do was reattach the door, slide in the pins, and it would be done and done well. He was hopeful, if not a little proud as he struggled to line up all the hinges. However, when he got the top one right, the bottom one would not fit and before long he was angry all over again. His measurements had been one quarter inch off so no matter how he tried, he could not re-hang the door. He was exhausted and wanted more than anything to just quit, but there was no one else to replace the door so quitting was not an option. He watched Sarah carrying quilts and pillows into the bedroom, as the children wrestled with the feather tick to get it up onto the frame. While he stubbornly stood half in and half out of the door, he watched Sarah take the children into the bedroom so they could stay warm together under the covers, and go to bed.

All his false bravado disappeared as the bedroom door shut against the cold. He sat down on the floor of the cabin with his feet outside the door in the snow and thought to himself that they were better off before he tried to fix it, "I should have just let it be," he thought to himself, "at least the door closed the way it was!" And that gave him an idea. If he couldn't figure out how to do it correctly, at least he could return it to the way it was before. In minutes, he had removed the hinge he had nailed on, lifted the door, and with one hand steadying the door, and his foot under the door lifting it into place, he managed to replace the pin in the old hinge, rendering the door at least closeable. As he locked the door behind him, exhausted, he turned and discovered the children had made up the feather tick for him to sleep in. It was scooted as close to the fire as was safe, with a pillow at one end, one blanket covering the tick, and another one on top, folded back and waiting for him to pull up over himself.

He walked around to the fire side of the inviting bed and thought that he had never been more tired in his entire life. As he pulled off one boot, he bumped something beside the bed and discovered a wooden box turned on its end, serving as a night table, and upon it was a now lukewarm cup of coffee and a fried potato and bacon sandwich Sarah had made for him. With a deep sigh, the enormity of their thoughtfulness washed over him, and for the first time he could remember, he allowed himself to cry. He cried for his mother. He cried for his sister and the years they had lost, and he cried for the little boy who missed getting to have a good father to teach him how to do things like fix a broken door. As he cried, he wiped his tears on his shirt sleeves and now they were both uncomfortably wet from the elbows down. He thought about taking off his shirt and hanging it in front of the fire to dry, then just held his arms out to the fire, knowing it wouldn't take long for them to dry. His thoughts wandered to the amazing phenomenon of how quickly water disappeared in the face of fire. Clothes hung to dry in front of a fire were dry as a bone in no time, and the water in a boiling pot had to be watched closely for fear of it boiling away. Water.

What was it Preacher said about water? That God leads us to still waters? Ben wished he had a Bible to read because he needed to hear that again. He needed to remember the sermon he had heard. He knew little about sheep, but remembered they weren't very smart, but surely that wasn't the Preacher's point. Ah, well. He was not going to chase any more endless thoughts around endless circles tonight. He had chased his tail for too long, and was exhausted mentally, physically, emotionally, and spiritually, and it was clearly time to rest. He remembered briefly thinking about how much more comfortable the bed was than the floor, and then he awakened hearing hissing noises, and various thumps and clangs.

For some reason, he couldn't move. His bladder was full to overflowing, he had a terrible taste in his mouth, and he couldn't sit up to save his life. He closed his eyes again, and when he opened them, he saw the faces of two children smiling down on either side at him. "G'morning!" Little Ben said with a smile. "We thought you was dead!"

Sissy reached across Ben's chest and swatted Little Ben and said, "Don't say that! What's the matter with you!"

"All right you two," Sarah said, "go set a place for Ben at the table."

Ben finally fought his way to the top of the thick feather tick and managed to swing his legs around to the floor. Apparently he hadn't moved all night and his limbs were paying the price for it now. As he sat on the edge of the bed and tried to get his eyes to stay open, he heard a "thunk" and looked over just in time to see a hot cup of coffee being placed on his little bed table by Sarah. He looked up and was rewarded with what he decided was the prettiest smile he had ever seen in his life, even better than Juanita's chubby smile, and he wondered why she was being so nice to him.

"Look!" Sissy caught his eye. "I put everthang away jist like you wanted it! Me and Ben took all the extra boxes and stacked 'em out in the woodshed, so now you can walk around in here all you want!" she said cheerfully.

"When did they do all that?" Ben wondered. As he turned to look out the windows he realized the sun had been up for hours and the light cut through his eyes like shards of glass. He felt for his boots so he could go outside and realized he was smelling bacon. Ummm! Bacon and coffee... his stomach growled and he hoped he didn't starve to death before he got back inside to eat.

When he returned he heard the hissing sound of cold wet potatoes sliding into a hot frying pan as Sarah announced, "Go on and sit down. Your breakfast will be ready in a minute." Little Ben retrieved Ben's coffee from the bed table and set it where Ben had sat before, then went to get himself a cup of milk that he took a drink of every time Ben took a drink of coffee.

Ben watched the activity going on around him and decided to enjoy the moment. This may not last forever, but after a good night's sleep, having a pretty woman smile at him while she fixed his breakfast was worth giving his undivided attention to. He ate bacon, fried potatoes, fried eggs, and fried buttered bread with homemade strawberry jam until he thought he would never be hungry again. As he leaned back to enjoy his coffee, his plate was whisked off the table and the table was washed off with a soapy cloth. Now that he was awakening, he began to feel badly about his behavior the night before, especially since everyone was being so nice to him this morning. He had to say something to clear the air because it wasn't in him to take all their kindness lightly.

"I'm sorry about last night," he said out into the air at no one in particular.

Sarah stepped in front of him, wiped her hands with her apron and asked, "Exactly what are you sorry for, Benjamin Waters?"

"For getting so angry I guess. I didn't like the man I was being last night, but it just seemed I couldn't stop myself from yelling at everyone."

Sarah said, "Alright, everybody come over here and sit down at the table."

As they noisily pulled out the chairs to sit down Sarah took a deep breath to say something, but Little Ben interrupted by shouting, "Sissy! You took MY chair!"

"These chairs got nobody's name on 'em, 'n I got here first!" Sissy screamed back making a fist and holding it up as a challenge.

"But I want to sit by Papa!" Little Ben pleaded.

"Stop it!" Sarah said turning to look at the children. "Here Ben, you sit in my seat and I will go to the other end of the table."

When it was all said and done, Sarah was at one end of the table; Ben was at the other, with a child on either side.

Sarah appeared to be the spokeswoman for the group. "Ben, when we got up this morning there was a bit of a lilt in the air. It could have been because we were excited about all the new furniture, right?" she included the children by nodding at them and allowing them time to nod back as if to say, "It could have been." They were all looking at him with one ridiculous, collective smile.

"Or it could have been that we were so happy to have so much food," again the nods of agreement. Ben had the feeling this had all been discussed prior to this conversation and they were about to announce the verdict.

"But there was more to it than that." Sarah's look to the children was downright conspiratorial as she continued, "You were about as angry as a man can get last night, and..."

"Yea, that is what I wanted to talk to you about." Ben interrupted, "I really feel bad about the way I..."

"No, no. Just wait. This is important. Just let me say it, and then you can go on," Sarah said with an authority that silenced Benjamin.

Ben nodded and noticed how uncharacteristically happy everyone looked as they sat there with goofy smiles on their faces.

"Now, as I was saying, you were about as angry as a man can get last night," she held up her hand to stop him from saying anything else, "and what did you do? You turned around and went over to fix the door. The day was half over, and you went over to work on fixing our door."

At that Ben felt a little embarrassed. It wasn't exactly as she had said, but he had agreed to listen, so listen he would.

"We all realized this morning that it was refreshing to have a man get angry and…" Now that it was time to say what she wanted to say, she couldn't find the words.

Little Ben's face became drawn and he looked more like an old man than the bubbly little boy who had been there just a moment before. "We thought you was gonna' beat us."

"I know, I'm sorry. I…" Benjamin was feeling really low at this point. If they wanted to punish him for his anger, they were doing a good job of it. He felt lower than dirt.

"But you didn't," Sissy straightened her arms out onto the table, palms up and said with a big smile, "You got real mad, but you didn't hit none of us!"

It was clearly a significant moment for them, had he been looking at it from their point of view, but from his own perspective, it meant they had been afraid of him all along. "I told you I would never hurt you," Benjamin said a little defensively.

Sarah got up, her smile gone, left the table, and began cleaning up the dishes while Sissy picked up the conversation. Her hands withdrawn to her lap, she looked down and said simply, "Well… men lie." He heard Sarah drop something in the kitchen and realized Sissy was speaking for all of them.

Benjamin felt overwhelming compassion for this little girl who had been forced to grow up far too soon. Without moving he replied, "Well, for future reference, I don't lie, and I don't hurt people," he said turning to make sure his voice was heard in the kitchen.

"Yea… Well… We believe you now. That's all," Sissy said with all joy gone from her voice. Both children were locked into their pasts, with memories so thick they couldn't see today, and Benjamin didn't know what to do, or what to say because he had worn himself out with worry the day before, and had no energy for taking on all this sorrow as well. He just wished the day could be carefree without all the worry he had inherited along with his freedom, so he finally said very quietly, "But, I do have something to share with you, that I feel I must tell you since we are living here together." Their frightened faces tipped up toward him.

"I actually have been known to hit children, and I must warn you, just so you know," his face remaining solemn as he spoke. Sarah returned to the room, dish towel gripped tightly in one of her fists, ready for battle.

He glanced at the faces again and saw Little Ben's lower lip quiver as he quickly continued, "I do believe I can hit children, even if they are laughing and running, with SNOWBALLS!" Instead of smiles as he expected, he saw them sadly considering how much pain a snowball could inflict.

"You children have never had a snowball fight?" His look was incredulous!

"Nope!"

"Well, you are in for a treat! Go get all bundled up and we are going to go have a huge snowball fight! But first we are going to have to build snow forts! Now surely you know how to build snow forts!" Benjamin searched their faces for some hint of recognition, but found none.

"Ok, let's go!" He jumped to his feet and began pulling his socks on, but the children still weren't sure of what was happening, until Benjamin shouted, "Boys against the girls! Come on Sarah! We can bundle up the baby and take her out into the sun in the bassinet." With that the children were finally sold on the idea and ran off to pack on as many clothes as was humanly possible. They had no idea what a snowball fight was, but if each of them was to have a grown-up on their side, it couldn't be that bad, and besides, Ben was smiling so they let go of their reservations and decided to go have fun.

They walked out into the snow ahead of Ben and Sarah who were getting the baby's bassinet set firmly on the frozen ground beneath the snow. The bassinet had long legs that made it table height, so the baby was far from the cold ground, basking in the sun. Ben left the job of tucking the baby in for Sarah to finish as he ducked down and made four snowballs, loaded them into his left arm and began pounding the children in the back of their heads with them.

Sissy was the last to turn around, so the last lightly packed snowball hit her right in the face. She stopped and looked for a minute like she was going to cry, but before she could react, Little Ben, who had caught the spirit of the event, squatted down and made a snowball of his own which he tossed back at Benjamin. For a full minute, snowballs flew in both directions, but with two on one, Ben was soon spending so much time defending himself he could not keep up making snowballs!

"Truce! Truce!" Ben shouted from behind his upraised arms, but one snowball landed on his arm, bursting into pieces and filling his eyes and mouth with snow! He fell to the ground and was immediately pounced on by Little Ben who sat on his back, while Sissy washed his face with snow. "Ok! I give up! Help, Sarah! Help!"

The two children and Ben looked up at Sarah and it dawned on them that she was standing beside the baby perfectly dry and untouched. They looked at each other and jumped up to make snowballs. Sarah looked a bit shaken, and cried, "No! Wait! Now, I have never done this, and I don't even know how to…" THWACK! The first snowball was to her belly and she turned her back to them for protection, dipped her head down, covering her face with her hands, and shouted, "WAIT!"

Ben gave the children a look that made them stop to see what she had to say. She turned back around and smoothed her dress down with her hands, carefully rubbing every flake of snow off the materiel on her coat, reminding Ben of an old schoolmarm. It had never occurred to Ben until now, that he had never seen her look disheveled. Even when they were staying in the cave she remained prim and proper under the worst of circumstances and for the first time, he wondered what position she had held in her prior life.

His thoughts were interrupted when she spoke, "Although I have been a witness to snowball fights, I have never actually participated. I would like to go over the rules of play..." THWACK! THUD! THUMP! Then, BOOM, BOOM, BOOM, the snowballs flew with great regularity, most making a direct hit on their target, and soon she was covered with snow, her hair knocked out of its bun, her hat in the snow, and not one square inch of her clothing without snow clinging to it.

"Ok, you rascals! If it is a fight you want, it's a fight you'll get!" Sarah shouted good naturedly. "Now, what is a snow fort, and how do you build them." The children were cheering and laughing as the girls began to build their fort on one side and the boys on the other. Snowballs were made and stacked, and strategies were mapped out.

The girl's fort wasn't nearly as big, or as well built as the boy's, and the girls didn't have nearly as many snowballs as the guys, but the ladies were ok with that. They were confident with their plan, so long before the boys were ready to start; the girls sat down behind their pitiful little wall and chatted.

The boys were feeling quite certain they had over-planned; after all, it was only girls they were going to battle. Benjamin was planning on overshooting his throws so any direct hits would have to be from Little Ben. And that wouldn't be too hard since their forts were fairly close together and the girl's fort was so low they really couldn't hide behind it.

The boys' fort, on the other hand, was large enough to hide five full grown men. There was a small hill rising out in front of their cabin which served them well. Ben started at the top of the hill and rolled huge snowballs three feet in diameter down to where Little Ben was, resting them against each other like pearls on a necklace. While Ben returned to the top of the hill to make another one, Little Ben packed snow between the huge snowballs, to create what appeared to be a solid wall. Before he made the fifth and last trip up the hill, Ben told Little Ben to start making snowballs and piling them in a stack between the two forts, but a little closer to their fort than the girls, "The more the better," Ben said as he looked over at the girls who were sitting behind a tiny wall, barely two feet tall, they had made by scooping the snow into a peak and patting it on both sides. They were sitting there laughing and giggling in an image that made Ben feel grateful, and warm, and healed at the same time. This was what he had wanted for his sisters, a life where they felt safe and had nothing to worry about because their mother was a strong woman, and in his daydream, also safe.

The gratitude in his heart just soared on the wings of an unspoken prayer as he looked up into the clear blue sky. He had no idea yet how to pray, so the angels spoke on his behalf praising his Shepherd and Protector for this unexpected day of joy. Never in a million years had he ever dreamed he would be a free man, and yet, here he stood, not only free, but blessed beyond imagination.

He stopped at the top of the hill and raised his arms to the sky. He had the odd sensation that his physical body had become invisible: his joyful spirit filled the space he occupied on this earth. For just a moment he embraced the Holy Spirit as if it had been beside him waiting a lifetime for him to turn and accept the healing and intense love God had for him, and he knew and understood that he was loved by a mighty and capable God of peace: a God so powerful and so forgiving, that it sought out even him, and lifted him from hell on earth, and set him down in the midst of beauty and peace. "He leadeth me beside the still waters," the scripture that had eluded him came bubbling up into his soul and he knew he would never forget it again.

He laughed out loud as he began rolling the last link in the snow fort down the hill toward those people he now realized he loved. He smiled as he watched Little Ben hunkered down behind the fort wall, and his girls sitting, talking in animated speech, punctuated with gales of laughter.

"Ready guys?" He shouted the alert and Sarah and Sissy rose up on their knees while Little Ben just made snowballs faster and faster.

Ben got behind the wall and shared a conspiratorial smile with Little Ben as he made a mental note to remember this moment as he recited all the wonderful times he had had, beginning with the visit with Lloyd and Juanita.

"GO!" Ben shouted as he and Little Ben began lobbing snowballs over the fort's wall without looking. Their goal was to get hit as few times as possible while inundating the girls with a deluge of snowballs. Then, when all of the girl's ammunition was spent, they would jump out of the fort and run toward them, pounding them with the stack of missiles Little Ben had left between the two forts.

Victory would come hard and fast and the boys would return to the house, dry and free from the inevitable snow down the collar the girls would be experiencing. They had even planned to make dinner for the girls so they could change clothes and sit down to a hot meal as soon as possible.

The boys were almost out of snowballs and ready to charge. "Ok," Benjamin said, "we will throw these last few and then jump out and run to the ones out in the middle. Ready? Go!" They jumped to their feet and came face to face with the girls who had decided they didn't care how many times they were hit, had faced the barrage of snowballs and advanced to where the boys had left them a neat stack of already formed ammo. Now all the boys could do was retreat and try to regroup, since they had no more snowballs, but the women were close enough to them to keep them defending their faces and necks while running toward the woods. The guys thought they had a reprieve when the pounding of snowballs stopped, and attributed it to the fact that they had found shelter under some low hanging tree limbs that were burdened with a massive amount of snow.

Suddenly the girls revealed an extra stash of superbly made snowballs they had been hiding in their gathered up aprons. They heaved them into the air, but to the relief of the boys, they were far too high to hit them. The snowballs made contact with the snow laden limbs, however, which obediently dumped their entire burdens of snow right down on the heads and necks of the unsuspecting warriors.

"Oh!" They shouted as pounds and pounds of snow beat them on the head and packed their collars, pockets, boots, hair, and even the tops of their ears with a wet heavy snow. As they came running out from under the trees, they found themselves recipients of the last insult. Each girl held one more snowball which found its target right on or close to their faces.

"We won," the girls said glibly as they turned and slowly walked back toward the cabin. The boys stood there in stunned silence until the girls dissolved in giggles and took off running just in case the boys decided to retaliate. Knowing they would not throw any snowballs toward the baby, they stopped when they got to her, and picked her up to go inside. The boys looked at each other and laughed at how completely covered with snow they were. Ben brushed the snow out of Little Ben's hair and ears as they laughed at the sight they must have been. They all returned to the cabin, wet and tired, and loving each other more than they even realized at the time.

The evening was warm and cozy. Sarah rocked the baby and sang sweet songs to her, and the children entertained themselves with a game of sorts that only they knew the rules to. They had changed into their new nightshirts and just looked so much healthier than they had been when Ben and Sarah found them. Another prayer of gratitude lifted itself from his soul and rose to the Heavens, but all Ben knew was he was feeling more blessed and happy than he knew a man could be. Yes, God had created another Adam and Eve, and had brought them to this Garden of Eden. But unlike the first creations, they had already tasted of hell, and were instead, incredibly grateful.

CHAPTER TEN

Just as the sun was setting, Benjamin began thinking of the things he wanted to accomplish the next day, the repairs he wanted to make, and the things he wanted to show Little Ben. He was making lists, and listening to the conversation Sarah was having with the children, when his thoughts were interrupted by a thud, and wondered for a split second if the door had fallen off. But with the door still intact he began to think of other options. Thud! Again it felt like something had hit the cabin, or fallen from the cabin, but he had no idea what it could have been, and he had no intentions of going outside just in case it was a bear 'come a'knockin'. The sounds subsided and he planned to have a good look at the entire exterior of the house first thing in the morning.

Suddenly a snowball shattered the window with a loud crash. Broken glass rained down on the floor, and the corner of the window sash jutted out at an angle. This time Ben charged the door and ran out into the night to see if he could find the culprit, but by the time his eyes adjusted to darkness, the guilty party was long gone.

Ben returned to the cabin, haunted by the dark shadows of guilt. Had someone found out about him and was telling them to get out? Again he wondered if he should leave this little family, so as to not drag them into his problems when he got caught.

In order to keep the children from worrying, Sarah put them to bed early, or at least that was what she told herself. Actually, her fear that she had been identified and would therefore bring trouble for Ben and the children had set her into a panic, and she wanted to have time to speak to Ben about her concerns, more for comfort than for answers. She lied to herself and said she just wanted to be brutally honest with him about her past, so he would move into the future with his eyes open. But the truth of the matter was, she just needed to talk to him, to watch his face as he heard what she said and to get his input. She was getting closer to him, and that was something that frightened her, as well. After all, he was a free man, and could leave tomorrow if he wanted. She had no hold on him and told herself she didn't want to be obligated to a man ever again, and now here she was manipulating the evening's events so she could spend private time with him. As she tucked the children in and left the room, her hand went up to her hair to be certain she looked presentable. "Stop it!" She meant to say only to herself. What on earth was she thinking?

"Did you say something?" Ben asked.

"Oh, no, I was just… uh… no, I didn't say anything." That was a close call. She had almost let her guard down and spent an evening enjoying the company of a man, knowing full well that she would regret it. "I think I will go on to bed as well," she said without looking at him.

He didn't blame her. He knew what she was thinking; that he was bringing trouble into the house, into her life and that of the children. And on top of that, he had no idea how to fix the window and had to ask for her help. *Will I always go through life half a man?* He wondered to himself. Here he was as tall as a grown man, and as old as a grown man, and yet completely devoid of any of the knowledge a grown man needed to survive.

"Uh… Sarah?" he could almost hear the gulp as he swallowed his pride.

"Yes," her heart skipped a beat. *Oh I cannot believe this*, she thought to herself. *Stop acting like a school girl!*

"What do you think we should do about the window?" There it was. Now she knew how ignorant he was; another low in his life, threatening to cruelly undermine his already dispirited self-esteem.

But she was pleased she had the opportunity to be alone with him, especially under non-threatening circumstances. "Well, we could use the lumber they brought for repairing the cabin and cover the window with that, at least for the night." she offered.

"Yea, I thought of that, but I hate to cut it up into small pieces because I don't know where I would ever get long pieces again and I may need some to patch these cracks."

"Well, we could nail them up there whole," she said. Then qualified her statement by saying, "Temporarily, of course." She was so frightened he would laugh at her; she felt the need to continue justifying her opinion. "Nothing says they have to be the right length. Then when we decide what to do with the window we could take them down." Sarah had never in her life been consulted in men's matters and had the feeling that Ben was going to tell her to mind her own business.

Instead he said sincerely, "You are so smart."

He could not have stunned her more had he hit her with a board. She felt elated that her idea was a good one, relieved he hadn't chastised her for stepping into men's territory, and surprised he had admitted so frankly that she was smart. Oh, for Heaven's sake! Why was she acting like this? She was baffled at her own behavior and yet when he asked her to hold the boards for him, she practically floated over to the window, pleased as punch to be near him, actually touching hands and shoulders while they worked.

They accomplished their task as quickly as possible in order to finish the pounding so the children could sleep. Sarah was amazed the baby slept through it, but the infant was exhausted from having been out in the cold all day, so sleep she did. By the time they were finished, all pretenses were gone. They enjoyed each other's company and no longer felt the need to hide it.

They sat at the table drinking coffee and laughing about the snowball fight, talking about Midgie and her crew, how much they enjoyed church, and how much healthier the children looked. It was friendship at its best. She found his deep voice to be soothing, and with every smile she blessed him with, his heart felt a little lighter. They had never talked before, about the children, or anything else. Now the conversation flowed easily. They were both rejoicing at the situation they were now in. And although they both interpreted it simply as lightheartedness, the truth was the Holy Spirit was busy at work restoring their souls.

"Hey, do you know the scripture the Preacher read Sunday?" Ben asked with no clue as to why he had thought of it. "You know, something about leading us beside the still waters and restoring our souls?"

Sarah said, "I am familiar with the passage, I mean I have heard it before, but I couldn't recite it, why?"

"It just really touched me somehow, in fact, that is where I came up with the name, Waters!"

Sarah laughed and said, "I wondered if that had been your real name. I was worried when I realized you had to introduce yourself and we hadn't talked about a last name. But I like it. I like Sarah Waters, and Ben Waters." She loved the way the names sounded, and more importantly, she liked sharing his name.

Ben said, "That day on the boat coming down here, I just felt such peace when I looked down into the water. I kind of forgot everything else that had happened in my life as I stared down into that peaceful river, just drifting along, not having to worry about where I was going or how I was going to get there. Then when I heard that scripture about God leading us beside the still waters, well, that just seemed like a good place to start, with the name Waters."

Sarah nodded as she listened to him speak, and was content just to revisit the trip on the Little Kanawha through his eyes.

"I want to get a copy of what he read. Do you have a Bible?" he asked hopefully.

"No, not with me," she said flatly. Thoughts of her past threatened to infringe upon tonight's sweetness, but she would not allow it. She had to go outside after drinking all that coffee, so she pulled on her coat, slipped her feet into her boots, and opened the door to find the sun just beginning to rise over the hill in front of the cabin.

"BEN!"

He jumped to his feet, afraid of what he was about to find, but when he got to the door he was equally amazed to find they had talked all night, and neither of them was at all tired. Suddenly, the baby, who had been rudely awakened by their shouts, screamed to be picked up and changed. "I'll get her, you go on outside," Ben said with the sweetest of smiles, and Sarah thought her heart would burst.

"Good morning all you children!" Ben shouted as he realized the baby had awakened both Little Ben and Sissy. "Little Ben, how about you and I fix the girls breakfast, and we will leave little Miss Sissy and the baby here so she can have her breakfast?"

"Don't you think it's high time we name her?" Sissy asked from the bed.

"Well, that's up to you, Sissy. But now that you've mentioned it, have you thought of any names you like?" Ben asked as Little Ben pulled on his pants and shoes.

"No," Sissy said, "but I'll think of one soon. Every human being deserves to have a name, don't you think? Even little ones."

Ben agreed, but by then Little Ben was ready to go, so they went out to the kitchen and Ben started frying bacon while Little Ben set about scrubbing potatoes. The sun just cleared the hill when Sarah returned to find the boys busy making breakfast.

She had just stepped inside the door, and was stomping the snow off her feet when she caught a glimpse of a rider coming up the road to the right of the cabin. Ben followed her gaze and the forgotten fear from the night before grabbed his chest and as he seized his coat and stepped outside, saying to Sarah, "Go on in and lock the door, Sarah."

Without a word, Sarah closed the door, slid the wooden bar across it, and went in to assist Little Ben in the making of breakfast. "Is Sissy awake?" Sarah asked conversationally, although her thoughts were with Ben and what he was facing. She began to revisit the fear she had felt the night before, that someone had recognized her and she was about to get caught. She wondered why she had stayed and brought all this trouble on Ben and the children when she knew full well that she had needed to run farther and longer if she were to remain free.

"Yea, she's feedin' the baby," Little Ben replied. Sarah had forgotten she had asked about Sissy.

"Oh, wonderful," Sarah said absently. She wished Ben would come back in and tell her what had happened out there.

"Ben," Abram said as he stopped his horse in front of the cabin.

"Abram," Ben said. Not wanting to mince words, Ben decided to face whatever the trouble was before Sarah and the children got involved. If they were going to take him, let them do it now while the children were in the house. Ben urged him on, "What can I do for you?"

Abram didn't bother to get down from the horse. He snapped his fingers and his boy, Denzel, jumped down from behind his father. "My boy here's got somethin' to say to you, don't you boy?"

The boy never took his eyes off the ground as he said, "Yes, sir."

"Well, go on boy before I give you another lickin'!" Abram was angry and the thought crossed Ben's mind that he hoped Abram was not now, or ever, angry with him.

"Yes, sir," Denzel continued. "It was me who broke your window, sir." He looked up at his father hoping that was enough, but Abram said, "Go on, boy."

"I'm awful sorry, and I'm here to make it up to you." This time when he looked up at his father, Abram seemed satisfied. "I figger a day's work should make you even, but you can have him longer if you feel it's needed. We mean to make this right by you, Ben."

Ben wanted to let the boy off the hook, but knew better than to stop a man from teaching his son responsibility. Besides, he could tell that Denzel had been crying, and he thought it as much a favor to Denzel to keep him out of his father's way for the day as it was to Ben. Ben said, "I think a day's work is just fine, Abram, and I thank you."

"As soon as we get to Jimmy's, we'll be replacing that glass, too."

"That isn't necessary, Abram…," Ben started to say.

"Yes it is, Ben. We want to make this right by you folks. The boy will be working off the cost of the glass, too, out at Jimmy's store."

"Well, I think that is a fair solution, Abram." Ben wanted to do something to let Abram know there were no hard feelings, and all he could think of was to shake his hand. As he stepped forward and offered his hand to Abram, he could see him visibly relax. "We have to work too close together, and have to rely on each other too much to have bad blood between neighbors, Ben," Abram said.

"I understand, Abram, and I appreciate your honesty," Ben smiled and Abram.

Satisfied he had solved the problem fairly Abram gave Denzel a stern look, then turned his horse around and headed home.

"Have you had breakfast, boy?" Ben said to the top of Denzel's head. Suddenly, the boy looked up and he said, "A little, sir." Ben laughed, remembering how hungry he was at that age. Yes, he had had breakfast, but he could eat again. Ben ruffled Denzel's hair, put his arm around the boy's shoulders and led him into the house.

Sarah and Ben shared a look as Ben entered with the boy, but no explanation was offered in front of Little Ben and Sissy. By the end of breakfast, Denzel had heard the entire story about the snowball fight, from the strategies, to the distance of the longest throw. Sarah was pleased that nobody mentioned who had won, it seemed to be the actual fun they all focused on, and that said a lot about the quality of people they were.

Denzel spent the entire time eating, but as soon as he finished, he took his plate to the kitchen and asked if there was anything he could do to help take up breakfast. Sarah assured him there was not, so he turned to Sissy and said, "I can throw a snowball farther than anybody else in the county. Why, I can throw a rock and knock a squirrel off a limb if I want to. I am the best there is at throwin' things."

"So what?" Sissy asked, totally unimpressed by his boasting.

"Sissy!" Sarah said firmly, take your plate to the kitchen and go get dressed. It is too late in the morning to be running around in your nightshirt.

Sarah looked at Ben, and Ben jumped to his feet and said, "Ok, Denzel. Are you ready to get to work?"

"Yes, sir," Denzel said with conviction. Ben saw Denzil as a young man stepping up to his responsibility, and was proud of the way he was taking his punishment. But then he realized he had no idea what to have the boy do.

"Uh… Denzel, do you have any idea how to fix a broken door?"

"Yes, sir, what's wrong with it?"

Ben walked over to the box by the door and said, "Well, this hinge needs to be put on it. I will help you take the door down."

Denzel looked puzzled and said, "Why do we need to take the door down?"

Ben had no answer for that, but luckily he thought of something to say, "Well, it's the top hinge, and…"

But Denzel turned and grabbed one of the chairs from the table, took the hinge from Ben, put six nails from the tin cup between his lips, slid the hammer under his arm and stepped up to the doorframe. Without a hitch, Denzel opened the hinge and placed it where it went against the door and frame. When he thought he had the door even, he nailed the hinge to the doorframe with two nails, and to the door with another two. Then he jumped down, scooted the chair back and carefully swung the door open and closed to be sure he had it placed correctly. Seeming satisfied with his placement of the hinge, he again climbed up and pounded the third nails into each side. Jumping down from the chair, he said, "Now what?"

Ben felt like screaming, and then was embarrassed that Sarah had seen him struggle all day with that door, and then fail to accomplish such an easy task. He slid a sideways glance at her to see if she was laughing at him, but she was overly busy washing the dishes and cleaning the entire kitchen and table with a little too much enthusiasm and focus.

"Good work, Denzel, now we have some repair work to do around here," he opened the door and ushered Denzel outside. "You walk around out here and see what you can find while I get dressed," Ben said, glad for the excuse to go back into the house. By the time Ben had put on his socks, boots and coat, Denzel was busy at work covering the cracks between the boards on the house. Having grown up there, Denzel knew of a storage building out back that had long ago fallen down so he went back to where it once had stood and began kicking the snow off it.

"What are you doing, Denzel?" Ben asked curiously.

"Well, if you didn't have nothin' else for me to do, I thought I might get some boards from this old building, and see if there was any hardware I could pull off 'em."

Ben said, "Oh, yeah, that would be fine, in fact I think I'll just help you do that."

They fell into a comfortable pace, randomly finding boards, a still intact shelf, and the rusty hinges from the door; they set aside to take into the house. It was like finding buried treasure, and soon they had salvaged almost enough wood to make a storage shed, or add on a room if they were careful.

"This is quite a find, Denzel," Ben mentioned, "Are there any other surprises around here I should know about?"

"Well, sir," Denzel said after pausing for a time, "I could show you where the well is. Snow won't last forever, and come spring, you'll be needin' water."

They climbed the small hill in front of the cabin, then another that was slightly higher. The meadow they were in stretched out several hundred yards, and was rutted by the wagons and sleighs that had traveled that way to the church. After a time, Denzel headed down to the left into the forest, where he pointed out the well that had been there for years. "It is the best well on the ridge," Denzel said. "Sometimes when our well goes dry, we bring the cows over here to water them."

"Well, I hope you know you can still do that, Denzel. And I appreciate your showing this to me!" He ruffled the boy's hair and continued, "You know, I think your breaking that window is the best thing that has happened to me in a long time!"

Denzel laughed and blushed, but he was secretly pleased that Ben wasn't mad at him. He just hoped his father would be as understanding when he got home.

On the walk back to the cabin, Denzel said suddenly, and without apology, "Your place is little."

"Well, it suits us," Ben said back to him.

"Well, I was thinkin' that the more little'ns come along, the more space your gonna need."

Ben found it amusing that Denzel just assumed there would be more children because that was just how it was in their house. While he was thinking about that, Denzel continued, "So's I was thinkin' a good use for some of this wood might be a loft. You can get more folks in there without adding' on, and it's warmer up there in the winter."

As they started down the last hill, cabin in sight, Sarah shouted, "Ben! Dinner is ready if you two are ready to eat."

As they stomped their feet on the porch, Ben said, "Reckon you could build that loft this afternoon?"

"Well," Denzel said, "I could get a real good start on it anyway. Then after my chores are done, I could come back and work on it a little every day until I got it all done."

"Denzel, you don't owe us that. You can just work on it this afternoon and that will be an end to your obligations."

"I don't mind, sir, I like working with my hands."

Before Ben could argue they opened the door to the smell of coffee and stew. Neither had realized just how hungry and cold they were until they stepped into the warm, aromatic cabin where they were greeted with the chatter of the children.

The day ended just exactly as Denzel had predicted. By the time his father came to get him, he had made a real good start on the loft, but there was much to be done. As he locked arms with his father and hopped onto the horse behind him, he said, "I'll see you tomorrow after chores!"

Before Ben could protest, Abram said, "How'd he do today?"

"Now that boy does a man's work, Abram. You should be mighty proud," Ben was glad he didn't have to lie, and he was pleased at Abram's reaction. That day's work had gone a long way toward mending fences between father and son, and Ben was glad to see that happen.

The evening was tense as the adults waited for the time when the children would finally be asleep. They should have been exhausted, but instead they were both looking forward to continuing the conversation they felt they hadn't finished. Ben wondered if that was what a marriage was--a lifelong conversation.

As the children settled in to their beds for the night, Sarah poured them each a cup of coffee and sat down as she placed the cup in front of Ben. "So," Ben said, "it appears that young Denzel was the one who broke our window." He could hardly wait to tell her that, and her reaction just egged him on.

"What?" she said surprised. She leaned toward him, filled with questions and intrigued.

"Yea, Abram brought him over here and made him apologize and work for a day to pay off his debt. They are replacing the glass as well, and Denzel has to work at Jimmy's to pay for the glass, too."

"Did you ask him why he broke the window," Sarah asked.

"No."

"Did you ask him why he was over here when it was getting dark, throwing snowballs at the house?" She was grinning like she knew something he didn't, which ruffled his feathers since he felt foolish enough for not asking him those questions in the first place.

"No! Why? Why are you asking me like that?"

"Don't you know?" She was teasing him because he was clueless.

"Know what? I don't get it."

"He fancies our Miss Sissy," she said smugly.

"What? Oh, he does not! What on earth makes you think that?"

"Because," Sarah said knowingly, "that is what boys do when they fancy a girl. Didn't you hear him bragging to her about how far he can throw a snowball?"

Ben still looked oblivious, and it made Sarah laugh.

"Men!" She said with a giggle. "I can't believe you can't see how starry eyed he was when he was talking to Sissy. You were right there! He was bragging about how he was the best thrower in the county! Surely you saw that."

"No, I sure didn't. But why would he break our window. That just doesn't make any sense at all."

"Well, maybe he was hoping Sissy would come outside," Sarah said, watching his face over her coffee cup as she took a sip. Looking for any signs of recognition, but finding none, she decided instead to change the subject before he became uncomfortable, "So, how long do you think it will take you to finish the loft?"

"Well, it should take a week or so, Denzel said. He is coming back every night until it's done," he said totally unaware that he just handed the proof of Sarah's argument to her on a silver platter.

Sarah's laugh was golden. "Oh yeah, he has it bad," she said as she threw her head back and laughed a joyous easy laugh. Ben didn't care if he was right or wrong, for as long as she laughed, life was good.

CHAPTER ELEVEN

Soon, it was Sunday again, and they found themselves excited to go to church. Whether it was for the fellowship of adults, or the feeling that they were a part of something bigger than themselves, they weren't sure, but they arose early, refreshed and eager to see Midgie and Abram coming up over the hill.

They were out of the cabin and waiting when the sleigh pulled up. Ben helped Sarah into the back, then took the baby from Sissy and handed it to Sarah. He then assisted Sissy as she climbed into the back and stood, looking for a place to sit down. Suddenly, Denzel nudged Maxine with his elbow, and she jumped up leaving a space beside Denzel for Sissy to sit.

This time Ben noticed. He was shocked at the revelation; and stood there staring at Denzel and Sissy as if seeing them for the first time. It was an awkward moment for everybody involved until Sarah said gently, "Ben, let's not hold everybody up!"

Ben snapped out of it and, mumbling, turned to pick up Little Ben and place him on the back of the sled. "Did you say something, Papa?" Little Ben asked.

"Nothing," Ben murmured as he jumped aboard and jerked as the sleigh began its journey.

He was very quiet all the way to the church, which amused Sarah. Once again, she couldn't wait to be alone with him so they could discuss the events that were unfolding. She had never enjoyed a man's company like she did Ben's, and it was all deliciously new to her. She found herself fantasizing about living this life until she passed from this earth rather than to face the fear and anxiety she would have to deal with if she planned to leave. She felt she had used up all her courage getting this far and just wanted to stay with Ben and the children forever.

For some reason, when they arrived at the church, they sat exactly where they had the first time they had been there: center row, in the back on the left. Ben went in first, then Little Ben, Sissy, and then Sarah was seated on the aisle with the baby. People nodded at them and smiled then turned as Preacher took his place at the pulpit. Ben wished he had a paper and pencil, and hoped someone there would have some he could borrow.

"Good morning, folks!" Reverend Morrison began with his usual broad smile.

"Good morning, Preacher!" the congregation replied.

"Well, this certainly is a blessed morning isn't it?"

There was a murmur as the crowd responded with various shouts of "Amen," and "Yes it is, Preacher."

"Well, didn't we have a blessing last week?" he said as he looked out at the congregation and acknowledged their smiles and nods. "Last week we had the privilege of being able to lift some of our fellow travelers on this earth, to care for them with an outpouring of love that went over and above what was expected!" The parishioners nodded with joyous smiles on their faces. Preacher continued, "We need to praise God for the opportunity to serve others as He served us, to care for others as He cares for us. You know, we are His hands and feet. He left this world and went to live with our Heavenly Father, leaving us to be His Shepherds on this earth, and if we do NOT do His work here, who will? Who will lift up the lost? Feed the hungry? Clothe the poor?"

Sarah and Ben looked at each other as the realization dawned on them that the Reverend was talking about them, and the outpouring of gifts they had been given. Sarah looked at the genuine joy on the faces of these humble people, and thought, Oh, so this is what Christ was talking about. She had never experienced the "love" and "serve" end of Christ's teachings. She had been bullied and beaten into submission by tyrants who meant to frighten the masses into repentance; first by her father who, in exchange for a higher ranking within the church, had traded her as if she were a fine horse, and then by her husband who threatened to kill her before he would allow a minister's wife to shame him before his congregation. She had been attending Midgie's church in order to maintain their charade, but for the first time her spirit was finding nourishment in Christ's words through the acts of this community and its church, and she found herself thirsting for more.

But for Ben, the experience was a reminder of the humiliation of being given all these things with no way to repay these folks. He wondered if the men would be waiting outside to speak to him regarding his debt. The longer he sat there the more uncomfortable he became. He wished he had his own sleigh so he could take them home right now. He began calculating the distance back to the cabin and wondered if he could even find it on his own. Then he thought of getting lost with the woman and children and felt the frustration wash back into his life just when he thought he was getting control of it.

"Brother Beck, would you like to testify to the glory of our Lord?" A huge mountain of a man stood up and said, "Well, sir! I just don't want to miss an opportunity to stand here before my neighbors and family, and say I love the Lord. When me and the Misses had our first baby six years back, we lost pert near everthang when a wild fire took our house and barn. We got out with our baby and the clothes we were wearing and that was about it. But the good folks of this church didn't leave it like that, because God had his hand in it." His eyes began to tear up and he pulled a big red bandana out of his hip pocket, blew his nose and continued. "No, the people of this church walk in His ways, and they reach out to those in need, and I am grateful for that. We never went hungry, never missed a meal. We were never cold, nor wet because one way or another we always had a roof over our heads. We lived with different neighbors at different times, and they fed us and helped us without a word about it. God put His hand of protection on us in a time of need, and I am grateful for the people of this church, who strive every day to do God's will, and I praise Him for His love. And I also want to praise Him for the opportunity to share his blessings with others this past week. You know, my heart was filled with gratitude when we received help from the people in this church. But it was filled with pure joy when I got to help others." The church was filled with affirmations, and he nodded his thanks again to all the people sitting around him, then sat down and put his arm around his wife who was crying.

Sarah noticed that nobody spoke of them by name, which would have been embarrassing. Instead the focus was God's blessings and the joy they all felt in sharing them.

"Anyone else have a testimony for us today about how God has lifted you with his people," Preacher asked as he looked around the room. "Sister Eileen? Yes, go ahead."

A small grey haired lady, with a little brown hat with dried flowers on it, stood and spoke softly. "When my husband died and left me with three small children to raise, I just didn't know how I was going to go on. I had three boys; newborn twins, and a four year old, and I just didn't know how I was going to feed them, let alone teach them boys to be men. But by the Grace of God, I am standing here before this congregation to say that He provided my every need," she said, pausing to collect her thoughts before going on. "Of course, the oldest of the three, Seth, enlisted with the Moccasin Rangers back in July of '61, and I know men take to war, but it is a hard thing for a Mama to face, so I am once again, standin' in the need of prayer." She stopped to wipe her eyes with her little white hanky, then held her head high and continued, "But, my boys are good men. They learned to hunt and provide for their families because of the Christian men who tuck it upon themselves to shoulder that responsibility in answer to the call of Christ to serve one another. In Acts 6: 1-15, Steven and six other men busied themselves with helping the widows, and so the men in this community did just that, and I am grateful for the Lord's hand in that. And my boys are grateful for that, too."

Warm smiles and nods came amidst the whispers of, "Bless you, Sister Eileen." Those seated nearest to her patted her on the back as she sat down.

Preacher smiled at Eileen, then looked at Mildred, and thought about how she had gone about alerting the community to the many needs of the Water's family. "I am reminded of Rebecca in the Bible," Preacher began. "Rebecca was a fine woman, a woman who already had God's heart, long before this story at the well. In fact, Rebecca had been walking with God, learning from Him, and doing His will long before Isaac even knew he had a need for a good wife. Yes, Rebecca was chosen by God long before Isaac was ready to be married. Rebecca had a good and generous spirit that brought her favor with the Lord our God, much like the good women of this community who have brought God's favor on their families." The Preacher looked at the men in the room and added, "Several of you men would not be here today, had your women not found favor with the Lord and TOLD you that you were coming to church long ago when you were sinners." Some heads nodded. "It was the same with Isaac. We men all need good women, don't we?" Ben looked at Sarah as the preacher continued, "Yes, we all need Rebeccas in our lives."

The congregation responded to that truth with murmurs, and grateful hugs from men to their wives.

"Now as you know," the Preacher continued, "Eliezer had been charged with the responsibility of finding a suitable wife for Isaac. So he got up and went to the central well in Abraham's birthplace. He put feet on his prayers! He didn't just lay there on his bed and ask for a wife for Isaac, he got up and went to the heart of Abraham's camp.

He took a gift of ten camels laden with goods, because he had the faith to believe that God would answer his prayers! Let's learn a lesson from Eliezer today folks. For he believed that God would answer his prayer... so God did!"

"Eliezer even had the courage and the relationship with God, that he could create a test. Because, Eliezer said unto God, 'God! Let it be that the maiden to whom I shall say, 'Please tip over your jug so I may drink,' and who replies, 'Drink, and I will even water your camels,' her will You have designated for Your servant, for Isaac. Genesis 24:14."

Now here, gentlemen, we must take time to recognize the person in the center of this story. It isn't Eliezer and his task to find Isaac a wife. And it wasn't Isaac who stood to become the father of all Jews. We men often fail to recognize the importance of the women in the Bible. But here is a woman above all women. Please listen with your heart. Preacher continued with his story as if it were the first time he had read it, "Then almost immediately, out steps a young girl who offered to draw water for him to drink, as well as enough water to fill the troughs for all his camels! In fact, Rebecca continued to draw water until all the camels there had had enough to drink! Can you imagine the hard work that took to draw enough water to sate the thirst of even one camel? And Rebecca did all this work, not because she was asked. Not because she wanted to take her place in our history, because she didn't even know she would have a place in our history. Her motives were pure, she wanted to help, and being physically able to help, she stepped up and volunteered to do more than was expected, proving her kind and generous nature and her suitability for God's will in her life. We often think of only the men called to do God's will, but clearly, Rebecca was a woman chosen by God, blessed by God, and favored by God."

"Do we have any Rebeccas here in this room with us today? In this community? Yes, we do. Each and every one of you ladies who stepped up this week and gave what food you had to give was a Rebecca. And why did you do that? Not because of the glory in it. Nobody knows to this day what part of that gift was given by each of you. Did you do it because you were helping your own? No, we were not just helping our own family members; these were total strangers we reached out to in need. They are family now because we are all brothers and sisters in Christ, but some of you hadn't even met them yet when you opened your larders to them. Did you do it for the payback? No, hopefully we will never need a helping hand, but if we do, isn't it good to know our neighbors love the Lord?" The room was buzzing with gratitude and energy. "No, you did it because that is what God asks of us, that we give freely of what we have, without concern for our own futures, and love our neighbors as we love ourselves." Preacher closed his Bible and held it against his chest with his left hand, thought for a minute and then added, "*That* was the gift of Rebecca. Rebecca had the heart of a servant. She did not need to be asked! She saw a need and filled it! She did it without worrying about running out of water, because she knew her God would provide! Her faith in God was SO ABSOLUTE! SO ALL CONSUMING!" He shouted, "THAT GOD, HIMSELF, WAS PLEASED WITH REBECCA!"

His voice softened as he repeated, "God, Himself, was pleased with Rebecca. What a powerful thing to say. GOD, HIMSELF, WAS PLEASED WITH REBECCA!" He walked around the front of the room as if in deep thought, and continued softly, "What I would not give to hear the words that God, Himself, was pleased with me." His eyes filled with tears as he continued. "And I know today, that God, Himself, was pleased with the actions of this community, *especially* the women of this church who, like Rebecca, were kind enough to offer what they had, to ones in need. And now, brothers and sisters in Christ, it is with great joy that we accept the Waters family into our fold." He looked them all in the eye, one by one, and said, "And I am sure that in the coming years, we will continue to meet the needs of this community, unconcerned of the cost, trusting in the Lord to provide, and trusting in each other, brothers and sisters in Christ."

Benjamin was stunned at the outpouring of love within the walls of this little log cabin church, but still was fearful that he might be approached by the other men in private for payment. His experience with grown men had been less than kind in the prison, and other than those inmates, his father was the only man he had known really well. Time would tell whether or not these men truly believed as the minister said.

"And in closing," Preacher continued, "I would like to know if there are any prayer requests or announcements that need to be made."

A big man named Carl, stood up and said, "Yes, Preacher we got some troubles up at the Markly place. Me and some of the men are going up to deal with it early in the week. We would like your prayers on the matter." Eyes of recognition darted back and forth and heads nodded as if a vote were being taken. "Go with God," Preacher said, adding his blessing.

Suddenly, Sissy stood up, shocking Sarah, Ben and Little Ben as they froze in their seats, wide eyed and in fear of what she was going to say. "I got a 'nouncement," she said loudly enough for God, Himself, to hear. Sarah touched Sissy's arm in an attempt to catch her eye and Ben's heart pounded so hard and fast, he thought it would explode. But Sissy would not be stopped.

"My baby's name is Rebecca, and I hope she will be as good as the one in the Bible," she said and then sat down with a plop. Ben broke out in a sweat, and Sarah had to struggle to keep her composure. They stared at their hands without moving, and Benjamin could feel his guts begin churning.

Preacher was glowing as he said, "Well, you know, Sissy, your parents don't have to raise that baby alone. It is the responsibility of the entire community to be certain she is safe, and has the right upbringing in the church in order to help her grow into exactly what Christ wants her to be. And I am sure with a big sister like you, she is off to a great start."

Stunned, Ben and Sarah stared without blinking into the backs of the pews as the last hymn was being introduced by the pump organ. Sarah's mouth was too dry to sing, and Ben suddenly needed to go to the outhouse. He looked at Sarah and placed the song book in the back of the pew, then headed for the back door. By the time he was finished at the outhouse, church was over and his worst nightmare appeared before his eyes. There were almost ten men waiting for him right outside the outhouse door, and he had no option but to walk toward them.

The first man to step up was Abram, "Ben, I want to introduce you to some of the neighbors." Filled with fright, Ben met all of the men, trying against all hope to remember their names. Stories followed about where they lived, and what they did for a living, but Ben couldn't relax and enjoy the stories out of fear: fear they were going to ask him for money, fear they were going to lull him into some false security and then injure him, fear that they were about to do or say something that might make him very uncomfortable, or worse, they had figured out who he was and were taking him into custody. His anxiety from the past reared its ugly head and made him want to bolt from their company.

Finally, one of the men said, "Ben, we got some trouble up toward Bear Fork. Can we count on you for some help tomorrow evening?"

Ben wanted to go into the limitations his leg put on him, or tell them he needed to know exactly what they were going to do before they left, but found himself saying, "Sure, whatever I can do." Was this what he owed them for the multitude of gifts? Were they going to do something illegal he was going to get dragged into, landing him back in prison? Well, the minister did give his blessings on it, so he would go along with them as far as he could travel without doing anything to jeopardize his little family.

"Great, I'll pick him up," Abram said to the group. "He is closest to me. Meet you in town about six, alright? Ben, I will pick you up about 5:30."

Ben nodded as his stomach knotted up into a tight ball. As the men dispersed, he saw Sarah and the children waiting for him beside Abram's sleigh. "Just a minute!" Ben called out to Sarah, "I need to speak to Preacher!" He turned and walked back to the church where he found Reverend Morrison standing in the doorway shaking hands, and speaking with each person leaving the church.

"Fine sermon, Preacher," said one short lady with a hat and little black purse. She turned to the five boys behind her and said, "Pay your respect, boys."

The boys stepped up and shook hands with Preacher, but knowing the spirit of little boys, he didn't wait for them to say what their mother expected. Instead he said, "Know any good fishing places around here?" Five heads shot up with smiles on their faces and all anxiety was gone as they discussed bait, lures, and locations of the best places to catch fish. Finally they said their goodbyes, and there was no one left but Preacher and Benjamin. Reverend Morrison looked Ben in the eye and stretched out his hand for a firm handshake. "Ben, we are so blessed to have you and your little family here. I would like to come by for a visit some time if that would be alright with you."

The thought of entertaining guests in their little cabin had never occurred to Ben, and the fact that it would be this Preacher was an honor beyond belief. This leader in the community wanted to come to their home just to visit. "Yes, sir! That would be nice. I won't be home tomorrow evening because I am going with Abram and some other men, but any other time would be fine."

With that, the Reverend's face became dark and he said simply, "Yes, I had heard the Markley's had some trouble up toward Bear Fork. Go with God then, son." This seemed to the minister to be enough information about the situation, although clearly it didn't calm Ben's fears in the least. The Reverend continued, "But, now, what can I do for you, Ben?"

"Well, sir. I was wondering if you could tell me that scripture about the still waters. I don't have any paper to write it down on, but I was hoping I could just remember it this time. It kind of stuck in my mind and gave me a hunger to hear it again."

Ben wondered if the preacher had time to do this, and was about to suggest they do it when he came to their home for a visit, when the pastor said, "It is the 23rd Psalms, son. Do you have a Bible at home?"

Ben was embarrassed and could feel his face flushing as he said, "No, sir. I would like to have one, but…"

"Well, you have one now," Reverend Morrison said as he handed Ben his black Bible.

"Oh, no, I couldn't," Ben protested, "This is yours. There is no way I could take this."

"It is the Lord's word, Ben, not mine. And if you will read it, and read it to your children, then it is fitting that I give it to you, and more importantly, it is fitting that you take it." Ben had the Bible in both hands now, with Reverend Morrison's huge hands covering his. "The word, 'Psalms' means 'songs,' Ben, and most of them were written by a little boy named David who was a shepherd, so he understood the importance of a shepherd leading his flock beside the still waters, and protecting them from the evils in this world, because without his guidance, they would die of thirst, or be slaughtered by the enemy. You know, Ben, sheep won't drink from bubbling water. They will stand right beside it and die of thirst. I know this about sheep because I own sheep. Christ knows our every need, and loves us enough to see to them. Just like David led his sheep, Jesus is our Shepherd and leads us to where He wants us to be, beside still waters so we can drink, and green pastures so we can be nourished. God brought you and your family to our community, Ben, and for that we are grateful." The Reverend's smile could brighten up the darkest of days, and his handshake and pat on the back made Ben feel better.

Ben couldn't help smiling as he hugged the Bible to himself and said his thanks to the man smiling back at him. He held his treasure to his chest protectively with joy in his heart.

After Sissy's antics at the church, the ride home was rather subdued for the Waters' family, but that didn't stop the others from laughing and talking with each other. Sarah focused only on breathing deeply, and Benjamin just hoped he could make it home to his own outhouse. Nerves had always seized him in his stomach, giving him the runs, or as the locals called it, "the green apple quick steps." He tried to control his urges by breathing deeply, and reciting his list of those things for which he was most grateful, but time after time, as the sleigh bumped along behind the horses, he feared he would lose control. Sissy's behavior at church combined with the upcoming trip with the men was more than Ben could handle. The overwhelming fear of what was going to happen to them now was like a monster that kept raising its ugly head in his thoughts, and peace was not to be found.

CHAPTER TWELVE

The second the sleigh was out of sight, and they were all safely inside the house with the door shut, Ben and Sarah took Sissy to task. "What were you thinking, Sissy? Do you want everyone to know this baby is yours? What made you say that in church?"

Sissy said, "I got somethin' for you'ins to think about. You do not own me. Just because we are playing like one big happy family, don't mean you own me and mine. I wanted to name her because she is MY baby and as her mother I have a right to name her! And stop saying, 'this baby,' 'cos she gotta name now, it's Rebecca!"

Neither Ben nor Sarah knew what to say. She did have the right to name the child, and the child was still hers. Sarah realized she had gotten so involved in playing the role of mother; she was beginning to think of all three children as hers. It was a dangerous thing to get lost in that role, and Sissy's words made her conscious of the fact that Sissy was free to take them away any time she wanted.

"Sit down," Ben said as he pulled out a chair at the table and motioned for them all to take their seats. Sissy just stormed off into the bedroom, leaving Sarah and Little Ben looking at Benjamin for guidance.

Ben just shook his head and began setting the table for dinner. He reverted to his Mother's behavior when his older sister had pulled the same trick, and simply went about his business, knowing full well that at some point she would have to come out of that room.

Little Ben, Sarah, and Ben prepared the food, filling the cabin with the smell of potato soup and cornbread. Little Ben regaled them with stories of Levi's slingshot and how well he could shoot it. "I want one," he announced just like any other little boy hoping to have his parent's approval for something that could potentially cause a lot of problems.

Ben smiled and said, "We'll see," bringing a smile to Little Ben's face. It wasn't that Ben needed time to think about whether or not he could have one. It was just that his mind was on more pressing matters and the promise of a slingshot would have brought questions about when he could have it and how to make one, that Ben honestly had no idea how to answer.

It was mid-afternoon before Sissy came out of the bedroom. She was not hungry; she was just bored in there. Nobody said a word to her, so she just pulled a chair up to the fire to warm herself. She was more than just a little cold, so she stood again, and backed up to the fire, hiking her dress up and holding it up behind her to warm her legs and backside.

Suddenly the tension was interrupted by a knock on the door. Ben walked over and opened the door to find Denzel standing there. "Could I speak to Sissy, please?"

At this point, Ben was having his doubts as to Sissy's trustworthiness when it came to their safety. She was angry and capable of saying things they would all regret, so he said, "No. Not this afternoon, Denzel. I am afraid this is not a good time."

Denzel looked as if he wanted to argue, but thought better of it. Sissy, however, had no problems with challenging Ben's authority and began shouting that nobody owned her and she could do as she damn well pleased. Ben looked down at Denzel and said, "Go home, son. Right now." Denzel opened his mouth to protest, wanting desperately to be Sissy's hero and take her side, but he recognized the look in Ben's eyes as the same look his father had just before he gave him a whipping for breaking the Waters' window, and wisely chose not to defy him.

"Yes, sir," Denzel said. He skillfully mounted his horse in one movement, turned, and left at a canter.

With a slam of the door behind him, Ben turned to face Sissy and found her to be insolent and ready for a fight. "Who the hell do you think you are?" Sissy shouted so loudly they feared Denzel had heard her.

"You do not talk to me like that, young lady," Ben said stepping closer and closer to her.

"Oh, so if you really don't hit children, just what do you think you can do to stop me? You are not my father! I do not have to do what you say, and I will talk to you any way in hell I want to!"

In one swift motion, Ben picked up the pan of melting snow they had set aside for washing dishes and dumped it over Sissy's head. The ice cold water brought an audible gasp from Sissy, and she took a step backward, reeling from the shock.

Ben spoke so softly and calmly that it unnerved Sissy when he said, "I don't hit children because I don't have to! I can make your life miserable in so many other ways you won't be able to count them." He again surprised her by gently, but firmly grasping her arm and leading her over to the bedroom that was already cold from having the door closed all day. With a gentle shove he pushed her into the room and closed the door behind her.

Sissy yelled and kicked at the door, pounding it with her fists. "There is no lock on here! You will have to stand there all day to keep me in here!"

Her protests were met by the pounding of a hammer as nail after nail went into the door. "Well, there's a lock on it now!" Ben said.

Finally, there was silence.

Ben put on his coat, opened the door and marched out into the snow to cool down. He walked up onto the hill above him and stood looking at the view, trying to calm himself. He knew this could be the end of the wonderful farce they had been living. Why had he allowed himself to believe they could pull this off? This was far too wonderful a life for a man like him, and he found that he was not surprised he was losing this sweet dream just as it was beginning to unfold. Nothing good came to people like him. Now if he could just figure a way out of this community without being discovered.

Before he had completely unruffled his feathers, he returned to the cabin fearing Sissy might get sick from being cold and wet, and hoping she had settled down and was ready to talk calmly.

But as he came back into the front room, he heard Sissy shout, "LET ME OUT OF HERE!"

"I would not enjoy your company right now, Sissy, and since I am in the only other room in this house, you may not join me," he felt his mother's spirit in him as he repeated the words he had so often heard her say to his older sister. In fact, everything he had said to her since their return from church had been said by this mother to his older sister, Rosemary. He had a new respect for his mother, and a new gratitude for his upbringing. His mother had handled each problem and disrespectful remark from all three of her children without the help of their father, and she had handled them well. No longer would he allow himself to linger on the wretched parent his father had been. From now on, he would only focus on his mother and the fine example she set for him. His new history would be that he came from a fine family and was raised well. The evilness of his father had poisoned him enough, and he would drink from that cup no more.

After nearly an hour, a small voice said, "Papa?" Sarah and Ben looked at each other, and then to Little Ben for assurance that he had not said it. Ben's glance at Sarah brought a tilt of her head and with eyebrows up, then she nodded her approval.

Bolstered by Sarah's attitude, Ben decided to take a chance, retrieved the hammer and, thanks to Denzel's exceptional teaching skills, began pulling out the nails he had put into the doorframe.

He was prepared for a disrespectful Sissy, but the one that stepped out was rather subdued.

Ben started again where he left off. He pulled out a chair and said, "All of you, sit down."

This time Sissy obeyed.

Sarah retrieved a blanket from the bedroom and wrapped it around Sissy. She had changed out of her wet dress, into her nightgown while sulking in the bedroom, but her hair was wet, and she was still quite cold and Sarah didn't want her to get sick. Sissy was humbled by the act of kindness in the face of her 'horble' behavior, and although Sissy hated it, tears began to form and slide down her face.

At the sight of that, Ben reached over and patted her arm just above her hand and that was Sissy's undoing. She bolted from the chair and threw herself into Ben's arms, sobbing and crying. Ben patted her back and whispered, "Shhhh! Shhhh! It's ok."

When she sat up there was a wet place on Ben's shirt from her tears. He smoothed her hair back from her face and said, "Talk to me. What is going on here?" She was still sitting on his lap, staring at the floor. All her thoughts backed up like a crowd pushing to get through a small doorway, and she just shook her head back and forth, unable to find where to start.

"Sissy, could we start at the beginning?" Sarah suggested. Sissy nodded without looking up. "Ok," Sarah pulled out Sissy's chair and Sissy got up and sat down in it. Sarah continued speaking, "This doesn't feel like something you just got angry about today. I get the feeling you have been angry for a long time, and it just found its way to the surface."

Sissy nodded her head again and they gave her time to think about what she wanted to say. Finally she said, "Well, you know the night Denzel broke the window?" She looked up to see them both nod. "Well, me and Denzel had planned to meet that evening, but earlier. But his Papa made him work later than he thought so he didn't get here until dark and I couldn't figure out a reason to get up and leave when I heard the snowball hit. I figgered he wasn't comin' so I'd already been to the outhouse. I had no idea he would come after dark and throw snowballs at the house, honest!"

Sarah and Ben exchanged looks. Sarah's was a knowing look, and Ben's one of confusion, so Sarah took the lead, "So you and Denzel like each other?"

"Oh, don't go makin' nothin' outa it! We're just friends. He comes up sometimes when me and Little Ben is playing in the snow, an' we just talk!" She looked at them and saw no disapproval so she continued a little more honestly, "But, well, I enjoy his company." She was looking very closely at her fingers that were intertwined on the table.

Sarah hadn't forgotten her original mission and continued the questioning, "So it doesn't appear that that is what made you so angry. I mean we didn't try to stop you from seeing him until this afternoon, so where did all this anger come from?"

Sissy's mouth tightened into a pucker and she tipped her head down. Sarah knew that right there, below the surface of that expression on her face was a volcano of feelings ready to come pouring out, if only they could get to them.

"Well, Denzel says we should get married. His Papa's got a little huntin'cabin off'n the woods and we could live there." Both Ben and Sarah's eyes widened.

"Do you want to marry him, Sissy?" Sarah asked incredulously as Ben jumped to his feet and began pacing around the cabin, hands on hips.

"I don't know what I want," Sissy said as she sat up straight in her chair. "I guess I don't know what I'm 'pose to do here."

"Well, Sissy, we are just finding out about all this." Sarah was at a loss for words. "Honestly, I am just completely shocked! I have no idea what to think, let alone what to say to you. Can you start at the beginning and tell us what is going on? We didn't even know you knew Denzel that well, Sissy. Do you love him?" Ben shot a look at Sarah that asked if she had lost her mind.

"No, this ain't about Denzel. This is about me and what I am doin' here. Me and Benji left off from th'orphnige 'cos we just wanted to get away from there. And, I guess, we din't think much about where we was goin', or what we would be doin' there."

Her words struck a familiar chord for both Sarah and Ben, and as Sissy continued, they found themselves coming face to face with their own private dilemmas.

"This is fun and all. I mean, I never got to have a Mama and a Papa before and you two have made it real nice for me and Benji."

"Little Ben!" her brother protested.

Sissy just rolled her eyes and continued, "And you've tuck real good care of Rebecca, too. But it just ain't real. As much as I would like it to be, it just ain't."

Ben was struggling to understand, sat down at the table again, and asked, "What do you mean this isn't real, Sissy?"

"Well, this little cabin is safe and warm, and we ain't gettin' hit or nothin'...."

They waited for her to formulate her thoughts.

"But, there's nothing' keepin' you two from just up and leavin'. You got money," she said gesturing at Sarah and continued by turning toward Ben, "and you're a man, you could up and leave tomorrow and we'd never see you again. That's what our Papa did!"

They could say not one word to comfort her, because they had wrestled with all the same thoughts, so they sat there in silence and allowed her to continue.

"But, me? Well, I'm not a grownup, and yet I got Ben and Rebecca to think about. And the only thing worse'n us bein' in that or'phnige would be us bein' split up in different homes or or'phniges. So I was thinkin' 'bout how maybe I should marry Denzel. Then at least I gotta home for us if'n you two up and leave."

They all sat there in stunned silence, lost in their own thoughts, with no idea what to say. Neither Ben nor Sarah had looked at their predicament from Sissy's point of view. To be facing the uncertainty they were facing as adults was unsettling enough, but to be a child in this situation, who was also responsible for the other two children, was horrifying. It was amazing Sissy hadn't snapped long before.

"Well," Ben broke the silence by stating the only bit of truth he could bring to the table, "I can tell you Sissy, that I have no intentions of leaving here right now."

"Right now," Sissy repeated snidely. She wasn't trying to be hurtful; she just knew that his statement in no way comforted her, because what she was looking for was something far more permanent than hearing his plans for the next few days.

Ben took a minute to think about what he really did mean by that and then he leaned forward, rested his elbows on the table and ran his fingers through his hair. Then he sat up and revised what he had said, "Ok, let me say it like this. Although I hadn't really put it into words, Sissy, I have been feeling a lot like you are feeling. Truth be told, I love it here. I love this cabin and this land, and I have had more pure happiness living here with you and Sarah and the children, than I have ever had in my life. And I love the people here, and the little log church we go to. So if I could, I would stay here forever."

Having said that, he needed to be careful not to assume they all felt that way. "But," he continued while looking at Sarah, "if you all don't feel that way, we need to come up with a plan for getting these children into a safe place where they can grow up with a family, because Sissy has no business getting married in my opinion. She needs to have a chance to be a child before she has to be a wife." He looked at her and smiled at her relief.

Sissy's little face just glowed, and Sarah was looking at him with a new energy as she said, "Well, I have to say that I wasn't really aware of my feelings on this matter until today, either. But now that you mention it, it has been weighing on my mind as to what we would do next. And as to what Ben said, I agree. I like it here very much, and if I could I would stay here forever as well. We all seem to have found a place where we can be ourselves, and I love the people here and our little church. There is something about this little community that is very healing, and, well, I just feel safe, something I haven't felt in a lot of years, either." She looked at Sissy and touched her on her arm, in recognition of what she had said earlier about never feeling safe. "So if we can agree that we will work together..." she looked around the table at the votes cast with smiling faces, and felt smiles bubble up from inside her.

"So, Sissy, it is agreed, we all like it here, right?" Ben asked as Sissy nodded enthusiastically as he continued, "Then I will say this. Now that we all agree that we like it here, and since staying here is what we all want, then I promise you that I will never leave this little family unless I am taken away by someone or something else."

At that, a hush fell over them as their pasts rushed into the room, choking out their joy. Circumstances and faces haunted them and threatened to suffocate them, as each one dealt with their own overwhelming memories and the fear of being returned to their past. Each one knew they had arrived in this place on shaky ground, and what they were trying to build here was, at best, fragile, and at worst, fraud. The thought of the good people of this little town finding out they were all imposters loomed in their minds as they looked out at each other across the table.

"Well, the way I see it, this is what we got," Sissy said. "And for me, this is the best I ever had, so I reckon I'm mostly just a'sceered a'losin' it."

Sarah's and Ben's eyes met and they realized they both had felt the same way. They had become friends, or maybe something more, and as hard as they had tried to ignore it and hold on to their independent personas, the truth was they both wanted to stay more than words could express.

"But what are the chances we can continue what we are doing here?" Ben wished he had the luxury of not talking about the difficult issues, but this one was far too important to ignore. Because this particular concern could cause the unhinging of their entire plan, he approached it prudently, yet honestly, "There are going to be times we will have to act as parents, Sissy, and to be honest with you, after today I am feeling a little less confident in your willingness to cooperate."

Sissy thought about that for a moment before speaking. Then said, "Alls I need is to know is what I am doin'. If I need to get married to give my brother a home, I will do it and I will be a good wife. If I am going to be your daughter, I'll do that real good, too. It's just the sittin' on the fence that was burning my butt," Sissy emphasized each of the last three words with a nod of her head indicating her frustration at not knowing the path she was walking.

"So," Sarah said, "What will happen if you get mad at us again then, Sissy? I must say I share in Ben's concern. I will tell you that there will be times I will correct you, and I will expect you to mind me. For example, I will not abide your using your rude language, and I will be correcting your grammar as well. In fact, I will not accept this position at all if you and I are to fight over which of us is the mother in this household, especially in public."

Sissy had to have time to process that information. It was not easy giving up the authority over Little Ben that she once held, and she sure didn't want anybody telling her how to talk, but after carrying the burden of trying to be a parent at such a young age, the security and freedom of being a child with parents was far too appealing to ignore. So if that was part of the package, she guessed it was worth it.

"I guess I wouldn't mind learnin' stuff, if'n I felt like I belong somewheres," Sissy finally broke the silence.

"But what if you get angry again, Sissy? Like you did this morning," Sarah still had her doubts as to how trustworthy Sissy would be in the future, and now that so many futures depended on her behavior, Sarah had to ask.

"I wadn't mad at you. I was feelin' like I had to walk one path or t'other, and before, outside the church, Denzel ask me if I was gonna marry him or not. He's real mad at his Pa for givin' him a whippin' for breakin' our window. Says he's too big to be whipped and he don't want to stay there no more. So's I was just..." Sissy's shoulders drooped. She sighed in resignation and said, "I'm sorry. I was trying to go down a path I didn't want to take and be a grownup about it all. If'n I know I don't have to marry Denzel to give me and Ben a home, then, well that makes all the difference." She looked at Sarah and Ben to be certain they knew she was sincere.

"And I can't say it'll be easy for me to give Ben over to you, but I can promise I will always behave in public, and keep our troubles private. I wouldn't do anything on earth to mess this up for Little Ben," Sissy said as she looked Sarah straight in the eye, winning her confidence finally.

"You keep talking about Little Ben, Sissy. What about the baby?" Ben asked. Sarah's slight movement attracted his attention and the subtle shaking of her head silenced him. He was amazed and delighted at how in tune they were when dealing with the children, and he was enjoying his first experience of walking in step with a grown woman. The feeling was exhilarating and he felt happy to be alive bringing a prayer of gratitude from the bottom of his soul, another first. He asked God that they might be given the privilege of raising these children. It was a lot to ask of a God he had never done anything for, but like the good folks of this community, he hoped to be a help to others in need. He wished he had something to offer Him, in exchange for the gift of allowing them to stay there, because a barter would feel better than one more debt to pay. But he reckoned that if God were to grant this one big request, he could be happy to spend his whole life trying to pay off his debts.

Sarah realized that for her, personally, to choose to ignore the risks the future might bring was fine, but these children needed to be aware of them. "In spite of the joy I feel about this arrangement we have come to, we have to face the fact that at any time, one of us might get caught, or all of us for that matter. We still have to remember who we are and maintain a watchful eye." Sarah paused briefly before continuing with the most difficult issue at hand. "And as much as I want to, I cannot promise you that this is forever, simply because of the fact that we might get caught. But I, for one, will do my best to stay here for the rest of our lives, even though we have no idea what will happen tomorrow."

Sissy was what the country folk called an "old soul," and once again her wisdom brought clarity to the newly formed Waters' family when she said, "Even *real* parents can't promise forever, Mama. All me and Ben's askin' for is a chance, n'if it falls apart, well…" she shrugged her shoulders and sat there looking at them as if the matter were settled.

Ben nodded his head at Sissy and then Sarah as if to announce that an agreement had been reached, then turned to Little Ben and said, "What about you Little Ben? Do you have anything to say about all this?"

Little Ben just shook his head, "no," and then asked innocently, "So, have you decided if I can have a slingshot?" Ben and Sarah laughed as Benjamin tousled his hair. Little Ben was already their child in his mind and he was happy not to have to think about the future any further than to consider the grand improvement a slingshot would make in his social life. Ben and Sarah knew he was going to be fine, as long as they were together.

Sarah stood and said, "And now I am going to check on Rebecca. She might need another blanket," she smiled at Sissy as she walked by, touching Sissy's shoulder as she passed, and Sissy smiled back, relieved to have the responsibility of the baby lifted from her shoulders and yet proud they were keeping the name Sissy had given her.

They had no idea what the future would bring, but at least they all had a clearer vision of the path they had agreed to walk together, and now they were no longer alone in their travels.

CHAPTER THIRTEEN

Ben did not have the calluses of a normal man when it came to living out in the real world; not the physical ones, or the emotional ones. When it came to waiting for the end of the day when Abram would come get him to deal with the problem at the Markley's, he had no defenses. He was a nervous wreck, and the food he had eaten that day was causing him to run to the outhouse repeatedly.

He refused any food at suppertime because he knew his trip in the wagon would be anxious enough and he didn't want to have to ask them to stop repeatedly.

He was out on the front porch waiting when Abram pulled up. "Hey, there neighbor!" Abram shouted.

"Hey," Ben shouted back nervously. Abram had brought his sleigh around to the door, and invited Ben to climb up and sit beside him. Fortunately, there was little conversation on the way to town, so Ben just enjoyed the view as the road meandered from hill top to hill top.

Ben was amazed at the sites of the journey, and like a child said, "Sure is a pretty view in these mountains, seems like you can either see down one side of the hills or the other, like around every turn is something new to look at."

"This is called a ridge road, Ben. It is carved out of the top of adjoining hills with as few'a curves as we can manage, so it does kind'a hug one side of a hilltop or another. In a minute we are going to start down town hill. It's pretty steep, and crooked as a dog's hind leg, but the horses are used to it." Ben smiled at the image of a crooked dog's hind leg. He loved the funny sayings these people had to color their world of speech. Someone could not simply run, they "ran like a scalded dog!" They didn't just walk to town, they "road Shank's mare." Apparently, Shank never had a mare, so the phrase meant "travel by foot." His favorite was, "It was as red as a pigeon's butt in pokeberry time!"

After several large ascending turns they began to descend at the place everyone called "Jimmy's." Jimmy's was a little store to the right of the road, with just enough room for a few horses to be tied up. Jimmy's house was up on the top of the knoll right beyond the store, with a magnificent view off both sides of the mountain. The road down to the town was steep in places, with many curves that brought them to a little valley, where the town was nestled into a gentle curve in the Little Kanawha River. Surrounded by hills, the little town lay quietly in the valley, looking like a picture in a picture book Ben had seen as a child.

It was there they met up with Joe Burson, who clearly was a friend of Abram's. The two men sat and laughed and talked freely about their school days, and the goings on of the Moccasin Rangers until several other men arrived and climbed into Abram's sleigh and headed off toward Bear Fork. Joe had enlisted in the Rangers back in July of '61, but was related to Bertha Markley, and had come home on leave to organize the men for this night.

The men were quiet, and filled with their own thoughts as they rode up the other side of the valley and out of town. It was dark when they got to their destination, and the men threw back a canvas revealing enough torches for each of them to carry at least one. When they got to the house, they formed a circle around the yard and lit the torches, holding them in front of their faces so those coming out of the house couldn't see who they were.

"Markley!" Abram shouted. "Markley, come on out here!"

After a time, a man opened the door and said, "Get off my property!"

Abram shouted, "Markley, we know that you been beatin' on your wife. Now we aren't here to interfere with you runnin' your home as you see fit, but we won't tolerate anyone beating a woman."

Markley stepped out onto the porch and closed the door behind him. "Y'all get off my property or I'll get my gun!" he shouted at no one in particular.

Joe Burson's voice came from the other side of the ring, "Markley, you and me have known each other all our lives, and there won't be no shootin' tonight.

"And there won't be any more beatin's here, Markley, or we are all comin' back, and we'll take a whip to you. You had better listen to us, Markley, 'cos if you hit her one more time, we're comin' back.

This time, Markley aimed his words at the man on the other side of the ring who had spoken, "Haze! I know who you are, and we are kin! I don't know how you can shame your kin like this!"

Haze replied, "You shame yourself, Markley. Every time you hit a woman, you are shaming yourself and our family, and we won't tolerate it. You better listen to them, Markley. They mean business. And they mean it when they say they'll take a whip to ya!

The ring of men began to walk toward the porch until the light was blinding for Markley. He held his arm up to block his eyes, as his cousin, Haze, stepped up onto the porch with him. With three other men behind him to keep him from returning to the house, Haze said, "Now, Markley, our women folk ain't gonna be happy unless we see Bertha for ourselves, so we can tell them how she is doin'."

Markley made an attempt to block the door, but the men were prepared for that. As they held Markley at bay, four men entered the house to speak to Bertha. When they didn't find her in the front room, two of them went to the kitchen, and two of them entered the bedroom, where they found Bertha cowering on the floor between the bed and the window. Her eyes were swollen and her lip split, and it appeared her right ear was nearly torn off. They had no idea the extent of her injuries, but were angrier than ever when they saw what he had done. They lifted Bertha to her feet, and helped her pack a bag, all the while hoping Markley would give them a hard time on the way out so they had an excuse to return the favor. They were itching for a fight, but knew their job was to get Bertha into the sleigh and covered up while the other men made sure Markley couldn't interfere.

Joe Burson stormed out onto the porch and stepped up to Markley menacingly. "We are taking Bertha with us, and I am hoping you try to stop us."

Markley said, "Now, Joe! We's kin, and you know how women can be..." In an instant Joe had him by the shirt, and it was all the other men could do to pull him off. The minute Markley was released, he ran off to hide in the shadows, while the men gently carried Bertha past him, and toward the wagon. Fortunately, since the men didn't know what they would find when they got to the Markley's house, they had brought pillows and blankets with them in case they had to rescue Bertha and remove her from the house.

"Ben saw them bringing Bertha out of the house, and the painful memories of his mother engulfed him. He ran to the woman and took hold of the blanket they were using as a stretcher to carry her, then hopped into the sled in order to help pull her up into the bed of the sleigh. They used the pillows and blankets to make her ride back as comfortable as possible, and were as tender and as gentle as any mother he had ever seen with her child. Before long they were on their way back to town with Joe holding her head and whispering to her that no one would ever hurt her again, as Markley shouted at them to bring her back. "You can't do this to me! I'll get you for this, Haze! You shamed your family here tonight, Haze!"

Haze was embarrassed, but not by his tears as he witnessed firsthand his cousin's brutality. Ben looked at Bertha's face and was transported to the time when his own mother had similar injuries. How he wished these men had been around to protect his mother when she so desperately needed them. These ordinary men had rescued the woman, and made it absolutely clear that Markley's behavior would not be tolerated, and they had done it without bloodshed. Ben had no idea where the woman would be taken, but he was sure someone was prepared to receive her in a place where Markley would never think to look, or at least he wouldn't dare to go. If they hadn't convinced Markley, at least *Ben* believed without a doubt that if Markley ever laid a hand on Bertha again, they stood ready to make good on their threat.

Again, Ben joined Abram on the seat and when they were far enough down the road to be certain Markley wasn't following them, the men began to speak gently to Bertha who was confused, "It's gonna be alright now, Miss Bertha, don't you worry about a thing. Now are you warm enough?" Ben was struck by the tenderness of these burly mountain men, who were perfectly willing and able, not only to threaten Markley, but also to carry out the justice Markley deserved, if necessary. Yet they covered Bertha gently with blankets, and made no attempt to hide their genuine concern for her.

As they rode along, Ben began wondering about this curious band of vigilantes. They had been so tightlipped about everything, he wondered if they were a posse, and if, perhaps there were a Sheriff on board who headed up the proceedings. "Is one of these men a law officer, Abram?"

Abram said, "No. No, we don't have a lawman in this area. We did have a fine one. Mr. Peregrine Hays, or Perry as we call him, was the Sheriff last year, but he got involved in starting up the Moccasin Rangers. So, no, we got no lawmen in this area, but still that don't mean we tolerate that kinda goin's on."

"Well, I was real proud to join you men tonight," Ben said. "It was a good thing you did, and you did it well. It could have been an easy situation for someone to get hurt in."

"Well, old Markley's bark is worse than his bite. Besides, most of the men here are kin to him and Haze, and he knew it. He wasn't gonna shoot nobody," and with that, Abram fell silent.

When they got to town they went over to a large two story home which had a porch full of people ready to welcome Bertha. There were several women holding torches so the men could see to get her out of the sleigh, some older boys standing by to get her bags, and two more men came out and helped carry her into the house. As the front door closed Ben could hear wails and sobs as the women saw Bertha's face. Abram took a big bandana out of his hip pocket, blew his nose and said, "Let's go. Bertha is with her sister now. She'll be fine."

Ben had recognized one of the men as the huge horse of a man he had seen at church. "Was that Hulse back there?" Ben asked Abram.

"Yea," Abram said. "Hulse is married to Bertha's sister, they were two of five Burson girls, so Markley ain't gonna bother her over here. He ain't gonna want to go up agin Hulse *and* Joe Burson." His little smile made Ben laugh as he thought of that cowardly drunk demanding that Hulse let him see his wife. Hulse could break ten healthy men in half if he wanted to, and Joe was the size of a small mountain so Markley would certainly be no match for them.

"Why didn't Hulse go with us?" Ben asked.

"Well, every man has his limits, Ben," Abram said wisely, "and none of us wanted to see Hulse swing for murder." With that Abram and Ben had a hearty laugh as the sleigh made its way across the snow.

Ben looked behind himself and realized the town was on the Little Kanawha, but he didn't see the dock, nor the little tent city he had seen when he arrived. "I don't see the boat dock we came in to," Ben stated.

Abram said, "Well, a little west of here there's a Union army camp where the boats dock when they bring supplies up from Parkersburg. I figger that's where you came in."

"Union army, huh?" Ben didn't want to admit he knew nothing about the war, not only because it presented him as uneducated, but also because it might prompt questions as to where he had come from, and what side of the war his people were on.

"Yea, most of this county has sided with the Confederates so far, but the Union moved in here back in the spring of last year, back in '61, and set up camp. Not everybody likes it neither. There is a man from Parkersburg, named Captain James Simpson who came down here and organized a company of men to fight for the Union. Most of the men around here wouldn't leave their families unprotected, but Simpson managed to get enough together to form a detachment big enough to take down to Camp Pierpont in Elizabeth. They call themselves Company C, 11th Infantry. I think they were mustered in as Federal volunteers right before Christmas. Were you here in November?" he looked at Benjamin for a response before continuing.

"No, we came here right before Christmas," Ben said adding no more information than was necessary.

"Oh, yea, that's right!" he said with a huge smile on his face. "Mildrid was fit to be tied 'til I could get her up there to see who was in Oakey's cabin! I believe it was Christmas Day when we first came up there!"

Ben wanted to ask who, and where Oakey was, but figured had he been renting the cabin that he should already know that. His thoughts were interrupted when Abram continued, "Well, there are some folks around here who weren't about to let the Union army, or any army for that matter, settle on our land, so they formed a group of vigilantes. Call themselves the Moccasin Rangers, and back, three or four months ago in November, just about a month before you got here, Conley's Rangers got into it with Simpson's men, and there were six or seven men killed up on Sycamore. You never met Perry Conley did you?" Abram looked at Ben just long enough to see him shake his head no, and then continued. "Conley's Rangers are usually farther south of here, down on the West Fork."

Suddenly, Abram's face lit up with a confounded smile, and as he shook his head left to right, he said, "Damndest thing!" Ben looked at Abram, surprised by the change of Abram's demeanor as he continued, "The meanest fighter Conley's got up there is a *woman* named Nancy Hart! Now, she's mean, I tell ya! She gets out in them woods and shoots to kill. But to see her, you'd think she was an innocent little country girl. She can sweet talk the secrets out of any man here, and then she goes off and tells the south what's goin' on."

"A woman *spy?*" Ben asked incredulously.

"Yea, she's a spy! They caught her last year, and she managed to convince them she had nothing to do with Conley, so they let her go! She came back with all kinds of information about the federal troops they were sending in to disperse the Moccasins. And she's a guerilla fighter, too. I'm tellin' you, she is meaner than any man they got up there! I wouldn't want to mess with her, and I'm bigger than she is!" Both men laughed as they sat there wondering what kind of woman could do such things.

Up to this point, Sarah had been quite an enigma for Ben. He saw her as very much the loving, gentle female, much like his mother had been, and yet also incredibly strong, confident, and extremely capable. Until he heard about Nancy Hart, he thought Sarah was the extreme. He started thinking of just how little he knew of women, and again his thoughts were interrupted as Abram went back to the topic of war.

"Right at the end of November, Captain Simpson brought about thirty men down the Little Kanawha looking for the leaders of these raids," he continued wistfully as if he was remembering good times with old friends, "They went right into their houses and arrested Pat Rafferty, and Jackson Wright… they just went door to door roundin' up men. Most of 'em took to the hills and Simpson's men just let 'em go. He knew better than to try to track men into their own mountains."

"Is he still around here?" Ben asked, concerned again about any trouble that might come up.

"No, they say he headed over to Arnoldsburg from here. That's the county seat. There is a small detachment still here in Pine Bottom, but that's mostly for keepin' supplies."

Ben was still of the mindset of a young boy as far as the outside world was concerned, and it frightened him to hear of fighting in this area. He had never held a gun in his life, and wondered if he should get one, and learn to use it. Although he had no idea where the West Fork was, he was happy to hear that Conley's men had mostly limited their fighting to an area deemed "farther south" of where he was living, and that the detachment down in Pine Bottom was a peaceful supply unit.

The rest of the ride home was made in silence. Ben realized the men had chosen tonight to go deal with Markley because of the full moon that lit the trail as they rode home.

As they pulled up at Ben's house, Ben jumped down off the sleigh and said, "Thanks Abram."

Abram said, "Around here folks are pretty tight lipped about their troubles. I reckon you'll keep this to yourself?" And with a tip of his hat he turned the sleigh and rode away in the moonlight. He hadn't waited for an answer, because it wasn't really a question.

CHAPTER FOURTEEN

Ben now had a much better understanding of the local people as he opened the cabin door and smelled the fresh coffee Sarah had brewed. "Oh! You're back!" Sarah said as she jumped up and poured Ben a cup of coffee. He sat down, but with his mind so preoccupied with everything that happened to him this evening, it took a minute to realize how nervous Sarah was as she hurried about the cabin.
"Wait! Wait a minute!" He wanted to grab her hand as she placed his coffee in front of him at the table, but remembered his promise never to touch her again, so instead he pulled out a chair beside him and said, "Sit down, come on, sit, please!" He patted the seat of the chair to encourage her. She did as he asked, but her eyes darted nervously at her coffee which was still in the kitchen. "Let me get your coffee, so we can talk," he said calmly as he stood up and gently walked into the kitchen, retrieved her cup and placed it before her on the table. He sat down again, and said, "You seem upset. Is something wrong?" He tried to move very slowly and behave in a non-threatening manner in part because he was aware of her fear of violence, and in part because of the horrible sight he had just seen. He did not *ever* want a woman to fear his presence, especially not *this* woman.

"No, I'm fine," she said, but for the first time since he had known her, she look flustered. Her hands flitted like two little birds from her face to her hair, to her apron, to her coffee, as if she had no idea what to do with them. He had become aware enough of her mannerisms to know that she was upset, but still was baffled as to what was wrong.

As he wracked his brain, trying to think of what to say, she was the first to speak, "So," she paused as she nervously sipped her coffee, "what kind of an evening did you have?" All evening she had practiced asking just the right question so as to not be nosey. What she wanted to ask was, "Where have you been?" and "What were you doing?" But she didn't feel she had a right to ask those questions, or *any* questions for that matter, so she just asked about the nature of his evening.

He planned to tell her all about everything that happened knowing it would go no further, but his thoughts were consumed with whatever it was she wasn't telling him. He watched as she held a ridiculously happy look on her face, but had no idea how to find out what was bothering her. He opened his mouth to speak, but nothing came out, because suddenly her cheery façade dissolved and huge tears appeared in her eyes.

She looked down and tried to regain her composure, but when she looked up and saw the concern on Ben's face, she broke down, "I didn't know if you were coming back or not," she said softly as the tears rolled gently down her cheeks. She didn't throw a fit, or sob and cry, she just said what was on her heart, knowing it was an admission as to how much she cared for Ben.

Ben sat straight up in his chair and said, "What have I ever done to make you think I would leave you not come back?" Surely she thought more of his character than that!

"No," Sarah said as she dried her eyes. She looked exhausted, and leaned back in her chair, her shoulders slumped and her head back as if surrendering to the forces determined to do her in. "That isn't it." She sat up straight with her elbows on the table, her hanky to her nose, and said, "I was afraid they had found something out, and they had either injured you, or taken you back."

Ben hadn't thought about the possibility of her worrying about that, and was glad he hadn't, or the day would have been much harder on him. Then he noticed the strain on her face, and realized she cared about him, and that she had spent a miserable evening agonizing about his fate.

In lieu of breaking his promise not to touch her, he simply placed his hand on the table beside hers, and instantly her hand was on his. He turned his hand over and completely encircled her hand with his. He was amazed at how tiny and soft her hand felt, and he had an overwhelming desire to protect her from any and all pain.

She felt incredibly safe with her hand in his. His hands were so huge and warm compared to her own; she felt she was completely hidden within his grasp where no one could ever hurt her. She relaxed and placed her other hand on top his and looked lovingly into his eyes. "I am so, so happy you are home," she said with a sniff. "I was so frightened, Ben. Frightened for you – and for us here at the cabin. I don't know what I would have done had you not come back," she said wiping her tear filled eyes again.

He was so touched by her words and the gesture of holding his hand, he could hardly breathe. He didn't want to move for fear she would withdraw her hand and the magic would be gone. He had never been as vividly aware of all his senses as he was at that moment and wished it would go on forever.

"Ok," she said withdrawing her hand from his so she could blow her nose. She felt braver now: brave enough to be bold, "So what did happened tonight? Is everything ok?"

He told her everything about the evening, from the silver play of the moonlight, to the frightening display of torches, to the rescue of Bertha, enjoying every minute of the telling. She was so easy to talk to. Her face encouraged him to tell more, and responded appropriately to every detail of his story. At times she would again touch his hand, sending a surge of pure joy through his spirit. He would love to spend a lifetime with this woman, and made a mental note to have a talk with God about that, first thing in the morning.

As they finished talking, they both realized they were holding hands, and looked deeply into each other's eyes. "Is this ok?" Ben asked.

"What? Is what ok?" Sarah's smile was curious.

"Our holding hands," she looked surprised and confused so he continued, "Don't you remember? You made me promise I would never touch you again."

She rolled her eyes and with a huge smile, she said, "Yes, this is ok." She immediately wanted to say that he was allowed to touch her, and she should never have made him promise that, but then again she was not comfortable with more than holding hands, so she stopped herself short. "In fact, I must admit I thoroughly enjoy holding hands with you," she said knowing at least that much was true. They sat there enjoying one another's company, and hoping they would have a lifetime together to do exactly what they were doing: smiling at each other and holding hands.

By this time, Ben had had more than enough coffee, so he got up to go outside. Turning from the table he was amazed to find the floor of the room covered with clothes. "What on earth is going on here?" he asked grinning in anticipation of her answer. She was full of surprises and he couldn't wait to hear what she was up to now.

"Well, I went through all the children's clothes, and mine, and yours, and took out the ones the children haven't grown into yet and put them over here," she was swaying around the room waving her arms indicating the placement of different groupings of clothing. I took our old clothes, mostly the ones we came here in, and put them in my grip for storage. I don't know if anyone could recognize us by the clothes we wore, but since we all have enough clothes from the church to do without those clothes…" She turned and looked up at him, noticing how much taller he was than she, and continued, "I thought we could afford not to use them." They were standing close enough to kiss.

They both began breathing harder as they looked into each other's eyes in the candle light. Their lips nearly touched, their breath quickened and their hearts pounded until, unexpectedly, Ben began to feel overwhelmingly inept and naïve; and Sarah began to panic. And just like that, the spell was broken and they both took a step backwards unable to make eye contact.

She turned to resume her sorting and he watched her moving from pile to pile, wishing he had the experience with women that most men his age had. He was about to sink into self-pity when he saw the bag she had brought with her, stuffed and bulging at the seams with their old clothes. How thoughtful that was to pack them away. He had never even considered the possibility that someone might recognize the grey winter prison clothes he was wearing. He struggled in vain to think if he had seen anyone else wearing that type of grey, and wondered if anyone had noticed.

"I really appreciate your packing up our old clothes. I would never have thought of that," Ben said humbly.

Eager to restore the easy banter between them, Sarah said gratefully, "Well, it was nice of you to say that." He just shrugged, which prompted her to continue, "Ben, listen to me, *this is important.*" When he looked at her she continued, "You have no idea how wonderful it is to have a man compliment me. And you do it all the time. I truly love how you simply say what you are thinking. Like around the table the other day when we were talking with Sissy about our futures; I would never have had the courage to say that I loved it here like you did. You were so honest with Sissy about your feelings in a way I can only wish I could be, and I am trying to learn to be that way, but it does not come as naturally for me as it does for you."

He looked down at her with genuine surprise on his face, and Sarah began to laugh. "What are you laughing at?" he asked with a hurt puppy look on his face.

"You are just so honest, and open! Whatever you are feeling is right there on your face. Then you speak it, clearly and succinctly. I have never known a man who compliments *anybody* about anything, but especially women." She could tell by his face that he wasn't convinced, so she continued, "You have complimented me more since I met you, than all the men I have known in my whole life put together, and it is important to me that you understand how good that feels; to be appreciated, and complimented. It means a lot to me."

He stood there in shock with nothing to say, so she began to flounder, "Ok! I am trying to compliment you, and tell you what I am feeling! Help me out here! This is not easy for me to do, I'm not you!"

"No, you just... Sarah, I have to say... well, this is the first time I have felt like I had... anything to offer you. For the first time since we met, I feel like I have value, and I just feel so good about making you happy, that... honestly, I don't know what to say. I guess, selfishly, I just want to stand here quietly, and enjoy it. I'm sorry if that isn't enough, but..."

Sarah looked at him in shock and said, "What do you mean this is the first time you felt like you had anything to offer me?" He shrugged his shoulders as he sat down in one of the chairs.

She knelt down in front of him and said, "I am just surprised to hear you say that. Do you truly feel that way?"

"Yes, I do." Being honest seemed to work with her, so he thought he would just put all his cards on the table. "You know I don't know how to fix things, and before this evening you and Sissy didn't want me near you. I have no money; I've had to rely on you for that. I had no idea what I was doing out there in the woods that first night, I don't know what we would have done without Sissy telling us where to go and what to look out for. Sarah, I have never ridden a horse, nor driven a sleigh or a wagon. I don't even know how to hunt. I am as worthless as tits on a boar hog, from my point of view." The tensions seemed to dissipate, and the barriers between them crumbled as they laughed until they cried over the phrase he had picked up from Lloyd. "Honestly," Ben continued, "I have no idea why you would even want me around."

Sarah thought for a second, got up and pulled a chair around so they were facing each other, "Then let me show you who you are from my point of view, ok?" She looked up at him through her eyelashes and smiled, while he took a deep breath and nodded.

"In the first place, you taught all of us how to have a snowball fight! None of us knew how to do that!" She grinned at his reaction when he rolled his eyes as if to say that was not an important contribution. "No! I am serious," she took his hands in hers and continued, "that was one of the most carefree and fun days of my life, and *you* did that. The children and I will remember that day for the rest of our lives." It pleased her that he smiled.

"And you are good with children, too," she said ignoring the face he made in disbelief. "Oh, I was *very* impressed with how you handled Sissy. That ice water over the head really took the wind right out of her sails without hurting her, other than her pride. I know so little about children, and I have no idea how to bake bread! But we do alright!" They both a good heartwarming laugh over that as they enjoyed their walk down their brief, but event filled memory lane. "*And*," Sarah stressed the word to indicate there was more to add to his worthy list of contributions, "you have made this house a safe place to live. I have not had that since my childhood, Ben, and I cannot tell you what a blessing from God Himself that is."

"Really?" Ben asked thinking of his mother and sisters and realizing just how powerful her words were.

"Yes, the day we girls were bathing and you and Little Ben stood way back in the field and lobbed snowballs at the door to see if you could come back in? That was a priceless gift to me, Ben Waters, and an amazing thing to teach Little Ben. You have a great deal more to offer than you think you do. In fact, I am realizing that each of us has something to give, and working together, we make a pretty good team!"

Ben's heart prayed, "Dear God, let me stay here with this woman for the rest of my life and I will do whatever you ask of me," In fact, he would have been happy had he just been allowed to sit there in that moment for the rest of his life.

CHAPTER FIFTEEN

Ben thought about her words over and over and each time he did, he felt a little better about himself. By Saturday, after another week of working and playing next to Sarah, he was afraid to go to church for fear he might jump up and preach a sermon on joy and deliverance! And he was far too shy to do that and then face the public afterwards. Even chopping wood in the cold went quicker with Sarah on his mind. He marveled at the thick calluses on his hands, and said out loud, "This isn't too bad for a city boy!" He was smiling in admiration of his calluses when he heard a scream.

"Mr. Waters, come quick! Pa fell through the ice and we can't get him out! His head's above water, but he can't hold on much longer! Me and Denzel can't get him out!" When Ben turned to look at the cabin, he saw that Sarah had heard the boy, too, and was out on the porch shouting, "Go ahead! We'll be fine!"

Ben ran over and caught arms with Elias, Abram and Mildred's oldest son, threw his bad leg into the air and was astraddle the horse before he could even think. This was his first time riding a horse, and it was a terrifying ride. By the road, the trip was twice as long as it was going straight down over the side of the mountain through the trees and underbrush, and Ben wondered if Elias knew about the cave, and the treacherous approach to it. Galloping at full speed in the snow and ice, tree limbs hitting him in the face threatening to knock him off the horse, coupled with the fear of falling over the cave entrance, and the terror of getting there too late to save Abram, had Ben's adrenaline pumping by the time they arrived. As he ran toward the lake, frantically looked for Abram, he heard Midgie sob, "He's gone! He slipped under a few minutes ago!"

He jumped off the horse and headed right to the ice covered lake where Abram had been entombed for several minutes. Having had no prior experience with this situation, Ben started to run out onto the ice but was stopped by Midgie who was sobbing and crying! "NO! You can't go out there like that! You need to walk on the boards!" Ben looked out at the frozen lake and saw several boards lying at odd angles on the ice. Carefully, he began walking on one like a tight rope walker, with his arms spread wide for balance. It was painfully slow, and all he could think about was poor Abram beneath the ice in that ice cold water. Ben remembered as a child getting his coat wet while playing outside, and the extra weight that it carried. *I'll bet he's clear on the bottom,* Ben murmured to himself. He turned and shouted, "Where did he go in?" and began taking off his coat and shoes while Elias came around the lake to point out the spot in the ice where Abram was last seen. Coatless and with bare feet, Ben dove into the water and began swimming straight down as far as he could go. His lungs ached for air and his hands were nearly frozen, but by waving his arms madly, his elbow made contact with a head. He turned and felt hair floating in the water, just as he had to go back up for air. The next time he went down, he knew he had to bring him up, or they would both freeze to death.

As his head broke through the surface of the water, he heard a blast of screaming and crying from Abram's family. "Go 'round to the other side and have boards ready to hand to me!" Elias nodded and ran to get the boards. "God help me," said Ben as he blew out all the air in his lungs, then breathed deeply and headed back down. *God I need your help. Please don't let those kids lose their father, and Midgie lose her husband. God help me find him. Help me, God. Help me*, he continued to pray as he made contact with Abram again, except this time it was his large, ice cold hand and arm. Ben took hold of the coat sleeve, put his foot against Abram's chest and pulled the coat off the arm. When his arm popped out, Abram's body rolled over quickly releasing the other arm from the coat. Ben dropped the coat to the bottom of the lake, grabbed Abram by the hair on his head and began kicking toward the surface.

Elias saw Ben surface alone, then turn and struggle with the body of his father. "Get the longest board and give me one end of it!" Through his tears, Elias managed to find the longest board and lay it on the ice near Ben. He wondered how Ben was going to get his father's body up onto the boards, but instead Ben just grabbed the side of the board and shouted, "Pull me in!" He held onto the board with his left hand as the biggest six of the children ran to help pull them to safety.

Ben was holding Abram firmly with his right arm across Abram's chest, even though his own arms had gone numb with cold. He kept arching his back to lift his head out of water, holding onto the board long after his hand started cramping, and gripping his right arm tightly so as to not drop his friend. He kicked his feet wildly, arms cramping as he arched his back in search of air.

"He's struggling again," he heard someone say.

He tried to open his eyes but a bright light prevented him from doing so. "Mama! He's wakin' up!"

He thought he had died because he saw an angel bending over him, her hair glowing in the light. "Sweetheart?" *Was that Sarah's voice?* "Oh Ben, please say something, honey."

Honey? Did she call me honey? And sweetheart? He was feeling pure elation as he drifted off again into the comfortable depths of sleep. It was the next day before he finally became awake enough to be aware of his surroundings. But this time when he awakened, he felt every single cell in his body throbbing. His arms were so sore they were unmovable, his back and hip joints hurt from lying still for so long, and his head pounded so badly he feared his brain would actually explode inside his head. He had a terrible taste in his extremely dry mouth, and could feel his eyelids scraping dryly on his eyes as he opened and closed them. The only thing that didn't hurt was his hair.

His groan brought a very disheveled Sarah to his side. Holding his hand in hers, she kissed his fingers and said, "Ben? Are you really awake?" She smiled and cried at the same time, cradling his face in her hand and rubbing his dry lips with her thumb. "You're back! Oh thank God you're alright."

She was a mess. Her eyes were red and swollen, her hair was in knots and she looked like she hadn't slept in days, but she was the most beautiful sight he had ever seen. Just looking at her made him hurt less. Oh, how he loved this woman, he knew it now, and the joy inside him turned slowly back into a warm, comfortable dreamy sleep.

But soon, those dreams turned into a nightmare as he felt himself suffocating underwater. He wanted to come up, but Elias and Denzel were both underwater as well, and he had to rescue them. He kept forcing himself to go underwater, but something was propelling him upward. Suddenly he sat up in his bed, wet with sweat and panting for air. Midgie rushed in and insisted he lie down again and Sarah picked up a huge pitcher and poured fresh water into a large basin. She took a cloth and dipped it into the water, wrung it out and sat down beside Ben "Shhhh. Shhhhh," she said as she washed his face. "You were dreaming. Everything is fine. You are safe right here in Midgie's house."

But it was so real, Ben had trouble shaking it. He panted and ran his fingers through his hair in order to force himself to become totally awake. "What happened?" he finally said.

"Abram fell through the ice," Sarah began, "and you went in to save him." She gave him some time to process that information before continuing, "You saved his life, Ben!"

"He's alive? Abram's alive?" he asked incredulously. It was coming back to him now; the horseback ride, the lake, the feel of the body when he touched Abram's ice cold hand. He shuddered at that thought, and wondered if there ever would be a time when he wasn't haunted by the feel of that ice cold hand floating out toward him in the dark, cold water.

His downturn in spirit prompted Sarah to say, "Midgie is heating some broth for you. Sit up and let me pile up some pillows behind you, but take it slowly. You might be a little lightheaded."

As he started to scoot back, he realized he was naked from head to toe. Humiliation rose from his toes up, bringing a bright red glow to his cheeks and ears. He could hardly look Sarah in the eye when she came back with the broth. His arms were sore and weak from hanging on for dear life to both the board and his friend, Abram, so he was doubly pleased when Sarah sat down to spoon feed him. There was no way he could ask her who had undressed him, so he managed to mumble something about the delicious broth, and Sarah told him not to talk. By the time he was finished eating he was exhausted, and with a full stomach he felt much better. He wanted to lie down again, but Sarah insisted he drink some water before he slept any more. "We could only give you sips of water until now, and you really need to drink this before you go to sleep again." Almost instantly after he drank the water, his headache began to let up, and he was happy to discover his eyelids moved more smoothly, without that raspy feeling. She was right, he did need water, and again he was grateful for having her in his life.

By the next afternoon he was able to go home, so they bundled him up like the men had done Bertha, and stacked up pillows for him to lean back on in the bed of the sleigh for the trip. Having to go around by the road, the trip seemed endless and by the time he got home, he was too weak to get out of the sleigh by himself. He was wishing they would let him sleep right there in the sled for an hour or so before he had to try to get up and walk into the house, when he heard a horse whinny, and then another.

There were several men from the church waiting at his house for him. Reverend Morrison, Haze, Hulse, Jasper Belt, Elisha Kearns, Beck, and Henderson Beall, another man whom he recognized from the trip to Markley's house, stepped into the sleigh and picked him up as if he were as light as a child. He hadn't realized they had put him on a flat blanket that was carefully placed to be used as a stretcher, exactly like they had done with Bertha. With two men on a side, and Reverend Morrison holding his head he appeared to be weightless as they lifted him easily out of the sleigh and began the short trip to the cabin.

"You're doing a good job, son." Preacher beamed down at somebody located at Ben's feet. He lifted his head just enough to see, and there between his feet was Little Ben supporting Ben's bad leg, running in order to keep up with the men.

The feather tick had been set up in front of a roaring fire and it looked so inviting Ben hoped they would leave quickly so he could go right to sleep. Against the wall behind the fireplace, next to the kitchen was a stack of firewood that went from floor to ceiling. It was at least ten feet long, and Ben guessed it would last them all winter. "You got enough firewood laid in for you 'til you get well, Ben, and Haze's boy and Denzel are going to keep you in fresh meat for a few weeks," one of the men said from the door as the men said their goodbyes.

"Is there anything else we can do for you before we go, Miss Sarah?" Hulse asked kindly.

"No, I don't think so. Thanks to you men, I believe we are set. But thank you so much for asking." She said as she turned to look at the enormous stack of firewood that had been a surprise for her as well when she had arrived. She looked around her little kitchen and felt happy and relieved to be home with Ben.

Ben raised his head and said, "How can I thank you for all this? I don't know how I can ever repay you!" Ben was so weak and emotional he feared he was going to burst into tears in front of everyone.

As the men opened the door to leave, Haze said, "You already paid us back, Ben, by helping with Bertha, and now by saving Abram's life. Now we are indebted to you." They left, closing the door quickly in order to keep Ben from getting a chill, leaving Ben, his family, and the Preacher alone in the cozy little cabin.

Preacher stood and said, "I am not going to stay long, because you need your rest, Ben. But I just wanted to have prayer with you, and thank you for being the fine man of God you are."

That did it. Ben's exhaustion dissolved any willpower he had and he began to cry, "But I am no man of God, Preacher. I am a sinner, and if you knew everything about me, you would never call me a man of God."

Preacher pulled a chair over to the side of Ben's bed and said, "Let me share a scripture with you that will show you how God feels about you, Ben. Its John 15:13, 'Greater love hath no man than this, that a man lay down his life for his friends.' Ben, that is exactly what you did for Abram. When you jumped into that water to save your friend, you were more God-like than human. Did you pray for God's help?" The Preacher smiled at Ben's weak nod. "Yes, you did because you, alone, would never have been able to save Abram. God went with you into that water; He sustained you, and He brought you out. God does not care about who you are or what you have done in your life; He loves you just the way you are. And you are a good, good man in the eyes of the Lord, Ben Waters. You have God's favor on you."

Ben was crying uncontrollably but the Preacher didn't mind. He just leaned over and placed his huge hand on top of Ben's head and said, "Oh, Lord we thank you for bringing Brother Ben and his family into our fold. We thank you for this man who willingly laid down his life for Brother Abram and we ask your blessings on him and his family. Heal his body, Lord, as no doctor can. Heal his soul and spirit and make him clean, washed whiter than snow, Lord, whiter than snow. We already know he is willing to do your work, Lord, we saw that when he was willing to give his own life to save that of Brother Abram's. We see that love in his family, Father, and we ask you to continue blessing them and lifting them up in safety and protection. We are all sinners saved by grace, Father, and we thank you for Jesus who laid down *His* life for *us* so that we can be free to live in love. We come before you to bring our gratitude, Jesus our Savior, our brother, and our friend. Amen." And with that he said his goodbyes, mounted his horse and left.

Ben was still crying, but they were not tears of sorrow, they were tears of release and exhaustion. Finally, when his tears were spent, he was completely worn out, but well fed, and more importantly, he was home. As he drifted off to sleep, he could hear the baby cooing, the children's soft voices as they played, and Sarah, humming in the kitchen, so he *started* to pray again for the privilege of living with them forever, but decided he had asked for that enough. It was time to begin thanking God instead, for granting his wish, because he was already living the life he had asked for. His prayers of gratitude were like a lullaby that rocked him into a deep, peaceful sleep.

CHAPTER SIXTEEN

Sarah could not be happier. She had discovered long ago that she enjoyed Ben's company, and recently she had even allowed herself to enjoy his touch when they were holding hands. But it wasn't until the riders pulled up and told her to come quickly because Ben had been pulled from the lake and was unconscious, that she realized she was starting to love him.

She had been angry with God for so long it seemed unfair of her to ask for his help again when worried, but her heart was breaking and could not help but cry out to God for help. Cali, one of Midgie's older girls had ridden up to watch the children, and gave her horse to Sarah. As Sarah rode down the treacherous path Ben and Elias had taken, she begged God to let him live; begged Him to watch over Ben and return him to her, and to the children. "God I know you are up there, and I know you have power. I know you have the power to save Ben for us, and I am begging you to intercede on our behalf, to keep him breathing, to keep his blood flowing, and to keep his heart beating."

After a while, her prayer shifted to anger as if everything in her soul pushed to be emptied out, not just the requests, but the frustrations and fear as well. "You are supposed to be the God of love! Well, I love this man so you should be happy to save his life for us. Please dear God, if you are the God of love, please have mercy on us and save this man's life. I know you can do it, but I am not sure you will do it because you seem to pick and choose whom you bless in this world. You bless men in this world who run roughshod over the women and children. You say in the Bible that there is no male, nor female in your sight and yet you allow horrible men to beat and abuse women in the name of the Lord! For years I begged you for mercy. I begged you to keep me safe, and yet the beatings went on." She was screaming her prayers now as she hunkered down over the horse she was riding to avoid being struck by a limb, while trying to keep her eyes on Denzel's horse so she wouldn't get lost.

She was out of control, and as her soul expelled the anger she found her thoughts returning to the present, even as she prayed, "So I took the matter into my own hands. You wouldn't help me, so I helped myself, and I got myself out of there. And I found a good man whom I love! And now you want to take him, too? Sometimes I feel like you are just one more man who is determined to make my life miserable! And I hate that! I hate the feeling that you are a man, so just like all the men I have met, you are going to step on my needs as if I am not important, because I am a woman! I want a God I can love and trust. I want a God who loves me as much as He loves men!"

She surprised herself at the angry words she had spoken, but she did not regret saying them, and suddenly, she found she had nothing else to say. She stopped screaming, stopped praying, and rode along in silence for a while, realizing she felt better than she had in a long time. She was experiencing some kind of elation that was heady and exhilarating. "I am being blessed," she thought as she rode along feeling as if she might just float off the horse. She enjoyed the sensation of her heart feeling light and began whispering, "Thank you, Father. Thank you for this blessing. Lord, I praise you for listening to me, and hearing my pleas." She tried to bring herself back to reality and worry about Ben, but found no worry in her heart. Instead she began praising God and saying, "Thank you, Lord. Thank you for saving Ben for me. I thank you, Lord, for hearing my prayers. Thank you isn't enough, but I don't have the words to express how in love with Ben I am, and how much I adore you at this moment."

As she pulled up to the Benson's house, Midgie came out looking concerned. She rushed over to Sarah's side to help her off her horse and to help her onto the porch. Once they were there, they stamped the snow off their feet, and Sarah asked, "Where is he?"

Midgie was surprised at how calm Sarah was, and felt a need to warn her about his condition. "Sarah," Midgie caught her by the arm and turned her to face her, "He's bad, Sarah. He isn't conscious, and may never be."

Sarah was amazed that her words did not upset her. She just had a peace that passes all understanding, and knew that no matter how long it took, Ben would be alright.

As she stepped into the living room she saw the strangest sight. There was Abram, lying in a makeshift bed in front of the fire, covered with a sheet and blanket, and a fur hat that covered his head and ears. The children were taking turns holding a blanket in front of the fire, then at the count of three the cold blanket would be removed and replaced by the warm one. The older boys would take turns warming their hands by the fire, and then gently rubbing Abram's feet and toes, sometimes elevating his legs and arms as if to encourage the blood to flow into his body and then back. They kept him in constant motion, talking to him and sometimes rolling him over on his side and pounding him on the back in the hopes of getting more water to come out of his lungs. The littlest one, Betty Sue, just stood back and held her worn tattered doll, and stared at her lifeless father as they struggled to save his life.

"We got a lot of water out of him," a pitiful Midgie said, "and he is breathing. Now it's in the Lord's hands," she let out a heartbreaking sob and then immediately regained her composure as eight children looked to her for comfort and stability.

"In the Lord's hands is a great place to be, Midgie," Sarah was surprised at just how much she meant that. Her smile was genuine and comforting to Midgie as Sarah took Midgie's hand and said, "God was with them in that water, Midgie, and He is with us now. Just trust that He has heard our prayers and believe that He loves us more than words can express." Sarah was pleased to find that Midgie's spirits had lifted a little at her words of encouragement.

Denzel took her to the room where Ben lay, still as death, and yet Sarah felt only joy in her heart. She looked down at him and smiled, knowing she would love this man tenderly and powerfully for the rest of her life. He was a gift from God and she would treat him as such.

But that was then, and this was now, Sarah thought to herself as she breathed deeply and looked around her little cabin. Her eyes feasted on Ben, lying by the fire, safe and sound, and her heart soared. She had the chance to care for the man she loved beyond belief, and the prayers of gratitude would not stop. Whether she prayed consciously, or her spirit was just joyous beyond words, she was living in a constant state of gratitude.

She was grateful for Ben's improvement, for Abram's life, for Midgie and her gifts of food and clothing, for the church, for her successful escape, and for each of the children. The new shelf Ben had found and put up for her in the kitchen where the cups and tin plates now sat beside three leather bound books, brought such gratitude from her heart that she could hardly contain it. "Thank you. Thank you," flowed from her lips as she bustled around preparing hot broth and chunks of the bread she had sent to town for. "Now that I am a wife and mother, I need to learn how to bake bread," she thought to herself with no feeling of dread or obligation. But this had not always been the case.

Before, she had been married to a very wealthy man who pressed his parishioners to make him even wealthier. He was the top man in a religious organization that arranged marriages and traded women like cattle. Her father was her hero until the day he announced that she had been "given" to marry a man who was forty years her elder. "Bartered" would have been a better word, because the arrangement made her father a very wealthy man. He had told her that she should be happy with the situation because the lower ranking church women would come in and cook and clean for them, affording her a life of luxury. Sarah spent the first few years trying to console herself with the thought that in her position, she did not have to learn how to do the mundane house chores, like baking bread and cleaning. Funny how life changes. Now she wished more than anything that she could bake a hearty dark bread for Ben to dip in his broth. She was a schoolgirl again, dancing around the kitchen daydreaming about baking bread for her husband, cookies with the children, and making dinner for Preacher some fine Sunday after church.

Ah! And there was another blessing she was grateful for: Reverend Morrison. She knew without a doubt that God had sent him ahead of the other men on the day they brought Ben home. She had gone home first to prepare the cabin for Ben's homecoming, and to let Cali go home. Cali took the horse Sarah rode home, back to the Benson's. And as Sarah stepped out onto the porch to thank her and wave goodbye, she saw the Reverend riding up.

"Good morning, Reverend!" Sarah was beaming.

"It is a good morning, isn't it Sarah! The Lord has been good to us, hasn't He?" Reverend Morrison said with that big heartwarming grin on his face.

"Oh, yes, He has!" Sarah said as he dismounted his horse and tied it to the post. "Come on in Preacher! I have hot coffee just waiting for someone to drink it," she said as she flashed a joyful smile at the Reverend, the likes of which he had never seen on her face before.

He knew something had changed her, because the look of sorrow in her eyes, even when smiling, was gone and a new joy flickered in them. He had seen that look a lot in his time as a minister. Life was hard and there was a lot of evil in this world, and it took its toll on the vulnerable. His guess was that Miss Sarah had seen more than her share of the evilness in man, and felt her soul had recently been restored. The old country preacher knew there was a time to preach, and a time to listen, so he closed his Bible and placed it on the table, scooted his chair out so he was facing Sarah, folded his hands, leaned back and said, "So what is going on in your life?"

She started by telling him which vegetables she was cooking, and about the broth that was warming, how good it would feel to have Ben home, and how much she appreciated having all the wondrous bounty that the folks from this community had provided, which brought her around to gratitude in general. She was so grateful for everything, and as she spoke she literally glowed with the Holy Spirit. Reverend Morrison could see it in her face and all around her. She walked taller and lighter and with a new confidence. After pouring the Preacher another cup of coffee and putting out a plate of whiskey cookies, one of the many gifts from the congregation, she poured herself a cup and sat down across the table from him. He smiled at the sight of the whiskey cookies, a staple there in the winter season. Little bits of dried fruit, and walnuts scantly covered with a mixture of flour and whiskey, and baked for many hours in a hot oven. They were dry, except for the moisture inside the dried fruit, but very flavorful and nutritious, and they would last a year without molding or going bad.

She had been raised to be a lady, and coached incessantly on proper manners for a minister's wife, so she forced herself to stop bubbling over with her newfound enthusiasm, and give the minister a chance to speak. When he didn't, she found herself again talking to him as if he were a long lost friend, chattering on and on with the encouragement of his wondrous smile.

Finally she ran out of words, and a comfortable silence filled the air. For the first time since she started speaking, she actually looked Reverend Morrison in the eye and saw the amazing depth of kindness, love, and acceptance there. She began taking long deep breaths and realized there were thick, heavy tears rolling out of her eyes and down her cheeks. She expected him to start shouting, "A moment ago you were sitting there telling me how happy you were and now you are crying like a child! You must learn to control your emotions, Evangeline!"

Instead he just continued in his silence, smiling at her, accepting her, which made her cry even more. She stood and went to the kitchen where she retrieved a cloth for her eyes, and when she came back, she said, "I don't know why I am crying. I am so happy, I just don't understand!"

"Well, tears aren't only for sorrow, Sarah, they are also a cleansing release. When we have hardships like you and Ben have had, and we face near tragedy, sometimes we cry even when things turn out alright. And sometimes we weep with joy! You have many things to be joyful about, Miss Sarah. Your husband was returned from what could have been a watery grave, and it was God who bought him out. That is a blessing, worthy of a great deal of powerful emotions."

Sarah sat down again, and stared at the table, deep in thought. She had been so blessed on the ride down to see Ben, and then had the joy of caring for him, and now, anticipating his return, that she hadn't had to face the horrible things she had said to God. But now, somehow, the layers of joy had been peeled back to expose the very angry words she had shouted at God, and she couldn't bear it.

Preacher patiently watched her struggle with the words she was trying to form, and eventually she looked up and said, "Could I speak with you about something?"

His huge smile lit up the room as and he said, "Of course." She stood up and started pacing back and forth behind the table, wringing her hands, again searching for the right words. Finally she asked, "Have you ever been angry with God?"

His face darkened and his eyebrows drew down frightfully when he said, "Oh, so angry! Many a night I have wrestled and fought Him until the break of day, just like Jacob in the 32nd chapter of Genesis."

Sarah had heard of Jacob, but had no idea he had fought God. She made a mental note to look up the 32nd chapter of Genesis in the Bible Preacher had given Ben. Again, she drew in her breath and said, "Don't you regret that? Being angry with God, I mean?"

Preacher knew her interest wasn't in how he felt; she was struggling with her own guilt, so he answered in a way that allowed her to unburden, "What do you mean, Sarah?"

"Well, when I was on the way down to Midgie's house, I was praying for Ben, and begging God to save his life. I just needed Ben to come home to the children and me, and I begged and begged for his life. Then I realized I was very angry with God for things that happened years ago, and I heard myself saying horrible things to Him, blaming Him for the sins of men, and screaming at him like a mad woman! When I needed His help the most, I was yelling at Him!" Her sobs interrupted her speech, but still Preacher waited patiently for her to continue. "I was screaming blame at Him for things He hadn't even done. I don't know what was wrong with me."

In no rush, Preacher waited for Sarah to once again gain control. As she wiped her eyes and blew her nose, he smiled that powerful smile and asked, "How did you feel after that, Sarah?"

She looked remorseful and laughed, then said, "Honestly, I have to say I felt good." She sat there smiling, and remarked, "I actually felt better for some reason." There. She had admitted it. She had felt better, and that was the truth. But then the words came back to haunt her, to make her feel guilty for her actions. "Does that make me a heathen, Preacher?"

His big burly laugh brought the smile back to Sarah's face. He said, "Our Heavenly Father is the Great Physician, Sarah. He knows the poison has to come out before a wound can heal. He has been waiting for that to come out and stop festering for quite some time, because he knew that until you ridded yourself of it, you were enslaved to the past, unable to move forward and accept the many riches he has in store for you. God wants to be your Father, your friend, and your confidant. If you are feeling something, or experiencing something, God wants you to talk to him about it. Don't worry about hurting His feelings," he said with that big smile again, "you can't surprise him with anything you do or say. He is a big boy, Sarah. He can take your anger."

He allowed Sarah to process what he had said. She watched her hands fold and unfold the cloth she was holding, and without looking up, she said, "Not everyone had a good father, Preacher. So saying God wants to be our father may not be all that comforting to everyone." She glanced up at him to measure his reaction to that.

"We humans are sometimes so limited in our ability to see God for the being He is, Sarah. The world gets mixed up in our thoughts about His nature, and we limit Him to our own understanding. But He is our one true Father, Sarah. Just give Him a chance to love you as you should have been loved, protect you as you should have been protected," he paused as she began to cry. "Bless her heart, Lord," he began praying over her. He placed his massive hand on top of her head and prayed, "Yes, Lord, be here with us in this moment and bring healing to her shattered heart." He continued to pray until she calmed down and wiped her eyes with the cloth from the kitchen. As soon as she was able, he continued talking to her, "Just give God a chance, Sarah. He will never let you down. From now on, He is your one and only Father. He gave Ben back to you as a welcome home gift," which brought a smile to her face again. "Just give Him one more chance, and I think you will be surprised." There was that healing smile again.

"Mama! Come see!" the children shouted as they came falling into the house covered with snow. "Look! There are some men ridin' up!" Sissy said.

"Ok, you children come inside and have some hot chocolate," Sarah said as she grabbed her coat and scarf. "And get those wet clothes off, the last thing we need is for you to get sick."

Reverend Morrison stood up and put on his black hat, riding coat and leather gloves, and went outside with Sarah to greet the men. As he got to the door, he turned and said, "That would be the men coming to help us get Ben into the house. Ben should be here any minute." And with another blessed smile, he left Sarah to return to the house and prepare Ben's bed.

CHAPTER SEVENTEEN

Ben was home and life could not be any better. He was sleeping peacefully in his bed beside the fireplace; the children were playing outside in the snow. Rebecca was sleeping peacefully in her bassinet, and Sarah was doing her best to learn how to cook. She made a mental note to purchase a cookbook the next time she saw one, and then remembered the scripture she had promised herself to look up. She found the Bible and sat down in a chair beside Ben and began to read. She was familiar with the Bible, but more as a weapon than a friend, so she decided to make an effort to read and see it as the folks in this community did.

That is how Ben found Sarah when he opened his eyes. She had been sitting there for hours reading the scriptures. She had sent the children outside to play in order to let him sleep, and they had come into the house exhausted and cold. Little Ben had fallen asleep on the bed in the bedroom where he was sitting with Sissy while she fed the baby. Benjamin thought Sarah was the most beautiful sight he had ever seen, sitting beside him with her apron on, her hair glowing in the candlelight as she read the Bible. How had he ever been so lucky? As quickly as that thought came into his mind, he replaced it with praises to God for giving him the gift of Sarah and the children. In his weakened state he began to cry again, and one huge sniff brought Sarah's head up as she smiled the most magnificent smile. She couldn't wait one more minute, so she dropped to her knees, grabbed his hand in hers, and said, "I love you, Ben Waters. I realized it when I was on my way to the Benson's farm and I begged God to let you live long enough for me to tell you that." She cupped his face with her hand and said, "I love you with all my heart, Ben. I do."

A weak smile spread across his face as he said, "I love you, too, Sarah." She kissed their intertwined fingers as they sat, enjoying each other's company. Finally, Ben groaned as he tried to sit up, bringing her back to the reality that he probably needed to relieve himself and to be fed. She helped him sit up on the side of the bed, brought him the white chamber pot, and turned to serve up broth, coffee, and bread. When she returned she was shaken by how much weight he had lost. He looked like bones inside the long nightshirt the Bensons had dressed him in, and his face was so gaunt, he looked like a completely different man. She was careful not to show her concern as she dragged the night table over to him, and served him his supper. "Can you think of anything else you would like to eat?" Sarah asked in the hopes that she could improve his appetite.

"No, not really," he said weakly. "This broth really hits the spot," he said panting for air. "I don't think I can eat the bread," he said worrying her even more.

"Well, just eat what you can!" she said cheerfully, hiding her concern as she walked back into the kitchen to see what might serve her well in fattening him up and giving him strength. Fear gripped her stomach as the thought occurred to her that she might lose him yet. "Give God a chance to be the Father you always needed," the preacher's words came back to her. "Whatever you are feeling or experiencing, God wants to be a part of it."

So she prayed as she chose a jar of home canned applesauce for his desert, and thought, *I am still afraid of losing him, Lord. After all your help, I am still afraid. Help me believe.* Maybe if she put some of that applesauce on his bread he would eat it. "Ben," she said as she rounded the corner of the fireplace, "why don't we try some of this applesauce…" But he was fast asleep again. The food scooted back from the edge of the table, he was covered almost to the top of his head with the heavy quilts they had been given. She returned to the kitchen, leaving the applesauce on the table in the hopes he would eat it the next time he awakened.

That evening, with the stress of the week's events over, fatigue hit the entire family. Little Ben and Sissy went to bed early, and after Sarah had done the evening dishes, she had only two chores left before settling down for the night; she had to empty Ben's chamber pot, and go to the outhouse herself. She put on her cape and gloves, wrapped a scarf around her neck, and pulled on the heavy fur cap Ben had been wearing when he got home. Ben's experience with having worn no socks the night Sissy ran off, had inspired him to make the rule that even when running outside for a moment, you should dress as if you were planning to stay all day, because if you fell, it might be a while before you were found. She picked up the chamber pot and headed outside. When she opened the door she saw a darkened sky, heavy with snow. She emptied the chamber pot and used the outhouse as fast as was humanly possible, but by the time she opened the outhouse door to leave, she could not see a thing. There was nothing but blinding snow. *A blizzard*, she thought to herself, *and no one knows I am out here*. Panic set in as she realized that it was possible that, with such poor visibility, she could miss the house my mere inches and wander out into the field, lost forever.

How far was it to the house? Which direction? Is it straight to the house? Or do I go to the right a little? How was she going to find it, and what if she missed? The snow was piling up on her boots and it struck her that if she didn't go now, she would never find her way. "The cabin is a big target," she said aloud to herself. She felt herself shudder as she thought that by trying to find the path to the front door, she might wind up in the field beyond the cabin. She decided instead to try to find the back of the house, and then once finding that, she could feel her way around to the front. As she walked forward, she had the illusion that she wasn't even moving. There were no points of reference to chart her progress, and although she knew her feet were moving, she could not see them for the snow. She took one huge step that sent her sprawling onto the ground, and when she stood up, she wasn't sure which way she had been headed originally. "Ok, God here is your big chance. Guide my feet, Lord, and lead me back to Ben." She lifted her head and tried to see if she could see the outhouse or the house, but there was nothing but blinding snow. The wind was picking up and she was getting cold. She had to hurry, but had no idea which direction to take. The only clue she had was her own footprints, so she dropped to her knees and crawled along the ground looking for any sign of her footprints, but to no avail. They had already been covered with pounding snow. Suddenly she remembered Ben telling her of the indentation in the snow that Sissy's footprints had made, like dragging his finger through his mother's sugar bowl. She crawled to the left of her and then the right, and caught sight of something that may have been a trail. She followed it back long enough to feel she had an idea of which direction to go, stood, and headed out with a strong gait to find the cabin.

  She was trying to remember how many steps it was to the outhouse, taking the biggest steps she could manage and counting them as she stepped, when suddenly she heard a roar that was so close to her right side she actually felt it vibrate, and smelled the moist hot air from a bear's mouth. She was so frightened she fell backwards into the snow, lost her bearings and ran in the wrong direction. Her tears were freezing on her face, but she tried not to scream for fear of notifying the bear as to her whereabouts. She leaned forward and ran head long into the blizzard resigning herself to the fate that awaited her if she didn't manage to outdistance the bear. She was getting hot and sweaty, the cardinal sin of survival in the snow, because after she cooled down, the sweat and dampness on her clothing would turn to ice, but she no longer cared. She had lost her way and had become hysterical in the process, leaving her no hope of finding the cabin.

  Her next step resulted in a blow to the head that almost knocked her out. She tripped and fell forward, bursting her lip open in the process. Her hands flew up to protect her body from falling, and came in contact with the solid and sturdy outside of the cabin. The cabin! She had found the cabin, and now all she had to do was find the front door. She imagined herself in the middle of the back of the cabin, and began feeling her way around to the left. When her hands felt the corner of the building she was please to discover that she was not in the middle, but rather closer to the edge. As she rounded the corner she stepped out into the fierce and cold wind which whipped her cape open, exposing the back of her neck to the cold, and chilled her to the bone. She kept stepping to the left, careful not to let the cabin leave her grip, farther and farther she went until her mind began playing tricks on her. Was this their cabin? It was too long to be the end of their little house, and for a minute she became so disoriented she almost decided she had run onto someone else's property.

The wind was so cold around her ears and neck; she stopped and put her face against the wall, and used her hands to pull her hood around so the wind couldn't hit her face for a just a minute. She wanted to sit down and cover up until the wind stopped, but then the thought of Ben lying in there almost helpless prompted her to try again. Finally, her fingers felt the corner of the building, and she knew that within minutes she would find the door. She sidestepped left again and again, knowing she had to stay in contact with the building if she had any hope at all. The wind was blowing at her back now, which helped her move a little quicker. This wall had the door on it, if she could just keep going. It seemed like an eternity, but she finally felt the trim on what she thought was the door, but to her dismay, discovered it was just another corner. She wanted to scream, but knew she had a very short time to live if she didn't push past her fears and find that front door.

Her saving grace was that she became angry. Had she allowed herself to dissolve in pity, she may have given up, but when she began to feel rage, a different attitude engulfed her. "I am going to find the door to this cabin if I have to go around it six times!" she shouted into the wind. "You are not going to defeat me, Satan; you are not going to take Ben and the children away from me!" She took three more steps and discovered her feet could go no farther. *The wood pile. I FOUND THE OLD WOODPILE! It is just to the right of the door, so if I can just make it around it*, she thought as she bent over and held onto the wood that Ben had stacked outside the cabin the morning before Abram's accident, never losing contact as she made her way around it.

When she found the door, her fingers were too numb to manipulate the clasp on it, so she used her elbows to hit the latch with an upward motion. Suddenly she fell into the cabin and landed on the floor with a thud. No one had missed her, which meant no one would have come looking for her had she not found her own way back. She was so warm lying there on the floor she was tempted to stay, but forced herself to stand to close the door and remove her coat. Quietly, she pulled a chair up to the fire to warm her fingers and toes, and became overwhelmed with gratitude for the warmth of the cabin. It was amazing to touch the wall in back of the kitchen, and know that on this side of that wall was warmth and life, and just inches away, on the other side of those boards where she had been just moments ago, could be certain death. She looked up at the boards that held up the structure she had taken for granted in the past, with a new appreciation. The old boards looked beautiful in the candlelight, and the word "home" was delicious on her tongue. Never in her life would she have believed she would be so happy with so little, and yet, happy she was.

She looked over at Ben sleeping soundly, and thought she should heat the broth, because he would soon be awake, and suddenly remembered she had left the chamber pot in the woods. "Back to real life," she thought dryly, kicking herself for leaving it out in the snow. Tomorrow after the snow stopped, they would all go looking for it, because she could not remember if she had taken it out of the outhouse or not. Maybe she had, but then did she drop it when she fell? Her mind was trying to remember when she heard Ben stir.

"Hi," he said with a big smile. This time when he sat up, he looked stronger, and sat up faster.

"Did you sleep well?" Sarah asked.

"Yes, I did, but you are going to have to stop insisting I drink so much water, I am about to burst."

"Oh!" Sarah smiled sheepishly, "about that…"

She didn't tell him about her entire trip, only that she had gone to the outhouse and left it somewhere. "But it is dark and snowing really hard so I don't want to go back out there until tomorrow, if that is ok with you." Sarah scrounged around and found another pan that would suffice, but was much larger than the chamber pot, so they had a laugh over the sheer size of it. He was so easy to get along with, she was beginning to drop her protective façade she had carried for so long.

She brought him a pan of soapy water so he could wash his hands, and was pleased that he not only ate the broth, but also downed two slices of bread with butter and applesauce on them. He started to lie back down, but Sarah said, "How would you feel about a bath?"

Sarah could see he was a little uncomfortable, so she added, "Why don't you bathe while I go put on my nightclothes, and I will wash your feet when I get back? I brought you clean clothes to put on, a pan of soapy water, and a pan of rinse water."

She got busy with the dishes while he washed his face and hands, and then excused herself to go change. She would go wash his feet when his bath was over, but she would linger in the bedroom, until he called for her. She sat on the edge of her bed, awaiting his call, when a sickening 'thud' told her he had fallen. She ran out into the room to find him flat on the floor unconscious. Apparently, he had stood up too fast and had fainted. She turned him around and supported his head and shoulders with her knee, and her left arm. As he awakened, his face was perilously close to hers and he thought for a split second of kissing her when he noticed the cuts on her forehead and lip, from the fall she had taken outside. "You have a split lip! What happened? Who did this to you!" He was shouting so loudly he woke up Sissy, and Sarah had to send her back to bed. "But first, Sissy, help me get him back onto the bed."

By the time they got him back into bed, Sissy had seen the cut on Sarah's lip and looked at Ben as if she could kill him with her bare hands. "No, wait!" Ben said to Sissy, "I had nothing to do with this!"

"I heard you yellin'! And then you was both on the floor!" Sissy drew back a fist and it appeared she intended to return the favor to Ben's face. "Don't you tell me you din't have nothing to do with this!" Sissy shouted back at them, awakening the other two children. Little Ben came out and Sissy, who was now being restrained by Sarah, proceeded to tell him Papa was beating up Mama. Little Ben was wide awake then and burst into tears as he jumped onto Ben and began beating his chest with his little fists.

"Stop! Stop it!" Sarah shouted. "Everybody back!" She had Little Ben's shirt in one hand, and Sissy's arm in the other trying to stop them from hitting Ben. "Now, stop it and sit down at the table, right now!

As they all took their places at the table, Sarah continued, "Now, I am going to start at the beginning and tell this story all the way to the end, and nobody is going to interrupt me!" She finally silenced everyone with a stern look, and continued, "Now, your father was taking a bath and he stood up too quickly and got dizzy and fell. I ran to him and was trying to see if he was ok, when he saw my lip and started shouting because he wanted to know how it had happened!"

A cacophony of questions erupted, and she said, "Be quiet and I will tell you the whole story."

By the time the story was told, everyone had forgotten about the accusations, and was focused on the grim outcome that could have happened. Little Ben had moved to Sarah's lap and had his arms around her neck, while Sissy cried silently at the thought of losing another Mama.

Ben began thinking about how he would fix it so that would never happen again while the children asked her questions about the bear. "Come help me get make some hot milk for everyone," she said as she dipped up Ben's broth and poured his coffee. "It is freezing in here! Little Ben, would you please stoke up the fire?"

Finally Ben said, "We are going to tie a rope from the front door to the outhouse. That way, all we will have to do is hold on to the rope to find our way back. And from now on, *nobody* goes to the outhouse without telling someone they are going. If you get up in the night, wake somebody up so we know you are out there. If the snow doesn't get you, a bear could, and we would never know what happened." He ate a few more bites of broth, bread, and applesauce, and then added, "No, from here on, we are all using the chamber pot at night! Nobody leaves this house during the night for any reason! Do you all understand?" Heads nodded vigorously in agreement.

Sarah was touched that he had put so much thought into it, and in an effort to lighten the mood, she said, "And *that*," she indicated with a nod of the head, "is the new chamber pot!"

Little Ben laughed and said, "That's big enough for me to take a bath in!" then immediately hoped he hadn't given Sarah any ideas about giving him a bath.

Sissy said, "I'm afraid I'll fall into it!" This sent them all into fits of laughter. Eventually, when Sarah went off to put the children back to bed, Ben lay in his feather tick and watched the blizzard going on outside the window. The thoughts of Sarah being out there, helpless and lost, frightened him, and he felt a renewed sense of fear in the face of their naiveté. He was too weak to worry, so he decided to just thank God for her safe return, the lessons they had learned, and the second chance they would now have for getting it right.

Just as the tiredness was beginning to swallow him up, Sarah came into the living room in her sleeping gown. She looked exactly like an angel with her long hair falling down around her shoulders. "Ben," she said softly. "I have a dilemma. I do not feel comfortable sleeping in the other room with you out here alone because you might have to get up in the night and you could fall again, and I might not hear it with the storm raging outside. And I am *way* too tired to sit up again in that hard chair all night."

He had no idea what she was going to suggest, but of those two options, he would much rather have her sleeping in the comfortable bed than to sit up in a chair one more night. He remembered waking up several times at Midgie's house, and seeing her sitting in a chair, always ready to care for him, so now he wanted her to rest, and he told her so.

"I am planning on resting, but just listen a minute," she said chastising him for interrupting.

"Alright, I am listening," he said folding his hands over his chest.

She moved over and sat down on the edge of the feather tick. "I was thinking that I would sleep out here with you. This bed is certainly big enough, and that way if you need anything, I would be right here."

Ben was touched beyond words. He was moved by the idea of falling asleep beside her, awakening to see her there, and maybe holding her hand as they fell asleep, but he was shocked she would trust him that much, a far greater gift of confidence than he had ever expected. "Are you sure about this?" he said.

"Yes, I am sure, Ben. After the last few days, I need to be close to you tonight and know that you are alright. I was so frightened that I would never get to see you again," the tears of exhaustion slid down her face as Ben scooted over, away from the fire, to make room for her, and threw back the covers in invitation. She sat down on the edge of her bed facing the fire, gathered her hair behind her back and deftly braided it down over her right shoulder, then slipped off her house shoes and swung her legs onto the bed. He was lying on his back on the left side of the bed, and Sarah was on her right side facing him, with her hands under her right cheek, her back to the warm fire.

She hadn't touched him when she slid into bed, so he made no moved to touch her, not even hold her hand. Eventually he rolled over to face her, and as tired as they were, they talked into the night, and fell asleep warm and safe under the blankets – as far apart from each other as was humanly possible.

Sarah awakened first, and found Ben lying with his back to her on the far edge of the bed. Oh, how she did love that man. She smiled at him and slipped over to relieve herself behind the curtain in the new chamber pot. Since it was still dark, she threw a couple of logs on the fire and went back to bed. About two hours later, the children began to stir. Sissy had fed the baby quite late at night after they had had their talk, so she was still sleeping, but the children were still up before dawn, which surprised Sarah since they had been up so late the night before.

"I can't believe it is still dark, Sarah said as she took a candle over to the window and tiptoed to see if she could see the stars, or if it were still snowing, but she couldn't see anything. Not even darkness. Instead she saw something like crinkled paper pressed up against the window. She didn't understand what she saw, so she went over to the door and opened it to find snow from top to bottom. The snow was completely up to the roof of the little cabin, so there was no way out without digging the snow out of the doorway, and even at that, they couldn't have gone anywhere.

When Ben saw the snow piled high, he could only think of Sarah out there lost, and regretted not having thought of the rule about not going out at night before. Well, he didn't have to worry about that right now, because it would be days before they could get out. Good thing they had the stack of wood in the kitchen, and such a big chamber pot! He had wondered why the neighbors had stacked the wood *inside* the house. Now he knew, and was grateful once again.

CHAPTER EIGHTEEN

What a great adventure! The children ran from door to window looking at the situation, and squealing with delight. In their entire lives they had never experienced anything quite like this! Sissy began drawing faces and stick people in the snow that was flat as a board in the doorway, while Little Ben began secretly making snowballs. It was probably his quietness that alerted the adults that he was up to something, so as he turned to toss the first one onto Ben's bed, he ran into Sarah who was standing behind him, fists on her hips. He was looking straight into Sarah's apron, and as his eyes slid up to her stern face. He stood there holding the snowballs in his now freezing hands. Suddenly, Sarah burst into laughter, gripped his hand and forced him to wash his face with the snow packed in his right hand. "No fair!" Little Ben said, but then he caught onto the joke and laughed with the rest of them.

The floor was covered with snow by the time they finished their antics, both kids were soaking wet, and the top of the snow, heated by both the heat escaping from the cabin, and the sun that was now beating down on it, was beginning to melt and create quite a puddle on the floor. "I must insist, children, that we close the door before that melts more and floods us with melting snow!" Sarah said with her newfound authority. Much to the children's chagrin, they were shepherded away from the door and told to find something else to do, and for a while, they played quietly in their room, while Ben and Sarah enjoyed each other's company, smiling often at the muffled laughter of the children.

But as the day wore on, the chamber pot screamed to be emptied, the children were bored and fighting, and Ben and Sarah were weary of the darkness. "Maybe we should try to burrow out," Sarah said. She had hated to bring it up, knowing full well that Ben would consider that his responsibility and therefore highlighting the fact that he was not able to get up and do it.

"I wish I could do that," Ben said with regret, "The kids aren't big enough, and I sure don't want you out there again."

"I am not a child, Ben! There is no reason on earth why I can't be outside! Please do not start treating me as if I am not capable!" Sarah said with great indignation.

She was about to continue her argument when Ben interrupted her by lifting one hand and saying, "Normally, I would agree with you, Sarah. But with that bump on your head, and the time you were out lost in the snow last night, I just thought you might be susceptible to getting sick or something. It may be days before we could get out of here for help, Sarah. I just didn't want to take any chances."

Her posture changed completely, knowing he was right. "Alright," she said reluctantly, "I guess that makes perfect sense," she admitted contritely.

Knowing her very well now, he refrained from smiling when he said very seriously, and very slowly, "But I will be careful in the future, not to insinuate that you are incapable, or weak, in any way." He paused for just a moment, then with an almost imperceptible grin, he added, "For any reason!" At the first recognition of a smile on her face, they both dissolved into laughter, and both their hearts filled with gratitude. His, for this lovely, strong woman who deigned to love him, and hers, for the patience, understanding, and steadfastness this man afforded her.

The magical moment was interrupted by an argument that was forming between the children. The fun of being snowbound had worn off, and boredom had set in. Sissy just wanted to sew, but Little Ben wanted someone to play with him. As one of Sarah's leather bound books began drawing Sissy's attention, Ben began poking her with his finger, saying, "Come on! Come on!

Come on! Come on!" Over and over he chanted until Sissy turned and swatted him, giving Little Ben the opportunity to burst into tears and run in to tattle on his sister.

"Alright, that's enough! I want you to get on your warmest clothes! We are going to dig our way out of here." Their eyes lit up and they squealed with excitement again, while jumping up and down, and clapping their hands. These were two happy children, not only because of the great adventure they were about to embark on, but also because they had spent the day listening to their parents laughing with each other and enjoying each other's company. Here in this little cabin, they had each other, and now the loving home they had only dreamed of in the past. Their joy was uncontainable. Sarah really wanted them to use that energy getting dressed, and digging the snow away from the door, but she couldn't bear to interrupt the spontaneous celebration that was going on. "Are you two happy?" she asked without even thinking about their response.

"Oh yes, Mama! We are very happy!" they said as they wrapped themselves around her waist, hugging her and looking up at her with adoration in their eyes.

"You know what? I am happy, too," she said as she knelt down to look them in the face. Have I ever told you two how very much I love you?" She was surprised when the looks on their faces turned from joy, to questioning, to huge rapidly flowing tears, in an instant. She almost fell backwards as they both lunged at her and hugged her neck. After a tearful moment, she decided that that was indeed something she needed to say more often. Every child, every human being for that matter, needed to know they were loved, and she would never miss an opportunity to express her love again.

As she stood up, she said, "Ok, now go get dressed. We have a lot of work to do." While she waited, she realized again that it was far too warm inside that cabin. The wood the men had chopped was perfect when the wind was blowing in through the cracks in the wall. But they were logs really, and far too much to put on the fire while the cabin was wrapped tightly with a coat of snow except for the back wall where two or three small cracks in the wall had escaped the mounting snow drift. But they couldn't let the fire go out to cool the cabin down, because there was no kindling to start a new one with. What she wouldn't give for a stack of smaller wood.

When the children came out, dressed like snow men, Little Ben announced he wanted to go first which brought on high pitched protests from his sister. But Ben decided since Sissy was taller, she could go first. Little Ben was comforted by the promise that he would be able to clear farther down the door than Sissy since he had to wait his turn. They chose a bowl to dip the snow with, and Sissy stepped up onto the chair, tiptoed, and filled the bowl to overflowing. "Now what do I do with it?" Sissy asked.

She had scooted the chair too close to the snow to bring it down in front of her, so Sarah suggested she pass it backward over her head into the waiting hands of Sarah, who tiptoed, and awaited the delivery of the first bowl. But as the bowl passed over Sissy's head, it tipped, and the snow spilled down her back instead.

Sissy screamed as she leapt off the chair, put her hands over her shoulders and tried to pull the back of her dress out. She jumped up and down in an attempt to dislodge the snow as it slid slowly down her bare back, lodging finally, and painfully, at her belt. Little Ben was thoroughly entertained as she squealed and stomped around, finally taking her coat off as she ran into the bedroom and slammed the door. Sarah had never heard a child giggle like Little Ben was, and she found it exhilarating. She laughed at Little Ben's giggles, but Sissy thought they were laughing at her, which brought her out stomping and throwing a fit at both Sarah and Little Ben.

Ben watched the entire episode from the comfort of his feather tick, and saw a rare opportunity for him to align himself with Sissy. "Come over here sweetheart," he said patronizingly, as he held out his arm. She stomped over and plopped down on his bed within the safety of his arm as he continued, "Now, I don't think it is fair for you both to laugh at Sissy!" This was a two sided blessing, because he both garnered goodwill from Sissy, and gave Sarah an opportunity to explain her intentions.

"We weren't laughing at you, Sissy. Little Ben was just laughing at the situation. We weren't happy it happened to you, but the way you hopped up and down when the snow was going down your shirt surprised us. And I was laughing at how hard Little Ben was laughing."

"Well, it wasn't that funny, guys!" Ben continued advocating for Sissy. "That snow was really cold!" Then with a twinkle in his eye, he said, "And besides, you dance divinely, Sissy!"

She realized then that he was teasing her, and with most of her anger dissipated anyway, she stood up and slapped Ben's arm gently and said, "Oh, you are as bad as Little Ben!"

Working together, they came up with a better plan for clearing the snow, and before long they had broken through, and the room lit up with the late afternoon light. Sarah wished they had pushed the snow away earlier in the day. But light was light, and she was thrilled to see it, so she encouraged the children to continue.

Little Ben was indignant about having to wait his turn, but almost as soon as he got started, his fingers got cold, his shirt and pants became wet, and he wanted to quit after working for only ten minutes. Sarah was fine with that because it was getting darker, which meant colder so she wanted the children to close the door anyway.

With the great adventure of the day over, the children were again restless, and Sarah remembered, and finally understood the complaints from her friends of the past. Those mothers had dreaded rainy days when the children were "confined to the house" for their play.

She was finding out a great deal about motherhood, and she liked it, even this part. She had discovered sleeping portions of her soul that had been awakened by loving these children, and she thought she could not love them more if she had given birth to them. Her thoughts were interrupted by fighting again, so she said,

"Now, while I get supper started, why don't you children go up and explore the loft Denzel and your father built. Again, she had called Ben their father, and again she watched for a reaction, but saw none. They were accepting life as it had been presented to them, and being children, they had not looked back. She was pleased that she and Ben were able to give them this home where they would be loved and cherished as all children should be, and stopped her thoughts short when they wandered toward the possibility of ever losing them.

The children were entertaining themselves by screaming and running up the ladder to the loft, in an effort to escape the imaginary bear that was chasing them. She smiled as they discussed which of them would go back down the ladder to get the "food" they had dropped on the way up. Little Ben was chosen to go back down the ladder and Sissy was to be the lookout. Sure enough, just as Little Ben's feet hit the floor, Sissy yelled that the bear was coming, and he rushed to climb the ladder, only to find Sissy wouldn't let him into the loft. A shoving match ensued, and just as Sarah was opening her mouth to shout warnings, she heard Ben's voice shout, "HEY! HEY! Somebody is going to get hurt! Stop that! Sissy, let him up there."

Sissy argued that the bear was behind Little Ben and if she let him up, she would have to let the bear up as well.

Ben said, "Well, help him up, and then pull up the drawbridge so the bear can't get in."

"What's a drawbridge?" That question brought about twenty minutes of discussion about castles, moats, drawbridges, knights, and eventually dragons, with the children sitting on the end of Ben's bed, absorbing every word. Sarah wondered how much education the children had had, and was pleased to find the children so interested in learning. She also wondered about Ben's education, but asking was taboo, so she would never know for sure. But he seemed very knowledgeable about the issue of castles, etc., so she was hopeful.

She almost had supper ready, so she said, "Ok, children! Go wash up for supper, and help your father get washed up as well." Without a word, they ran to the white enamel pans they had saved snow in for washing up, washed their hands, and then took a pan of water, a wash cloth and bar of soap over to Ben.

"I am so proud of you for doing what your Mama told you, and remembering to bring me a pan of water as well!" He remembered the pride he felt when Lloyd complimented his work, and added, "You two are growing up to be fine people." Sarah looked up just in time to see the children beam.

During supper they discussed their new plan for digging their way out of the cabin, and once again they had a good laugh about how quickly Sissy got undressed, but this time, Sissy laughed, too. Their eyes shined at the sights before them as they looked out into the candlelight and saw Sarah with her golden hair and brown eyes, Ben with his dark black hair and blue eyes, Sissy and Ben glowing with youth and now, good health. After they ate, Sarah brought the baby to the table so as a family, they could continue the fellowship.

"So this is the Waters family, huh?" They all nodded and smiled in agreement, and Ben continued, "Do you all like the name?" He had meant the name "Waters," but Little Ben thought he meant the name "Ben" for the both of them.

"I like being a Junior!" he said brightly, so Ben acted as if that was what he meant in the first place. I do, too, Little Ben! I think it suits both of us! Don't you?" Little Ben nodded his head quickly several times. It was certainly easy to please this child.

"Papa?" Little Ben looked up in adoration at Ben. "What was your Papa's name?"

Ben hated to lie, but the stakes were too high to give that kind of information to one so young. So he said, "Lloyd."

"What was your Mama's name?" Little Ben continued.

"Juanita." And there it was; another part of his history rewritten. He and Sarah made eye contact across the table, and Sarah, in an attempt to change the subject said, "What was your Mama's name?" she said to both children.

"Mama," Sissy and Little Ben said simultaneously, with an incredulous look as if to say, "What are you thinking? Of course our Mama's name was Mama!"

Both Ben and Sarah laughed at their response, then Sarah eased the tension by saying, "I don't know why I asked such a silly question."

Sissy patted her on the arm and said, "Its ok. We all ask silly questions sometimes." Sarah appreciated Sissy's grace, which brought up another matter Sarah wanted to discuss.

"Sissy, I wanted to talk to you about something. Do you know what grace is?"

"Yes," Sissy replied, "It's what you say before you eat."

Sarah smiled and said, "Well, yes it is, but I was meaning more like the grace God gives us all."

"Oh, then... no," Sissy admitted.

"Well, grace has many meanings. It can be to have mercy on someone, very much like what you just did for me."

"What?" Sissy said completely confused.

"Well, I was embarrassed because I had asked such a silly question, and you just said that it was alright because we all ask silly questions sometimes. You could have made fun of me and said mean things, but you didn't, you gave me grace and made me feel better."

"Oh!" Sissy said with a look of surprise on her little face.

"Grace can also mean elegance, or refinement, or poise and beauty. It is a word filled with charm and loveliness, and it reminds me of you."

Sissy had been drawing circles on the table with the water ring her cup had left on the bare wood, but upon hearing that, she looked up at Sarah with a very serious look on her face and said, "Me?" She was clearly shocked that so many nice things would bring her to Sarah's mind, and was having a tough time seeing herself in that manner, especially after a day of fighting with her brother.

"Yes, you," Sarah proceeded slowly since it might be the only time she would ever get Sissy to sit still and listen to her.

"You were willing to give up your future and marry Denzel in order to give your brother a home. That is very grace-filled, Sissy." She watched the wheels turning inside Sissy's head and knew she had never even considered herself a hero. "In spite of the hard life you had before running away, you cared for your brother and Rebecca, and you never complained or demanded that you have your way, at their expense! You are one of the most grace-filled people I know."

Sissy sat with her elbows on the table, and her little fingers in each side of her mouth casually. She never took her eyes off Sarah as big tears welled up in those big eyes and rolled slowly down her face.

Ben said, "I agree, Sissy. I have to tell you that I had no idea what to do when we got to the Braxton's and they weren't there. It was you who told us we needed to climb the hill to be away from the road because we had no idea who would come along. You know far more about surviving than I do Sissy, and I admire that very much." He sat up a little straighter and said, "And I agree with your mother," he said taking Sarah's approach to finalizing the changeover, "You are one of the most grace-filled people I know, too. I would go as far to say that you are one of the finest and strongest human beings I know, as well."

Sissy was in tears, unable to speak, so Sarah continued, "Sissy is a nickname some people give their sisters, so I was thinking that someone might ask you what your real name is," she waited for Sissy to process that and then added, "And I was thinking that, had I been lucky enough to be your real mother, I would have named you Grace." Sissy's stare was unreadable prompting Sarah to make a caveat, "Of course, if you want, you can just tell people your real name is Sissy. You don't have to change it at all if you don't want to, or you may want to choose a new name for yourself. That would be fine with us, wouldn't it, Ben?"

Ben shook his head in agreement and looked at Sissy hoping to see some sign of her reaction to Sarah's words. Instead, Sissy burst out of the chair and into Sarah's lap, threw her arms around her neck and said, "Oh, thank you, Mama! I love it! Can we start calling me that right now?" she said as she placed her head on Sarah's shoulder.

Sarah had her hand on the back of Sissy's head and her other arm around her waist. The hug made her feel something she had never felt before in her life; a love so deep she did not think she could survive without it. It wasn't that she loved Sissy more than Ben; it was that she loved her in addition to Ben. They were a family and she was beginning to know and understand just what those words meant. All those years she had benefited from the independence that money and an absentee husband provided, came crashing in on her, filling her with regret. While she had tolerated the stories her friends told her about their children, she wished she had been a more attentive listener, and hoped her disdain for their lifestyle had not been obvious. For she was now realizing what a fool she had been.

CHAPTER NINETEEN

Sissy sat down at the table and pointed to each of them, starting with Little Ben and said, "Little Ben, Papa, Mama, Rebecca, and me, Grace." She laughed and clapped with joy, and Ben remembered the pitiful little forms they were on the boat, and his desire to change all that. How incredibly grateful he was to his Heavenly Father for allowing him to show these children kindness. His thoughts turned to the 23rd Psalm and the section about restoring his soul, and said, "Sarah, would you mind reading the 23rd Psalm to us?"

"Certainly not," Sarah said honestly. She would never have believed she would look forward to reading the Bible after the beatings, when her husband would read passages about how a wife was to be obedient. She had hated the Bible and turned a deaf ear to his sermons Sunday after Sunday. But by the time these thoughts had crossed her mind, she had come to the end of the table where the Bible was and felt herself smile at the sight of it.

"Here we go," she said with a twirl that moved her skirts around so she could sit down without having to use her hands to tuck her skirt under her. With the Bible in one hand and the baby sleeping soundly in the crook of her other arm, she had trouble finding the scripture. Ben offered meekly to look for the passage, but had never had any instruction on the use of the book, and was discomfited at the thought of looking for the passage with everybody watching.

Sarah said, "Psalms is usually in the middle of the Bible, unless they have a lot of different information in the back to help you read and understand the Bible as a whole," she said directing her comments to the children as if she hadn't noticed Ben's awkwardness. From the corner of her eye, she saw Ben holding the Bible between his knees, and putting the backs of his thumbnails together in a measured attempt to find the center of the book.

The children were beginning to watch Ben's feeble attempts with impatience, so as he continued to split the Bible open and look for the Psalms, she decided to distract them with more information about the Bible. "The word 'Bible' means books, a collection of books. And Psalms is one of the many books in the Bible." She glanced at Ben and saw him open the Bible and then close it again, so she continued her lesson, "And each book is divided into chapters, as most books are, but then the lines in the chapters are numbered so you can find the specific one you want." Another glance at him told her he had been successful!

"Ah! Here we go," she said as she leafed through the pages and located the 23rd chapter of the book of Psalms. "Thank you, Ben, for finding that for me," she glimpsed at him briefly as she said that, and then had to stifle a laugh because his face was beaming exactly like Sissy's and Little Ben's when he had paid them a compliment.

"The 23rd Psalm," she began. "The LORD is my Shepherd; I shall not want."

"What does, "shill" mean?" Sissy asked.

"The word is, "shall," and it means, "will." I will not want." Sarah said patiently.

"That's silly! Why din't they just say will?" Sissy was not amused.

Sarah said, "There are far more words in our language then we ever use, Grace," she watched Sissy grin at the use of her new name. "And it is my job to teach you as many of those words as possible, so you can have a good grasp of the English language. So let's start again."

"The LORD is my shepherd; I shall not want," Sarah read.

"Wait, what do you children think that means?" Ben asked.

"I don't know," Little Ben wanted to say something because Ben had asked, and if Ben was involved, Little Ben wanted to be involved. "I don't even know what a sepred is."

Ben and Sarah looked at each other and Sarah nodded at him to go on.

Ben started, "Well, if you remember, Rev. Morrison spoke of a shepherd as a person who takes care of sheep, and sheep aren't the smartest animals in the world, so if they didn't have someone to guide them, they wouldn't know where to get food or water. Sheep won't drink from bubbly or flowing water, so the shepherd has to know where the still water is or they will just die of thirst." He paused to look at their faces to get a read on how well they understood what he was saying. As soon as he was satisfied they got the meaning, he continued, "So who do you think our shepherd is?"

"We ain't sheep!" Grace said indignantly. "We don't need no shepherd!"

Sarah decided to leave the grammar lessons for later, and speak directly to the subject. "But if there is a being out there who loves us SO much that He wants to guide us and help us, wouldn't that be nice to know?"

"I reckon," she said looking down at the table dejectedly.

"Well, think of it like this," Ben said thoughtfully, "you were all alone in Parkersburg, hiding, and skinny, little Benji hiding in the bushes, and stealing food to stay alive. Winter was coming and you had no coats or a place to live for that matter. And look at you now." Sissy looked up at him acknowledging the point he had made.

"Do you want for anything now?" he said hoping she would understand the words he had chosen. "Do you go hungry anymore?" They both shook their heads, "No." He continued, "Do you have enough to drink?" They nodded, yes. "Do you have a warm place to sleep, with people around you who love you and take good care of you?" They nodded more vigorously. "Well, it was God who brought us here, because He loves us and HE is our Shepherd. Would you please read those words again, Sarah?"

She opened the Bible and resumed her reading, "The LORD is my shepherd; I shall not want." The words finally made sense to Sarah. After having read them mechanically hundreds of times over the years, they began to reveal their meaning to her, and she shared that meaning with the children. "Think of all the needs God has met for us. He provided this cabin, and the food we are eating, all the furniture and clothes. We have everything we need, and without our having to pay for it, which we could not have done on our own."

Ben was the next to share his new insight, "And none of us were planning this, were we? Did any of you plan to meet us and come here and live like this?" They chuckled and shook their heads as if to say, "Never in our lives did we think we would be here."

"So what we are saying is, our God, our Shepherd who loves us and wants the best there is for us, gathered the five of us together, just like a herd of sheep, and brought us to a place where we needed nothing. We want for nothing." There was complete silence as the reality of his statement gave them each a new perspective. "The LORD is my shepherd; I shall not want." Ben enjoyed just saying the words out loud, and had the thought that it was worthy of memorization, so he encouraged the children to repeat it after him. "Now, let's try to remember that, ok?"

"Go on, Sarah," Ben said.

"I will start over, and I want you all to say the first line with me."

They all said in unison, "The Lord is my shepherd; I shall not want."

Ben said, "I'm sorry to interrupt again, Sarah, but I think it is important to say that God loved us enough to bring us here before we even asked him to. I didn't even know there was a Shepherd until recently, but He brought me here anyway, and gave me each one of you, and this place to live. I think if He did that before we even asked, that we should be able to trust Him to always lead us, don't you think?"

The thought made Sarah relax a little. She had her mother's voice in her ears telling her that she had been lucky all her life, but someday her luck would run out. Had she seen this as just her good luck? And if so, didn't luck run out? Sarah had been living in the fear of just that, but here in the scriptures, it told her something completely different: that it had nothing to do with luck, and everything to do with God's hand protecting and guiding them on their collective journey. "Yes, I think the only way we can live sanely, is to trust our Shepherd. It isn't our good luck that brought us here, it was our Shepherd," Sarah said with the authority of both a Mother and a leader.

"The Lord is my shepherd; I shall not want," Sarah continued. "He maketh me to lie down in green pastures."

Ben interrupted, "Little Ben, what do you see when you look out our front door?"

"SNOW!" shouted Little Ben, happy to have the right answer finally.

"Well, yes, you do see snow right now," Ben laughed and continued, "but this summer, what is going to be outside our door?" Little Ben stared blankly, clearly unable to think of even one good answer.

Sarah came to his rescue and said, "Well, by this summer, that big field out there will be covered with green grass, so it will be a green field, or a green pasture. He did just what He said He would; He led us here to lie down by green pastures. And it isn't just the grass that makes that so wonderful. He led us to this community who helped Him meet our needs by giving so much to us. I think that is what is meant by leading us to green pastures." Ben nodded his head in agreement.

Sarah continued to read, "He leads me beside the still waters," then looked at Ben with a twinkle in her eye.

Ben responded by saying, "I don't know about you all, but I really enjoyed the ride here on the clear calm waters of the Little Kanawha River. I had been on a train, and had traveled by foot, and I had a pretty rough time for a while. But then I remembered what my father had told me about traveling, about how safe it was to travel by water because the bears couldn't get you, and there were only the people on the boat to deal with, so bands of robbers couldn't catch you out in the woods alone. I found it very healing to watch the waters as we traveled and I felt safe and calm for the first time in my life. In fact, that is where I got the name, Waters."

Ben smiled at the children as they clapped and giggled at the revelation because it was yet another secret they would share. "So when it says that our Shepherd would lead us beside the still waters, well, that means something to me. Because the still waters had an impact on me before I had even read the words we are reading now," Ben said as he nodded to Sarah to read on.

"He restoreth my soul," she read without noticing the subtle change in Sissy's face.

Nothing Sissy ever did escaped Little Ben's scrutiny however, and he said, "What's wrong, Sissy Grace?" Sarah found the combination of the two names endearing.

Sissy Grace said, "What does, 'storth' mean?"

Sarah had to look back at the Bible to discern which word she was referring to. "Oh," she said as she glanced at the page again, "Well, 'restoreth' means to rebuild, or fix up," she said unhappy with her explanation. She struggled with the true meaning of the word as she thought it was meant in the scriptures.

"Actually, it means more than that," she said, closing the Bible on her thumb, and searching for the right words. She paused as she prepared to explain the difference in what she had said, and what she thought the scriptures meant. "We took lumber and fixed up this cabin, and even rebuilt some of it. But it isn't anywhere near what it looked like when it was first built. So we actually just fixed it up. But to restore something, we would have to bring it back to the same condition it was when it was new. This scripture says that God restores our souls, He doesn't just fix them up He makes our souls as new as they were before we had hard times." They all thought about a time before... a time when they were innocent and pure, and loved living. Could it be true that they could feel like that again? Could God really restore their souls to the original quality?

Ben said happily, "You know, I feel that my soul has been restored. Better than restored, really. I am happier now than I have ever been in my whole life."

Sissy Grace said, "Me, too! I feel happy, too. I am happy that I don't have to be the Mama anymore, and I get to be a child for a while." She immediately felt remorse and look at Little Ben and said, "Sorry, Little Ben."

Little Ben scooted closer to Grace, took her hand and laced his fingers in with hers, smiled up at her and said, "That's Ok, Sissy Grace. I am happy that we both get to be children now. I like having a sister to play with."

Sarah smiled and said, "This is amazing. I think our souls have been restored, and we didn't even know it was happening." She was astonished at the fact that this scripture seemed to be speaking directly to them, and then stunned to think God had brought the five of them to this point, to this table, with this scripture in their hands. She expressed her thoughts, mostly to Ben, but the meaning was just as clear to the children. The realization that God had brought them together, equipped them to survive, and even to thrive here in the midst of this bitter winter weather with the help of this loving community was beyond understanding. They had been blessed, and the reason was there in her hands. She read the words again, "The LORD is my shepherd; I shall not want."

She had gone from an uninspired reader of the scriptures, to an overwhelmed participant in the living Word. Overpowered by her emotions, she felt incapable of continuing the reading, promised the children more tomorrow, and sent them off to bed.

"What's wrong?" Ben asked, noticing the change in her demeanor.

She nodded toward the bedroom indicating her desire to wait until the children were asleep to talk. "I just want to get the dishes done up so we can relax," she said with a smile.

"Could I help you?" He asked, secretly hoping she would refuse his offer due to the fatigue settling in on him.

"No, no! I want you to rest, it won't take me but a moment," Sarah needed time to gather her thoughts, and fell into the routine of washing, rinsing, and stacking the dishes. She needed time to process what she was thinking and feeling as she was accustomed to doing, alone with her thoughts. But instead, she discovered to her surprise, she had a strong desire to discuss it with Ben. She had always been an independent thinker, relying on the input of no one but herself. But now it seemed she really didn't know what she was thinking about any given subject until she talked to Ben about it. She valued his insight and trusted his kindness. In fact, that was what she loved about him the most, his ability to think independently, express his thoughts clearly, and yet accept the ideas of others without feeling threatened as a man.

She was about to credit her good fortune in meeting this man, to luck, when the idea that God had brought them together and to this place reoccurred to her, making her heart race and her head swirl. She finished the dishes quickly, slipped in to check on the children and change into her night clothes, then returned to find Ben already sleeping soundly.

She knew he needed his rest, but was greatly disappointed that she couldn't discuss with him this issue that was burning at her soul. She wasn't at all tired, and couldn't sleep if she did lie down, so instead she paced the floor wishing someone would awaken so she would have some company. She thought about stepping outside to look at the moon and then lifted her arms in futility when she remembered they were snowed in, and smiled, quietly saying, "So, here I am in the belly of a whale! Well, God, you have my undivided attention." There was nothing left to do but read the passage again, and this time she heard it not as the mindless rhetoric she had heard recited in church, nor as the teacher reading it to the children. This time the words vibrated off the page and felt so personal when she read them, it was as if she had written them herself.

She found herself smiling at every word, every phrase that had become living words to her. She had feared falling directly into the pits of hell if she ran away from the "church" she had been raised in, and instead ran away and fell headlong into the loving arms of God, Himself. This Bible now in her hands had revealed to her the truth about God's love for her. No wonder she had never been allowed to read it. Very crafty on the parts of the high ranking officers of the church, to keep everyone far away from the truth, and make them believe that only the six highest ranking men in the organization could interpret it. Their religion was invented by men, and God had delivered her from it. As she sat there with her head back and eyes closed, she could actually feel the burdens lifting from her tattered soul. Almost in a dream world, she could feel His presence in her heart as she allowed Him to move about freely in her life, lifting the burdens, mending her broken heart, healing her spirit, and leaving pure joy in their place. She hoped the feeling would never go away, because in that moment of understanding she knew she would never be afraid again. Through this window of insight she could see with great clarity, how much He loved her and how worthy of her trust He was.

    She felt the dreaminess of sleep come upon her, put the Bible down on the end table, blew out the candle and carefully crept onto her side of the bed, far from Ben. With her back to him, she returned to the blessing she had been experiencing, and fell into a deep healing sleep.

CHAPTER TWENTY

The children were up early catching Ben and Sarah still asleep. The baby was sleeping since Sissy had just fed and changed her, so the children decided to cook breakfast for the family. Little Ben stoked up the fire while Sissy went quietly to the front door for snow to melt so she could scrub the potatoes. Soon, the wonderful smell of frying potatoes and coffee filled the air.

"Good morning!" Sarah said as she yawned and stretched lazily. Perhaps she should have jumped out of bed, apologized for sleeping late and leaving her chores to the children, but instead said to herself, *the children seem happy, so I guess this is how we do it in our family.* The thought made her laugh since personal freedom was a new experience for her, and she became giddy with the idea that those five people got to make up life as they went, have it as they wanted it, and love each other while doing it.

As she made her way over to the chamber pot, which they had placed as far from the kitchen as possible in that tiny little cabin behind a curtain of thick blankets, she realized that one way or another, it had to be emptied, today! Coming back from that chore, she washed her hands, kissed the children on the tops of their heads, and said, "Do you want me to take over?"

"No," said Sissy. "I am not useless. Had it not been for you and Papa, I would be a married woman right now, keepin' house and fixin' breakfast for my husband and Little Ben. I think I can handle fixin' breakfast for you every once in a while." She smiled and unexpectedly, Sarah saw her as much older than before. She guessed that Sissy, having had a reprieve from being the mother of a baby and a nine year old boy, had reverted to some childlike behavior, creating an illusion that she was much younger, and her stunted growth from poor nutrition encouraged that false impression. But the truth was, she could have been a wife, how old did she say she was? Fourteen, the day after Christmas? Oh, no! They had forgotten her birthday. They should have done something for her, made special cookies, or a cake. But then they were just glad to be warm and have anything to eat. Next year, Sarah would make it special. Next year, she thought. She loved the sound of that, the thought that they could all be together in a year, or ten years just filled her spirit with such joy, it was reminiscent of the night before when she read the scriptures and sat with God, enjoying His company for the first time ever.

Finally Ben began to stir just a little, but enough to send a joyous Little Ben over onto the feather tick, bouncing and chattering away to the man who was barely awake. "Me and Sissy is fixin' breakfast for you and Mama!"

"Are fixing breakfast," Sarah insisted. "And it is, 'Sissy and I,' not me and Sissy. Think of it like this; it is selfish of you to think of yourself first, and *put* yourself first, so you would never say, 'me and sissy.' Put others first and say, 'Sissy and I.'"

Little Ben looked at Benjamin with a face that was bewildered and pleading for help. Sarah collapsed into a chair, laughing happily, and said, "Come here, Little Ben." The boy thought he was in trouble, so Sarah took his hand and said, "How do you feel about hugs?"

He opened his mouth to say something, but instead threw himself into her arms, then sat on her lap with his arm around her neck. Sarah said, "Often I have wanted to give you a big hug, or hold you on my lap, but I didn't know how you felt about being hugged." Then she stopped, looked around the room and shouted, "Waters family! How do we feel about hugs?"

Sissy said, "I like being hugged, except…" she looked at Ben and dropped her head indicating her discomfort with being touched by grown men.

Ben said, "No problem, Sissy! I will always have big friendly hugs ready for you, and if you want one, just come get it. But if you don't, well that's fine, too. Because every woman should get to decide who she hugs and who she doesn't hug. Is that fair?"

Sissy nodded and smiled, happy to have been given control over her own body. She thought she couldn't be happier until Ben said, "And I want you to feel free to hug your Mama, or your brother, or your sister all you want, without any obligation to me. I wouldn't want you to be cheated out of hugs on my account."

She looked at him through narrowed eyes, wondering if she had misjudged him. "Well, he talks real good, I'll give him that," she said bringing laughter from both adults. Then thought to herself, but time will tell. She returned to her cooking as Ben winked at Sarah, warming her heart. She was going to enjoy getting used to feeling good about life.

After a delicious breakfast, Sarah announced that she and Ben were going to do the dishes, so the children could go play out in the snow. "We are going to have to clear a path to the outside today," she said, "So get bundled up as much as you can." But she was talking to the backs of their heads because the minute they heard they were going to get to play in the snow, they were headed to the bedroom to get dressed.

Ben rolled over on his back and stretched, spreading the blanket out with his feet.

"Come on lazy bones. You need to get up and move around a little or you are never going to get out of that bed," Sarah said playfully.

"ZZZZZZZZZZZZZZZZZ!" Ben's attempt at feigning sleep brought a bubbly cascade of laughter from Sarah, followed by the hearty deep laughter of Ben as he looked at her with great love in his eyes. It was music to the ears of the children because they were part of a family that loved to laugh.

Ben's legs were a bit wobbly, but he was careful and made it to the chamber pot just in time. "Are you by chance having the children dig us out of here so we can empty that chamber tub?" he asked with a big masculine smile.

"Oh, yes, indeed!" Sarah said with a smile that welcomed him into the kitchen as well as her heart.

As Ben picked up the dishtowel used for drying the dishes, he said, "I'm glad we had that little chat about hugging." Sarah wondered what to say, but before she could formulate any words, he said, "So now we need to talk about how the adults in this house feel about kissing."

She turned to face him with a slight grin on her face, but saw the children coming out of the bedroom and gave him a look that indicated the conversation would have to wait. "Alright," she said to the energetic children, "are you all dressed up warm and dry?" The children stood for inspection while she made certain they were dressed warmly from head to toe. "Ok, here are two dishpans. I was thinking you could dig your way out with these, you know, scoop up the snow and throw it out away from the house? Now stay together, and no snowball fights without us!" With that the children grinned, pulled two chairs over to the door and began digging.

Since there was no place to throw the first few pans of snow, Sarah had them put it in all the pots they had available, for bathing later much to Little Ben's disappointment. But slowly they progressed to the point where they could actually get outside, and then they were gone.

As the last foot disappeared out the top of the snow, Sarah turned to Ben and said, "Now, where were we?"

Ben said, "I believe the subject on hand was how the adults in this family feel about kissing," Ben tried to look very serious, but the little boy in him showed on his face. He knew she was embarrassed, and he was being bold, but much to his pleasure, she was woman enough to hold her own in any conversation, and she was not backing down from this one.

"I would like a moment to tell you how I feel about that," she said with a mischievous smile. "And then," she continued, "I would like a moment for rebuttal."

They both laughed at what she had said, and then Ben asked, "You want a moment to refute what you just said?" She giggled and glanced at the door to be certain the children weren't listening.

"Yes, I do," she said as if that were the most commonplace of events.

"Fine," Ben said and then waited curiously.

"Sit down," Sarah said as she pulled out the chair. Ben stood where he was so she pushed passed him to pour him another cup of hot coffee. When she turned around, he was still standing so she said again, "Sit down!" When he didn't move, she took his arm and led him over to the table and said, "In the first place, this is your first time out of bed and I don't think you should be standing up this long. In the second place, I don't think I can say all this with you standing there looking down at me like you want to kiss me."

"I do want to kiss you," Ben looked down at her with that grin that drives women mad, forcing her to close her eyes completely, or succumb to the kiss right on the spot.

Without opening her eyes, she shoved his shoulder and said, "SIT!"

He took his seat and sipped his coffee with an indulgent look on his face that told her he was listening, but still planning on getting that kiss.

Again she closed her eyes in order to fend off his charm, and turned to walk around, being very busy so as to not lose her nerve.

"I admit," she began, "I do, so, want to try kissing you," she said trying to avoid looking at Ben.

"Go on," he said as if he were an elderly professor encouraging a young student to continue with her assignment.

She looked at him with feigned annoyance, and then continued. "But…" she tried to form the words, and the struggle became obvious on her face, so Ben got up, poured her a cup of coffee and pulled out a chair so she could sit down.

"You know," Ben said, giving her a minute to regroup, "one of the things I like best about us is that we can talk about anything. Whatever it is, just say it."

She decided to just pour it all out, and trust Ben to make sense of it. She sat straight up, looked him in the eye and said, "I may enjoy kissing you," she began, "But I may not like it at all," she said as a matter of fact. "I may shove you away and go lock myself in my room and cry all day." She took a deep breath before continuing, "I honestly don't know how close I can get to you, in that way."

Ben sensed that she was very serious, and he sat still, giving her his full attention.

"Ben, things have happened to me, at a very young age, that…" she began panting as if she were reliving some horror in the past, her face changed and she took on the appearance of a trapped animal trying to get free.

She didn't have to say one more word. Ben sat his cup down, leaned toward her and placed his hand on her arm, and said, "Its ok. Its ok." She was appalled with herself for crying like baby, but she couldn't stop herself. He put his arms around her, and she felt so safe that she just exploded with tears, in spite of the fact that she was telling him she may never be able to be a wife to him. But there was nothing she could do, the dam had broken and it all had to come out no matter how long it took. *God knows all the poison has to come out before healing can begin*, she heard Preacher's words come back to her as she lay there against Ben's chest, being rocked back and forth like a baby, and sobbing as the memories flooded back.

As she sat up and blew her nose, the children came sliding back into the house with rosy cheeks. They stopped and looked at Sarah, then stared at Ben accusingly, their fists balled up ready to fight.

Ben and Sarah laughed at the drawn down eyebrows of the children, then Sarah recovered by saying, "It is alright, children," she laughed and blew her nose again. "These are good tears, healing tears. Your father is a very good man, and you do not need to be afraid of him hurting me. Come here." The children came to her knee obediently, so she held one each of their hands and said, "In the first place, your father has been nothing but kind to us. I think it is time we begin to trust him a little, don't you think?" Little Ben nodded vigorously, but Sissy smiled with only half a smile and rolled her eyes. "Sissy, your father deserves the same second chance we all got when we came together. I don't expect you to trust him until you feel like it, but I would like for you to think about giving him a chance, alright?"

Sissy didn't look up, she just nodded her head yes, so Sarah lightened the mood by saying, "Well, now! Is the world still out there?"

The children began chattering about how bizarre the world looked. There were whole trees missing under the ocean of snow, and the little place under the limbs of the trees where the boys had tried to hide from Sarah's and Sissy's snowballs had turned into a small fort with a sliding board down into it. Both adults enjoyed the animated reenactment of lively events that included the use of the dishpans for sleds.

"So you haven't shoveled any snow yet?" Sarah asked. The children responded with silence and looks of shock. "You forgot?" They both nodded seriously until the all four started giggling. "There isn't any hurry at all, you kids just go out and have fun."

"Wait," Ben said, "Why did you come back in?"

"We was wonderin'," Little Ben began, but was interrupted by Sarah.

"We *were* wondering," she corrected.

"We were wondering if you knew where you dropped the chamber pot. We was..." A look from Sarah stopped him and made him think, "We were gonna to try to find it."

"Good boy!" Sarah said tousling his hair. "I have no idea where I dropped it, and I don't think you will find it until spring thaw, but I can tell you exactly where to look for it." The children listened intently. She spoke very deliberately "It is somewhere outside the cabin, under the snow." The children gave her a dry look, clearly indicating they did not enjoy the joke; and while the grownups laughed good naturedly Little Ben and Sissy turned and went back up the snow path and disappeared out the top of the door, pulling it closed behind them.

Sarah sighed heavily as Ben turned her to face him. "Listen to me," he said as he placed his fingers under her chin and lifted her face toward him. "I am happier right now than I have ever been in my life. If we never get any closer physically, than we are right now, I would die the happiest man that ever lived on this earth. You do not owe me anything, and I do not expect anything more from you than you are able to give comfortably." He waited for the words to find their target, then said, "Now. May I be brutally honest?"

She smiled at the now familiar phrase he used, then nodded yes, but became subdued as she noticed the pain etched on his face.

He paused for a minute as if collecting his courage, stood and walked around with his fists in his pockets. With his back to her, he took a deep breath and said, "Bad things don't just happen to girls, Sarah," he said honestly, and painfully. He had to look at his feet to brace himself against the onslaught of humiliation engulfing him as the memories came flooding back to him as well.

Sarah watched him, afraid to breathe. She sensed that this was extremely difficult for him, and allowed him the same grace he had given her; she waited silently for him to manage his feelings and then speak when he was ready. She watched him breathing deeply in an attempt to hold back what she guessed was tears, or anger, or both, and after several long minutes, he spoke.

"To be perfectly honest, I don't know if I could ever be a husband to you, in every way. There are years and years of bad things, that…" His breathing quickened and she could feel the tears of a broken heart, long before they began gathering in his eyes. She rushed forward to hold him in her arms, as he had done for her just minutes before. He cried as hard as a grown man would allow himself, then turned abruptly and walked around while regaining his composure. "I feel like a fool," he said finally, pulling a handkerchief out of his hip pocket to blow his nose.

As much as she wanted to lecture him on the fact that both men and women should be allowed to cry, and how he had been through a lot, and how sorry she was for his misfortune, her own spirit told her he just needed to move on, so instead she said jovially, "Well, aren't we a pair!" And it worked.

He laughed and looked at her with great compassion and said, "Yea! We may be the only couple on earth who live together their entire adult lives and never even kiss." His smile turned to seriousness as she slowly walked over to him, and hugged him again. The best of feelings washed through his soul. Just to stand there with her in his arms, relaxed and feeling loved, was the most magnificent sensation ever experienced. In his heart he knew that might be all he was capable of, and that was enough. If he could just have the privilege of holding her in his arms from time to time throughout his life, he would know he had been blessed.

She looked up at him and before the two of them could think about it, they kissed. His arms tightened softly around her and drew her near, and she relaxed and sank deeply into the kiss. For a split second, she began to panic, but then told herself that this was Benjamin, the kindest, most gentle man she had ever met, and allowed herself to be carried away by the exquisite closeness to him.

They broke apart from one another, pleased with the victory over their pasts, and as thrilled with the kiss as two young school children. They grinned at each other all day, to the point where the children began asking what was going on.

"Grownup things," Sarah said to Little Ben. You mind the little boy things, and we will mind the grownup things." Her stern face dissolved into a playful smile as she looked at Benjamin, and Benjamin confused Little Ben even more when he smiled first at Sarah and then him. Little Ben had no idea what was going on, but he knew there was a secret that he had not been made privy to, and he was unhappy about it.

CHAPTER TWENTY-ONE

It was time for dinner, and exhaustion took its toll on Ben as he ate. He had wanted to go out with the children to move snow, but Sarah insisted he go back to bed. Despite his protests, he was happy he obliged when he felt the softness of the pillow and feather tick draw out his fatigue, and he slept for hours without moving.

By the time he awakened, the children had made a virtual sliding board into the house, and while it appeared to be great fun entering the house in that manner, when Ben stood, he recognized that the heat of their bodies sliding over the snow had turned the ramp to solid ice, which would cause water to pour down into their cabin like a waterfall when it thawed. It was almost dark when the children begrudgingly returned to the doorway to tear down their playground slide. "Start up a little higher and then dig downward away from the house. That way when it warms up, the water will roll away from the house," he said, pleased the children were obeying him.

"By the way," Ben said, "does anybody know what day today is?" he asked as he stretched his arms and back. Having no idea how long he had slept he was completely disoriented. He was surprised to find that he had slept right through an entire Monday, Tuesday, Wednesday and Thursday. He had come home on Friday, and in answer to his question, today was Saturday. "I want to go to church tomorrow," he announced as he returned to his bed.

Sarah, not wanting to argue with him simply said, "And I hope you can do just that."

He had heard everything she had meant with those words, and smirked at her over his shoulder.

"We might can't get out'a here," Sissy Grace chimed in.

"Yea, it might snow some more," Little Ben said hopefully.

Ben smiled and said as he looked at Sissy, "Well, IF we can get out of here, and IF the Bensons can get here to pick us up," he continued as his gaze shifted to Little Ben, "and IF it doesn't snow anymore," his eyes shifted to Sarah, "and IF I am well enough…" He waited as he looked around the room at all of them, "I want to go to church!"

"Alright, Ben," Sarah said noncommittally.

Ben added, "In other words, we'll see, right?"

"I don't want any chance on earth of losing you," she said tenderly, ending the conversation. The sting of not being allowed to go was tempered by the feeling he had when she tucked him in; he felt cared for, and loved, so the protesting stopped.

After supper was done, they gathered round to read more of the 23rd Psalm. Before reading it, Sarah noticed a note written in the margins of the page. She assumed it was the writing of Preacher since the Bible had once belonged to him, so she found it worthy to be read aloud, "The word, 'Psalm,' means, 'song,'" She looked up at the faces of those nodding in acknowledgement of that interesting fact. She continued reading, "When King David was a little boy, he was a shepherd, and wrote many of these songs, or Psalms." She looked up at Ben and said, "Isn't that interesting?"

They all nodded, so she continued, "So we are continuing to study the 23rd Psalm, or the 23rd song! It is interesting that a little boy who was a shepherd wrote this don't you think," she said as she looked at Little Ben, who moved his head up and down most vigorously.

"So, the first part, we discussed, about how the Lord is our Shepherd. So we talked about the five of us as sheep that God gathered together like a little herd of sheep and brought us here, remember?" Sarah said with a smile.

Little Ben laughed, "So we are the herd of Waters!" They all smiled at the viewpoint of a child in these matters, and Little Ben was pleased with their responses.

"But we are more than sheep, we are God's children, and I believe He brought us together so we could protect each other and be happy," Sarah said truthfully.

Ben picked up the instruction of the children by adding, "More proof that this is true, is that we really don't want for anything. God has provided this bed, and the food, and the house through the people who believe in Him and do His will. I hope in the future that I can do that for others, that I can be the feet and hands of God when someone needs help."

"But isn't that what you did already, Papa?" Little Ben asked in all innocence and pride. "'Cos you let God use your hands and feet to save Abram!"

Ben was touched when he looked at himself through this little boy's eyes. He was a hero to Little Ben, although Benjamin had a hard time seeing himself as anything but an imposter, a murderer who was fooling the people around him. Yet when he saw himself through his son's eyes, he saw what others in this community saw, and hopefully what God saw: a good man, capable of doing extremely kind acts. The last thought elevated Ben's spirits to a frightening level. Unaccustomed to the feeling of goodness he experienced when he thought of himself, he felt the urge to sabotage his elation by thinking, "Yes, but when they find out, they will see me for who I really am and then everyone will know what God already knows about me. I am a murderer, an escapee, a liar and imposter, and a sinner of the worst kind." He was grateful his spirits collapsed into the pits of despair, because he was far more comfortable with despair than joy, and was now ready to go back to listening to the scriptures.

"Yes, Little Ben, your father did allow God to use Him to save *Mr. Benson*, not Abram. You must call your elders by Mr. or Mrs., not by their first names. You, too, Grace." When Sarah saw her little mouth pucker, she added, "Because that is what all your new friends at church do, and you don't want them to think you are not polite, do you?"

Viewed in that light, it made perfect sense to Sissy whose frown was replaced with a smile as she said, "Ok, Mama!"

Ben continued by saying, "So, He led us, his children, to this meadow, by way of the still waters of the Little Kanawha River. You know we all have things in our past that we have to deal with, and I was really wrestling with some things that had happened to me as a child when we got on that boat. I found the still waters to be healing for me and, as you know, that is where our last name came from," he said, delighted at the children's expressions. "Long before I ever heard this scripture, I felt the peace that the still waters brought to me, on that boat ride."

"When I think about that boat ride, I think about the BEAR!" Little Ben shouted.

"Me, too," Grace said sadly, "'cos I wished the bear would just kill me and get it over with." They all started to laugh until they realized she was dead serious. A hush fell over the room as both Sarah and Ben realized there was a possibility that Sissy had actually been so unhappy she would view death as a release.

Ben was trying to think of a way to address the issue, when Sarah spoke up, calling on her natural ability to move forward in life, and said, "Do you still feel that way, Sissy?" And there it was, the part of her he had loved from the first, her ability to put the past behind her and move into the future confidently without a backward glance. *Those who are behind me*, was a phrase of hers that came to mind. How he wished he could wrap *those who are behind* him into a neatly wrapped box and pack them away as she did.

"NOPE!" Sissy said smiling from ear to ear! "I'm happy now!"

He had a lot to learn from the two women in his life, and he couldn't help but wonder if that ability to move on without being anchored to the past was just a female trait. He took one step toward feeling sorry for himself for the lack of experience he had with life in general, and then stopped himself, and tried to collect in his mind all the events that had happened to him since meeting Lloyd and Juanita. *I have to remember that this is my life now,* he thought to himself. *These new memories are the foundation of my new life with Sarah and these children, my life in this community, and my new walk with God,* Ben thought with great resolve. The only chance he had at happiness in this world, was to train his mind to focus on the good, and to drop his past into the sea of forgetfulness. When the other issues crowded around and threatened to enter the equation, Ben resolved to allow His Shepherd to deal with those issues. After all, He had gotten them this far, He could handle the rest, and with that one thought he began his journey completely immersed a new level of self-esteem that was neither too lofty to be comfortable, nor so low he was again lost in despair. He listened to Sarah read the scriptures from a better vantage point. He was no longer the sheep that was left behind, nor the shepherd who was responsible for everything, but the very loved and cared for child of God, and just as Sissy Grace, Little Ben, and Rebecca were made to be the children in a home, Ben found peace and safety in his place in God's plan, safe in the care of His Shepherd.

"He restoreth my soul," she read with such a heartfelt depth of understanding that the entire family was drawn in to the spirituality of the message. They were all feeling restored, so the message took on a fiercely personal meaning to the Waters family.

"He leadeth me in the paths of righteousness for His name's sake," she continued.

"Yea, though I walk through the valley of the shadow of death, I will fear no evil, for thou art with me," she said as her face lit up with recognition. "This scripture sure was true for me as I walked through the valley of the shadow of death with you, Ben. And I find the wording interesting as well. I always thought this meant at *my* death. But walking beside someone who might die, in the *shadow of their death,* was a terrifying place to be; perhaps even more frightening than facing my own death, actually. But, I prayed and prayed on the ride down there that you would be alright, and suddenly a peace came over me, and I felt God's presence just as sure as I feel the presence of everyone at this table. I wasn't afraid any more, I just somehow knew you were coming home with us, and I felt truly grateful. This scripture is amazing.

As she sat there with the Bible closed across her thumb, she looked back in retrospect and saw her life with Ben as a well-orchestrated dance, bringing them together, in perfect timing with God's plan. But her thoughts were not only about the good in the scripture. She was dreading the reading of the next part, because they had been read to her in her darkest times, and evidence that God wanted her to be beaten into submission. Finally, she picked up the Bible and continued, "Thy rod and thy staff they comfort me." She had nothing to add.

Ben said, "What does that mean?" The communal shrugs sent Sarah back to the Bible.

"Thou preparest a table before me in the presence of mine enemies," the look around the table was one of doom. "What does that mean?" Sissy said cautiously, "Are they coming for us?"

Sarah and Ben locked eyes, but Sarah was the first to speak, "I am not sure what that means," uncertain of what to say to her, she just encouraged them to finish the reading and continued, "'thou anointest my head with oil; my cup runneth over.' Well that certainly is true! Our cups do run over, we all have everything we need and more."

She hoped her dodging of the issue would help ease all their fears as she finished with, "Surely, goodness and mercy shall follow me all the days of my life: and I will dwell in the house of the Lord forever." There was another hand written note there, but Sarah just wanted the children to go to bed and for the day to be over, so she closed the Bible and said, "Alright, it is time for bed now." The children bounced out of their chairs and headed to the bedroom with smiles on their faces.

Sarah, not wanting to return to that scripture until she had a better understanding, vowed to come up with something different to read to them tomorrow night, and made a mental note to go thru the books and manuscripts she had brought with her as she tucked the children into bed, and joined Benjamin for their comfortable evening of conversation together.

Sarah was feeling wonderful, but knew that Benjamin needed to go to sleep early if he were to go to church the next morning, so she encouraged him to go to bed, and agreed to continue their conversation while lying face to face, though far apart on the feather tick. As she fell asleep, she whispered a little prayer of thanks for all the wonderful blessings she had in her life, and asked at the end that God would prevent Ben's trying to go to church for at least a week. Call it women's intuition, or just plain worry about losing someone so dear, she dreaded the day that lay ahead. Every day that slipped by saw a stronger Benjamin, yet Sarah was not convinced he was strong enough to travel to church, sit up all morning, and then travel home again in the cold.

"Please listen to reason," she said to Benjamin, the next morning as he dressed for the journey. "If you wait one more week, you will be sure to be strong enough, but to go today is to risk getting pneumonia." Her pleas were to no avail. He was going and that was all there was to it.

She knew better than to insist, and refused to nag, so she stood there waiting at the door with the children, while Ben rested on his feather tick dressed and ready for church.

He giggled as the smile she reserved for the children turned to disapproval when she looked at him over her shoulder, and he hoped that Abram would be with the Bensons when they arrived, supporting his decision to go, mainly because Sarah would be impossible if Abram weren't with them.

He heard Midgie singing hymns long before he heard the jingle of the horses' tack or the chatter of the Benson children, and sat up slowly to steady himself for the journey. He hadn't made it to his feet when Elias and Denzel entered the cabin to assist him to the sleigh. "Good morning, boys," Benjamin said to the two strappin' young men as he stood to meet them, and pulled on his jacket. They didn't say a word as they each wrapped one of Ben's arms around their necks, and grabbed a leg, picking him up in one fell swoop and carrying him to the sleigh before he could protest.

CHAPTER TWENTY-TWO

He had traced Jesse this far, Hoover, a bounty hunter, had attributed more to luck than skill. The chain gang Jesse was working on had been within eyesight of the train track so it was only common sense that the prisoners would have escaped as stowaways on the train, headed either north or south. His partner had headed north to track down any news of the escapees whereabouts, and had found three of them already. *No tellin' how many of 'em came south*, he thought to himself. He figured quickly how many could still be on the loose; there were three Arly caught, the five they caught hiding in the woods, the one who got off the train and went to his home in Virginia, and the old man who hadn't even tried to run, made a total of ten already captured. That made five still on the run, and it was conceivable they had all come south on the train.

The one old man who had been in prison nearly sixty of his seventy-seven years of life, had had no desire to run, and therefore was the only one remaining to tell the officers what had happened. The prisoners had not been the initiators of the event as was first thought. Just a handful of common robbers had ambushed the three armed guards as they huddled together around the fire, drinking coffee and telling stories while the prisoners worked in clothing that was barely adequate. The robbers had killed the guards, taken their guns and cash, thrown their keys to the prisoners, and taken off into the trees squealing like pigs, whistling and laughing at their good fortune.

Hoover had stopped at each stop and questioned everyone who worked there about the men and their descriptions, but no one had recognized any of the men until he got to Parkersburg, where his questioning brought him to a man named, Sergeant Lloyd Calvin. "Yes, I did see a stowaway named, Jesse," he said reluctantly confirming what other dock workers had already reported. The other men had never been invited to the boss's house, and wondered what was so special about this cripple that he had worked for only a few hours and then left to find the Sergeant's house for a home cooked meal, a slight not easily forgotten.

Hoover had the feeling this man was trying to protect the inmate, but he seemed to be truthful when he said he knew nothing of his whereabouts, since Jesse left in the middle of the night from his barn where he slept. Anyway, Hoover, certain he was going to get nothing else out of the man, thanked him and left.

Hoover had been a bounty hunter most of his life, and he had a sixth sense for when people were trying to hide something from him. He suspected a greater relationship between the Sergeant and the boy, probably because of what the other men had reported, but he let the matter drop and began questioning the locals about what other modes of transportation led from that area.

There were two major roads leading out of Parkersburg in opposite directions that had been built originally to move soldiers easily during the Revolutionary War. One was the Winchester-Parkersburg Turnpike that covered the northern part of the state, and the other was the Staunton-Parkersburg Turnpike that went down through Charleston to Winchester. Common sense told him they would not head northward, back toward New York, and with no particular place to start, finding someone who had gone southeast would be almost impossible. Hoover stood looking at the river, thinking that if he were Jesse or any of the others, and had gotten this far, he would cross this river and head west in order to be as far from New York City as was possible. "Can you lead me to the boat docks?" he asked a young man in a tattered uniform.

"Yes, sir," he said tiredly. "Right down that a'way," he pointed and then walked on with no offer of more assistance.

As was his custom, Hoover began passing around the information on all the prisoners, but Jesse in particular, and was rewarded with stories of how a man with a bad leg had saved the life of a young girl, and the lady with him had called him, "Jesse." He had become a hero in these parts, so everyone seemed to know he had taken the boat "clean to Creston."

This was the best chance he had at the moment of getting the reward for the capture of one of the inmates, so he got a room, and boarded the boat heading for Creston the next morning. The captain of the boat remembered Jesse's awkward gate, and reported that he hadn't actually disembarked there, that he, his lady friend, and their two children had gone on ahead to Pine Bottom.

He smiled as he landed in Pine Bottom and realized it was a place steeped in poverty. *This was going to be like taking candy from a baby*, he thought to himself. *I'll just lock him up, get myself a hotel room with a hot bath, and be on that train back by Tuesday!* He thumbed through the roll of bribe money in his pocket, as he pulled his cigar out of his mouth and spoke with great formality to the woman who was hanging clothes on a line, "Excuse me, Madam."

She looked him up and down, decided she didn't like him and said with her back again turned to him, "This ain't no whorehouse, and I ain't no Madam." Then with one swift movement she retrieved a military weapon of some kind, shoved it into his belly and said, "Now, I don't like you. And I don't talk to people I don't like. So's you best be movin' on a'forn I blow them fancy store bought duds clean off'n your body."

He needed no further urging. As he turned he saw several women standing outside, or just inside their tent flaps holding various weapons, clearly ready to use them. He had underestimated the readiness of these women to protect themselves and their friends from the riffraff coming off the boats that landed there. Perhaps this was going to be just a bit more difficult than he thought.

He walked through the center of the tent city to the other side, slipping and sliding in the mud and snow, with the hopes that when he got there, he would find a road leading to a larger town. Instead he found trails that went in many directions; too many to explore this late in the day. He turned and saw only tents behind him since the women had all gone inside, and shouted to the vacated campsite, "The best way to be rid of my presence is to point the way to the nearest town."

After a brief pause, one arm emerged from the first tent he had visited, and pointed east.

By the time he found Pine Bottom, he decided the shoes he had worn were worthless, his pants were heavy with mud, and he was even colder than ever now that the sun had gone down. He had never in his life been where money could not buy him a hot meal and a room for the night and he decided he never would be again if he could help it. Word had already spread from the tent city to the town that he had gotten off the boat and was obviously from the city; two strikes against him from the beginning. No one knew what he was up to, but they knew it was no good and were unwilling to assist him in his ventures.

Door after door was opened by the man of the house who was holding a gun with both hands, and several times, their sons had weapons as well. It wasn't until he knocked on the door of a woman who had been recently widowed that he found himself surrounded by a group of men, led by the biggest human being he had ever seen in his life.

Hulse wanted this man out of town, and began by stepping closer to him in a menacing manner, and announcing, "State your business."

Hoover attempted to befriend the giant by using the techniques he had used so effectively in the past, "Howdy, sir, my name is Hoover," he said as he held out his hand, but stopped in a cold sweat when he heard sixteen guns cock all around him as each and every man stepped a little closer. He knew to lay all his cards on the table if he wanted to live, "I am a bounty hunter, and… "

"Get me some blankets and biscuits," Hulse called out to the woman behind the door. The door opened and, with a toss, the blankets fell onto the porch, followed by a loaf of homemade bread. Another man retrieved them and gave them to Hulse. "We are a Christian community here, Mister. And for that you should be thankful. But we don't cotton to your kind comin' here, peckin' around like a chicken hawk. Now you take this bread and blankets and head on out'a here. You can leave by boat tomorrow morning."

Hoover took the blankets, tucked the bread under his left arm and turned to walk away. "And don't you never come back, neither." He had no idea where he was going to sleep, but he wrapped the blankets around his head and shoulders, grateful for their warmth, and began eating the bread ravenously. Before long, he had found a place out of the wind, on the porch of a store that was locked up tight to camp out on for the night, and was doing his best to make the blankets stretch around his entire body.

"Psssst!" He thought it might be a mountain lion, or a bear, or some other beast he had heard stories about. He tried to tell himself it was his imagination, but he heard it again, unwrapped himself and stood up. "Psssst! Over here, Mister!"

He looked to his right, and in the shadows saw the wormiest looking man he had ever seen. "State your business," Hoover said loudly and with the hope that it sounded half as intimidating as when the giant said it.

"You got money?" the man said.

Hoover knew what to do with a man who wanted money, and he knew exactly how to handle him. "I may," he said, wondering whether anyone would come to his aid if this man were to rob him. "Come up here on the porch so I can see you."

"Nope! I can't do that. You gotta know there are men watching every move you make. If they sees me talkin' to ya', I'm a dead man. No, sir, we's gonna do our business just like we is."

Hoover thought about that, and decided to take the advice of someone who understood the people in this area. "Alright! I am a bounty hunter and I am looking for a man named Jesse who passed through these parts a few months ago."

"Mister," the dark figure said quietly, "squirrels don't piss in this neck of the woods without the locals knowin' about it." Then he added, "But you gonna have to do better'n that with the tellin' of it, cos' with the soldiers and all, we got men comin' and goin' all the time."

"Well, this man has a bad leg. His Pa broke it when he was a boy, and wouldn't spend money on a doctor to set it. His foot points in the wrong direction, and he kind'a drags his leg behind him some."

There was such a long silence that Hoover thought the man had either run off, or fallen asleep. "Are you still there?"

"Yea, I'm still here, I'm just a thinkin'," he said, lapsing into another silence. It seemed to Hoover to be an eternity before the man answered. "Now, I heard tell of someone with a bum leg somewhere, but I just can't remember where he landed."

Hoover took that as a request for money, and slid a one dollar gold piece onto the edge of the porch. A filthy, grimy hand reached out and grabbed the coin, then a voice said, "Well, I thank you for that, Mister, but that ain't it. I know about where he is, but I can't think to tell you how to find him."

"Do you know where he is or not?" Hoover was losing his patience with this man and was too cold and too tired to care whether or not someone did do him harm.

"I can take you to Preacher Morrison in that area, maybe he knows."

"If I find him, there is a five dollar reward in it for you," Hoover said, hoping the amount would be enough to elicit his support.

"I want my five dollars right now, Mister," his voice had become lower with the nasty stench of underlying threat in it.

"You are out of your mind," Hoover said. He waited for the man to argue, but was met with only silence. He waited and said, "Are you still there?" Silence again. "Wait!" he shouted out into the night. "I'll give you the five now, but if we don't catch him, I'll find that big man over there and give him a complete description of the snake that assisted me. I don't think in a town this size that he will have any trouble figuring out who you are."

Again he heard nothing but silence, but was too angry to bargain any more. After several minutes the man in the shadows said, "Fine. The only way you won't be followed is if you head back down to the river. I will meet you there with a mule and take you from there."

Hoover stood up and bent over to get the remainder of the bread. As an afterthought he took the blankets as well, wrapped them around his shoulders and ambled quietly out of town. About a mile down the road, he heard the same, "Pssssst!" He stopped and waited for the man to step out of the shadows. Within minutes, they were riding out of town and headed for the ridge road that led up the mountain, north of Pine Bottom.

CHAPTER TWENTY-THREE

The next morning Reverend Morrison found Hoover sleeping in the one of the pews of the church, warmed by the fire he had built in the potbellied stove. Preacher immediately recognized the man's clothes as those of a city slicker and put up his guards as to the man's intent. As the Preacher went about his morning preparations, bringing in a supply of wood, building up the fire, and leaving song books and Bibles in the seats, the man awakened and looked surprised to see he had company.

"Good morning, sir!" Hoover said with all his well-practiced charm as he struggled to sit up. He was stiff from being so cold the night before and then sleeping on the rock hard pew.

"Good morning." Preacher said with a guarded smile. "Do you need a ride somewhere, sir?" Hoover noticed the man was cordial, and yet offered him a way to leave their community, a gesture that was absolutely clear to the bounty hunter.

Preacher sat in one of the benches and listened intently as the bounty hunter told his story, and then said, "Before you can say anything to the fine men and women of this church about the man you are looking for, you must speak to the elders about this."

"This man is wanted by the Federal Government, Reverend," Hoover shouted as he came to his feet, "and if you do anything to interfere with bringing him in, you will be held responsible!" Hoover was showing a side of himself he had tried to hide when he was attempting to glean information from the

Holy man. He was livid, his face red as a beet, anger seething from every cell of his body.

The country Preacher stood up and said softly, "I suggest you lower your voice." Hoover backed down when he realized the Preacher was a nearly a foot taller than he, twice as broad through the shoulders, and no stranger to hard physical labor. His acute ability to size up a man quickly told him that just because the Preacher was kind and gentle most of the time, didn't mean that was all he was capable of. Raw fear pounded through his veins, rendering him speechless as the Preacher took one step forward making Hoover fall back into his seat pitifully.

The Preacher spoke quietly with the men as they entered the church, and smiled at the women and children as the families trickled in, filling the small log church to the limits. Hoover was so intent on examining the gait of each man as he entered, it took him by surprise when two of the biggest men he had ever seen appeared beside him, escorted him to the front and positioned him beside the pulpit in a chair facing the congregation and began speaking to him in subtle tones. Once they had made their instructions clear, they stood beside him like sentries as everyone stared at the newcomer suspiciously, instead of catching up on the news as usual.

The Benson children entered the church and opened the doors widely to allow their brothers to carry the two men in. Abram was brought in first, and seated close to the stove. Next in was Ben, sitting on the crossed arms of the boys, with his arms around their necks in order to stabilize himself. Once seated, Sarah and Midgie brushed the snow off the blankets over their legs and fussed over them until they both protested enough to get them to stop while being greeted with pats on the backs and words of welcome and encouragement from the friends and neighbors in the congregation.

After the first hymn was sung, Preacher began by saying, "I want to start this morning's service by turning to the scripture I have chosen for today, Romans 8:1," he paused as the pages of their Bibles flipped noisily, and when they stopped he continued.

"There is therefore now no condemnation to them which are in Jesus Christ, who walk not after the flesh, but after the spirit." He walked around the front of the church and allowed them to think about those words before he continued with his sermon.

"Now all of us are flesh and bone, are we not?" Heads nodded and murmurs encouraged him to continue. "So what is Paul talking about in his letter to the Romans? How can we not walk around in the flesh?" He smiled at the children who were sitting on the front row staring up at him, intrigued by the riddle he was posing. "No, the key word here is 'after' the flesh. Paul says there is no condemnation to them who walk not AFTER the flesh, but AFTER the spirit."

"So what does that mean?" Preacher continued. "Well, have you ever known someone who puts all their faith in worldly things? Things that pass away? How many of you have known of a man who puts the love of whiskey above the needs of his family?" Heads nodded as they thought of those they knew presently in that state. "And how many of you know someone who would turn on a fellow human being for the price of gold?" Preacher waited for a minute, and in that silence, Hoover began squirming in his seat. "Why, we have an example of this in our own Bible in the 26th chapter of Matthew, don't we? Did not Judas betray our beloved Jesus for a sack of gold?"

"Yes, Judas walked after the flesh even though he had experienced Christ firsthand, because THE DRAW TO WALK AFTER THE FLESH IS POWERFUL!" he shouted as cries of "Amen" rose from the congregation. He returned to the pulpit, opened his Bible and laid it out in front of him so he could see the scriptures. Placing his hands on either side of the pulpit, he straightened his arms, leaned forward and said, "It is human nature to walk after the flesh," he continued, "to follow that which brings good fortune to us, regardless of who it hurts."

Hoover felt his neck burning and the heat rising into his face. Surely the Reverend had prepared this sermon long ago, and his own interpretation of it was just a fluke. He became extremely uncomfortable in that room, and wished he were not sitting in front of the church where everyone could see him. He felt as if every single person there could see to the bottom of his soul, and he wasn't particularly proud of what they might find there.

"I think the worst part about walking after the flesh, is that you have no one to tell you your value except those others who are also walking after the flesh. Who do your neighbors say you are? And if you aren't wealthy enough for them, or tall enough, or come from a good enough family, then where do you go to see yourself more clearly, and in a better light? There is nowhere to go, for if you are walking in the flesh, then flesh becomes your master, and a cruel and fickle master it is."

"But for those of you who are walking with the Lord, following after the spirit," he paused, then continued, "and with the Lord, as it is said in Psalm 42:1, 'As the hart panteth after the water brooks, so panteth my soul after thee, O God!', YOU SHALL BE FOUND BLAMELESS!" he shouted!

He continued to shout from the pulpit, "THE DIFFERENCE BETWEEN WALKING AFTER THOSE THINGS OF THE FLESH AND THOSE OF THE SPIRIT, IS THAT IT DOESN'T MATTER WHO YOU ARE, OR WHO YOU WERE, OR HOW MANY WORLDLY RICHES YOU HAVE!" he paused, knowing what he was about to say was going to land on fertile ground, then continued softly, "because if you are safe within our Lord, Jesus Christ, then you are found to be blameless. And being blameless if far better than having riches, isn't it?" Heads nodded in understanding. "Because when we look to our Father, he does not condemn us. He says, 'You have been found blameless, go my child and live in abundance!'"

He laid the Bible down on the pulpit and stepped out into the crowd and said, "So now you who are walking in the spirit, don't look to those who are in the flesh to say who you are. You are not who they say you are. Look instead to the Heavens and ask God who He says you are! Because the answer will be that you are His," he said as he began shouting again! "REDEEMED BY THE BLOOD OF CHRIST! And THEREFORE, YOU are found to be WHITE AS SNOW! WASHED IN THE BLOOD OF JESUS!"

His voice softened again as he added, "As you leave this church today, I want you to take this with you. Remember who you are! You are a precious child of God."

At that the Waters family looked at each other. For so long, the words, "remember who you are," were words of condemnation and warning. Remember that you are not as good as they are. Remember you are just pretending to be one of them. Remember, if they find out, we will all be taken back. But the words the pastor just spoke made it perfectly clear to them that God was their judge, and that they had already been found blameless. Sarah, Ben, and Sissy had tears in their eyes as the realization hit that they were truly loved because of God's undying grace. It wasn't anything they had done, or not done that gave them value, their value was found in the love of Jesus their Savior, and their Shepherd. They were at first embarrassed by their tears, but discovered they were not alone. Grown men all over the church were pulling bandanas out and blowing their noses, and women were wiping tears with their little hankies, that were hand crocheted around the edges.

Suddenly, Preacher turned and walked briskly to the front of the church, and with outstretched arms said, "And now by the Grace of God, may we walk hand in hand together after the Holy Spirit, knowing we are all sinners, saved by the Grace of our Lord and King. Amen"

The crowd began to search for their hymnals as Preacher said, "Now if I could have your attention before we begin to sing, please. Brother Hoover here needs our help in locating someone he has been searching for, and I promised him just a moment with you."

Sarah, Benjamin, Sissy, and Little Ben each individually froze in absolute terror. They were paralyzed with fear and struggled to breathe as Preacher stepped back to allow Hoover to stand and say exactly what he had been told he could say, and nothing more. The large men on either side of him had made it perfectly clear there would be nothing said that would frighten the children, and they would tolerate no threats of any kind. So

Hoover stood up, more concerned at this point with getting out with his life than catching Jesse.

Just as he began to speak, the pressure became too great for Little Ben. He burst into tears and climbed over onto Ben's lap where Ben comforted him as best he could. In his weakened state, Ben knew he could not prevent them from taking Little Ben and Sissy away if that was who the man was there for. He wished he could protect them from this moment, and felt helpless knowing he could not. He glanced over at Sarah and their eyes locked with the knowledge that neither could see themselves going on without the other. "Please God, let them take me," Benjamin prayed, suddenly realizing his first worry was not about himself, but about the children and Sarah.

Since the words, "prison," and "murderer" had been banned, Hoover said, "I am looking for a man who is missing from upstate New York." He paused to choose his words carefully, and then said, "His name is Jesse McFay and he's a cripple. His leg was broke as a child, and never set, so he should be easily identified by his leg that he drags behind him." Benjamin's heart nearly stopped. He felt his head draw down in disgrace as he sat there before God and everybody, being exposed as the fake he was. And yet, unbelievably, in addition to the total and complete humiliation he was feeling, there was room for even more pain as he felt himself flinch at the word "cripple." Even though he had absolutely no regard for this man, it hurt as much when he called him names as it had hurt when he was a child. "It doesn't matter who they say you are," Benjamin heard inside his head, but he could not help but sink into despair as those kind people who had helped him so much, out of pure Christian devotion, learned that he was an imposter.

"There is a right sizable reward for his return, which I would be happy to share with the lucky one who gets to me first with the information I need to find Mr. McFay," he said with a lilt to his voice. Money was a language in which he was fluent, and he was used to getting the most results when it was the language of choice. Yes, now Hoover had them where he wanted them, and his confidence was coming back.

Benjamin looked down at his fingers and wondered which of his loving neighbors would be first to turn him in when he heard Hoover speak. "Yes, sir," Hoover said as he tipped his head back to see the face of an unidentified person seated in the back. It was then Benjamin realized someone had held up their hand to speak. "Yes, you sir, there in the back," Hoover said as he pointed indirectly with the hand holding the cigar.

"Now, I am just a simple man, sir," a man named AJ, spoke so softly, and so painfully slowly, Hoover wanted to scream. AJ continued, "Now, you are going to have to tell me a little more about this Jesse feller. We don't get many newcomers here, so we need to know 'zackly when this man would have come into our little community. 'Cos most of us growed up together and have knowed each other for years! Why, ole Catch over there," he pointed to a man who raised his hand in the air and smiled at everyone, and then continued, "Why, me and Catch fought over that woman he is married to when we was just boys! I got his front tooth, tho', so he din't get away clean free!" Hearty laughter filled the room as Catch stood up, used his hat to wave at the crowd and smiled a big smile to show the missing front tooth!"

Hoover tried to speak again, but was interrupted by another man who stood up and said, "And the three of us is brothers!" The man pointed to the two men and their families who were sitting in the rows behind him. "Ain't none of us ever been to New York, let alone come back from there crippled!"

The church filled with a boisterous laughter Hoover found impossible to speak over. Just as the noise began to die down, Benjamin's heart sank, as Abram stood slowly, pointed at Benjamin and said, "And one time, when I was a little bit younger, and a whole lot stupider than I am today, I was dumb enough to walk out on a frozen lake, and I fell through the ice. My friend Benjamin here pulled me out, and didn't ask a penny for it!"

"Didn't slow him down none, tho'!" said a man who had stood up in the back so he could be heard. "He got eight kids and one on the way!" The room filled with laughter again, and Ben realized with a sobering jolt, that they all knew. Everyone in this room already knew who he was, and what he had done, and they were protecting him. Nobody was lying, Abram was indeed a "little bit younger" when he fell through the ice, than he was today.

Benjamin's heart raced as he became conscious of the fact that they had probably known from the beginning. God's Grace caught in his chest as he remembered what Abram had said the night he dropped him off after going to the Markley's, "Around here folks are pretty tight lipped about their troubles." He wondered if that was why he had been included in Bertha's rescue. Was that their way of showing their understanding of the situation? These people may not have the embellished life of some, but they were certainly not ignorant. Some of them traded for a living and probably had been to Parkersburg now and again and had heard about the bounty on him. He was wondering if they had any idea about Sarah and the children when another voice interrupted his thoughts.

"Now, we are a pretty tight knit group here, Mr. Hoover, so if this stranger would happen to come into our midst, what are we supposed to do with him?" a man's voice from the right side of the church asked. Ben glanced sideways at the man whose face looked very serious indeed.

Now this, Hoover could handle without thinking about it. "Well," he said, "just tell your local lawman about it and make sure you give him your name so I can pay you well for your information."

At this, a real character named Paul, stood up and spoke just as 'serious as a judge', "Now, we don't happen to have any lawman in these parts, Mr. Hoover, so should we just kill him if we see him? I mean is he wanted dead or alive?" Everyone there knew Paul, and they knew he would rather eat skunk than help this outsider, so they played along with him by looking equally as concerned at the bounty hunter, pretending to be eager to hear his response.

"No, no! Don't hurt him, just hold on to him until I can get back here to pick him up," he said, knowing the bounty would not be paid if any harm came to the prisoner.

At that point, one of the women stood up, stomped her foot, and said vehemently, "Well, if he is that bad, I don't want him living in MY house, and we have no jail!" She was greeted with a loud rumble of concern and nods of agreement from all the women in the church as they stood in mass, and shouted their concurrences.

"I say we just kill anybody we don't know from now on, just in case!" another said, bringing the entire congregation to its feet in a din of confusion, and frustrating Hoover to the point of yelling, "NO! NO! YOU CAN'T DO THAT!" He tried several more times to shout, unsuccessfully, over the pandemonium that had erupted.

After several minutes, Reverend Morrison stood up with his black Bible under his left arm, and held his right hand high in the air. The room fell silent instantly. "Well, Mr. Hoover, you have had your say, and now while we close the service with the hymn written by a woman named, Charlotte Elliott nearly thirty years ago, Mr. Walker, and Mr. Arnold are going to escort you back to town and stay with you until your boat leaves tomorrow morning." The giant men stepped up and grabbed hold of Hoover's arms, prepared to remove him bodily if necessary.

Mr. Hoover had taken their guff this long, but was not about to be treated like a prisoner with two armed guards, and said, "I beg your pardon, that will not be necessary," he huffed as he yanked his arms away from the men beside him, grabbed his lapels and jerked on them in an effort to straighten his coat and regain at least a small modicum of dignity.

"Yes, sir, it is necessary," said John Arnold, "you know there is a lot of wilderness out there, places where a man could die and his body would never be found. We wouldn't want that to happen to you, now, would we, Mr. Hoover?" The veiled threat was hardly veiled. He looked at the Preacher, and out at the faces staring at him and knew he was going to get no further with his questioning. He would do as the men "suggested," leave with these two massive men, and never return. There were four more convicts out there who would be a lot less trouble to bring in anyway.

As the men left the church, the Preacher held up his arms and began the singing with his beautiful, rich voice, "Just as I am, without one plea, but that thy blood was shed for me, and that thou bidst me come to the, Oh, Lamb of God, I come, I come."

The Preacher made an alter call for anyone who had not accepted Christ as their Lord and Savior, or anyone who had a need to come forward in prayer. As they sang the last verse almost everyone came forward, including Benjamin and Sarah, with Abram and Midgie right beside them. As they prayed and emptied their hearts of all their burdens, they felt hands on their backs, shoulders and heads, and they heard prayers of gratitude to the God that saved them both from the frozen waters, and brought them back to their families.

Benjamin said a prayer of great thanks to God, for bringing him to this place where he could have a second chance, in the midst of people who worshiped a God of love and forgiveness. The words of the song prayed with him as he sang, "Just as I am – and waiting not, to rid my soul of one dark blot, To Thee whose blood can cleanse each spot, -O Lamb of God, I come! I come!"

Church was over, and before Ben and Sarah could turn to face the congregation, they were swarmed with folks warning them there would be no more swimming until spring, pounding Benjamin on the back with thanks for saving Abram, and asking Abram if he had learned anything about walking on ice. The church was joyous, happy, and noisy beyond belief in their celebration of life, for not only had God brought Abram and Benjamin back from the brink of death, they had duped the city slicker and sent him packing, tail between his legs. They may not have all the riches of city folk, but by God, they were family and families stick together.

Epilogue

The ride home was joyous and filled with laughter. Sarah leaned comfortably against Benjamin under the warmth of the wool blanket and breathed a sigh of pure contentment. Here she was, surrounded by people she loved, in the back of an open sleigh, a far cry from the carriages she was accustomed to, on her way to a home that was little more than a shack, and she had never been happier. Her eyes went from person to person, drinking in their smiles, their giggles, and the love that passed from Abram to Midgie and back again as they chatted comfortably, cuddled up together under another wool blanket on the other side of the sleigh.

She thought about Denzel and Elias, and suddenly saw them, not as children, but as young men. Her stomach clenched at the thought that they might get caught up in the war, as her eyes wandered toward Little Ben. She began calculating how many years it would be before he could become a soldier, and prayed for a quick resolution to the horrible conflict that already taken the lives of so many of their neighbors.

Feeling as though he had not been breathing for several moments, Ben took a deep breath of the brisk, ice cold air, and wondered if it were getting colder, or if his illness was causing him to shiver. He was not only cold, he was exhausted and felt so short of breath that he was actually a little light headed. He weakly turned his head to see if he could see the cabin, hoping against hope that it would be just moments away, but his thoughts were interrupted when Little Ben came climbing over the other children in order to get under the blanket between Sarah and him. He was grateful for the added warmth when Little Ben had to move to Ben's lap when Sissy Grace also came to sit between them.

Ben looked at Sarah, and was pleased at how happy she seemed, and decided not to mention the cold that was growing inside his chest, and his inability to get enough air. He just prayed he could make it back to the cabin before he became dangerously ill, and wished he would have listened to Sarah and stayed home one more week.

They rode along in silence, each one deep in thought, as the Benson children laughed and teased each other. Sarah was not certain as to the effect the war would have on their community or their own little family, but for now, on this day, she was grateful for their blessings, and thankful for this particular serving of God's daily bread. She smiled as she looked at the sleeping faces of her three children, completely unaware of Ben's fight to remain conscious as he sat beside her.

Ben just hoped his foolishness would not cause him to lose this second chance he had been given, and prayed that God would give him one more gift of Grace, for the sake of Sarah and the children. Finally, he could not fight it any longer, and slipped into a deep, deep, sleep.

CONTACT INFORMATION

BOOK TWO is almost ready for release!

If you would like to receive an email alerting you to the release day, please share your email with me at:

Bit.ly/livingwatersseries

Your email will never be given out, and will be used ONLY for alerts about my books. Thank you so much for reading my book! Also, if you would like to chat with me, please join me at:

https://www.facebook.com/sharonturnerbooks

Blessings!

ABOUT THE AUTHOR

Sharon Turner is a native West Virginian who has a deep love for the beauty and history of the state, a deep respect for the wisdom of the mountain people, and a profound love for God that colors her world, and everything she writes.

She was raised singing shaped notes at her church and at home, and only converted to the round note system used today, when she went to what was then Fairmont State College, where she received a degree in Music Education. She also has a Masters in Communications from West Virginia University.

She and her husband now live in the Eastern Panhandle of West Virginia and have two children, four Grandchildren, and rescue small dogs.

Story telling is a large part of West Virginia culture, and Sharon is a direct descendant of several winners of local Liars Contests, where many men, women, and children compete by telling the tallest tale they can manage. But story telling is not only used as entertainment, it also provides a living history of their past. Many of the stories she will be using in this series, are ones told by people living in her county, who remember the stories handed down from generation to generation, about actual events that occurred during the Civil War.

Many descendants of those who fought in Calhoun County, are involved in the annual reenactment of those events, and represent their ancestors who fought there.

It is her hope that she can give the world a better view of the rich cultures that exist in West Virginia, as well as insight into God's deep and non-judgmental love He has for us, His children.

Made in the USA
Lexington, KY
17 August 2017